# The Ninth Realm

MICHAEL CHATFIELD

Cover Art by Jan Becerikli Garrido
Jacket Design by Caitlin Greer
Interior Design by Caitlin Greer

eBook ISBN: 978-1-990785-00-9
Paperback ISBN: 978-1-989377-99-4

# 1

## A Higher Stage

E rik jumped to the side, and Rugrat fired through the opening. The creature slammed backward with the shot, a tombstone floating above it.

Erik sighed and released the power running through his body. The walls of the room they had been fighting in broke apart and fell away into the floor, revealing an arena around them. A new version of the training dungeons. Only Lee Perrin and their guards were in attendance.

Erik checked his stats and recent gains from the fighting at Kushan.

588,045,746,157,831/1,168,160,000,000,000,000,000 EXP till you reach Level 105

| Name: Erik West | | |
| --- | --- | --- |
| | Level: 104 | |
| | Race: Human-? | |
| Titles: | | |
| | From the Grave III | |
| | Blessed By Mana | |
| | Dungeon Master V | |

| *Reverse Alchemist*<br>*Poison Body*<br>*Fire Body*<br>*Earth Soul*<br>*Mana Reborn IV*<br>*Wandering Hero*<br>*Metal Mind, Metal Body*<br>*Sky Grade Bloodline* | |
|---|---|
| Strength: (Base 90) +88 | 1958 |
| Agility: (Base 83) +120 | 1218 |
| Stamina: (Base 93) +105 | 3267 |
| Mana: (Base 317) +134 | 4700 |
| Mana Regeneration (Base 340) +71 | 264.04/s |
| Stamina Regeneration: (Base 162) +99 | 59.52/s |

*Damn, that is a lot of zeroes.*

"Heard you ran into some Avegaaren students the other day." Lee Perrin stood, walking toward them, as Erik drank from his canteen.

"We did?" Rugrat asked, getting off George's back as he transformed into his demi-human form and stretched.

"The group of five that defeated Aziri."

"Ahh, well now I know why they were surprised I didn't know who they were and didn't bow or scrape for them." Erik wiped his mouth with the back of his hand.

"Might that have something to do with your increased use of my training arena?"

Erik shrugged.

Lee stood in front of them. "I hear that two fleets have set out to hunt down the remaining dragons."

"Probably to provide support. The Mission Hall put a large bounty on the heads of the dragons, dead or alive. Every Hero is going to be running over to claim a part of the resources," Erik said.

"I never realized how strong a Ravager or Devourer could be. It was just like you said. Aziri seemed to blend into the elements, with them becoming an extension of himself."

"To have that sort of control, though." Erik shook his head.

"A Ravager becomes a Devourer when they have cultivated their primary element to the Celestial Grade. Unlike creatures and people in the Ten Realms, a Ravager has to figure out their own path to utilize that power. They don't have elemental cores."

"But they do have a bloodline?" George asked.

"Correct. Some will have some latent memories through their bloodline that can assist them. Most don't. Many are killed by the elements they consume. It would be like tempering without healing concoctions and instead of the cultivation following a set path, you have to create the path, the changes to their bodies. Many are mutated by the elemental influx."

"Hmm, so they have greater flexibility to the alterations made to their body, but very few make it through the process. That makes it seem like humans. When we cultivate, is there a plan within our bodies, like mana and the elements know what changes to make?" Erik asked.

"Ah, well, the Ten Realms were created to train us. Wouldn't it make sense for them to give us a path?"

Rugrat grunted. "They're not exactly giving out cultivation manuals."

"No, but I think that's intrinsic to the Ten Realms. It must be teaching our bodies, if not our minds, how to deal with increased amounts of mana and elements in our bodies."

"Sounds rather mysterious." Erik raised an eyebrow.

Lee smiled. "I went to the Ninth Realm and heard a great number of things, but I wasn't able to enter Avegaaren."

Rugrat stepped forward. "Do you really think that we have a chance?"

"I think both you and Erik might. You have the raw power."

George tilted his head to the side.

"I still have much to teach you. You have mastery in one element, but you haven't cultivated it to the peak, and although you unlocked your bloodline, you haven't cultivated your mana nearly enough. While Avegaaren might teach you a lot, I don't think there is anywhere in the Ten Realms with the ability to increase someone's cultivation as fast as Alva," Lee said.

"That Ninth Realm spear user at Kushan had the same cultivation as me. But he was so much stronger. Did he have a secret cultivation art? Formations?"

"No, their trick is much harder to learn and use than that." Lee turned to Erik. "Avegaaren trains the strongest fighters in the Ten Realms. *Never* underestimate a student from Avegaaren. Cultivation is rarely what they rely on to win their battles. Also, it seems almost suitable as I have run out of things to teach you and you're making connections I haven't made before such as elemental resonance." Lee smiled. "You have trust in one another, and you have rudimentary ability, but you have become reliant on a great number of things, and I'm not enough of a teacher to teach you. The teachers I would send you to pale in comparison with those in Avegaaren in terms of combat."

"Before we jump to the Ninth Realm, which'll cost us a whole Celestial mana stone, we should talk to Egbert. We have information from across the realms. Surely we can learn from that."

"Things like fighting are hard to learn from books, but that would be a good place to start. I have another class. I'll see you all later."

George scratched his head while Rugrat frowned, chewing on his lip.

"Come on, he'll be hiding in the library," Erik said.

Egbert was attired in neon flamingos and a deep blue shirt with a fedora and red shorts, sitting in a beach chair with a coat rack next to him with his cloak on it, and a stack of books at his side.

The only window in the room looked out of the library tower across Alva's bustling living floor.

Erik knocked on the door as Egbert raised a finger, finishing his paragraph and putting in a marker.

"What are you three doing breaking into my tower of solitude for?"

"Had a question for you." Rugrat glanced around the room, unsure of where to stand. There were full bookshelves that had turned into teetering towers on the floor.

Erik navigated the room carefully, catching a pile of books that started to tile dangerously. He held onto it, making sure it would remain standing before moving again.

"You know of Avegaaren?" Rugrat continued.

"Yes, the academy of the Ninth Realm. Most accommodating people. You get to the Ninth Realm by completing the Eighth Realm Trial directly, or by finding your why, then you can use a totem to gain access to the floor. Children are not allowed to be born in the realm. Only people with a reason for why they fight may enter the realm. To join the academy, you need to challenge one of the ten thousand people in your grade—broken down by age to gain attendance. Crafters—"

"Woah, woah. Okay, calm it down. Just wanted to know if you'd heard of the place. Wanted to know if you think we can train to the level of people from Avegaaren with the information we have."

"Ah." Egbert nodded knowingly.

"Some inner competitiveness? Well, yes, you could if we have a few hundred years. They not only have information in books, but they also have people who have actually done the things in the books. Reading about it is one thing; doing it, that is another matter."

Erik and Rugrat shared a look.

A book tower collapsed. Everyone looked at a wincing George.

"Sorry."

"No worries." Egbert waved his hand, using a spell to put the books back into an equally unstable arrangement. "I actually wanted to propose that we send some people to the Ninth Realm and as our resident realm scouts. I can't think of two that would be better suited." Egbert smiled.

Erik raised his eyebrow. "I sense you want more than just us moving around the Ninth Realm."

"Well, as a purveyor of fine books—" His arms encompassed the room. "—I am always interested in information, and the more information we have, the faster our students can progress. While we might be a few centuries behind Avegaaren in terms of information, if we were to have two fine students that kept meticulous notes, it wouldn't be so hard to bridge the gap. Then we would only require the practical experience."

Erik glanced at Rugrat, who shrugged.

"What else do you have to do except to play emperor? You can train, fight to your heart's content, and your lives won't be on the line. You can finally learn how to use your powers to their limit."

"Seems that this Tenth Imperium holds the reins of Avegaaren. They recruit from there, at the least, possibly control it."

"From my own sources and Elan, he is such a resourceful fellow. The Tenth Imperium is an institution that might be as old as the Realms. You know their connection to the Associations and the Mission Hall. They are the only group with a force in the Tenth Realm. I'm not sure for what purpose, but it seems that there is fighting to be had in the Tenth Realm."

"What makes you think that."

"Why do you fight? The Eighth Realm Trial. Only if you fight, will you reach the Ninth Realm. It is clear that they want people that will fight. It is why the strongest crafters remain in the Seventh Realm."

"What are they fighting?"

"Well, we don't know about Ravagers and Devourers, but it's clear their students do with how they dealt with Aziri."

"But…" Erik frowned. "Wait, Ravagers are just mutated mana beasts, right?"

"Ravagers might have similarities with beasts in the Ten Realms, but they are not from it. Tread carefully with the Tenth Imperium. We have fewer answers and more questions regarding them."

Rugrat, Erik, and George walked in silence up the street toward their home. Storbon, scanning around them.

"Don't feel bad about wanting to go to the Ninth Realm," George said. "Lee was right. I need to train more and get stronger. I talked to Davin already. Being another Fire element beast, he's in the same way. I'm looking forward to training with him."

"Thanks." Rugrat patted him on the shoulder. "You can still come with us up there."

"All the training equipment is here, and it costs a Celestial mana stone to get there. Bit rich for my blood right now. I still need to work off the other stone." He smiled as they reached the front door.

"How are we going to tell Momma?" Erik asked.

"Tell me what?" she said, opening the front door.

"If we should call you Mayor Rodriguez or not." George grinned. "Ow!" A spoon appeared and disappeared in short succession, leaving him holding his head.

"That's Momma to you! Delilah and I were going over plans and started making dinner. Go and get cleaned up. You smell like the training arena and Egbert's books! Storbon, if you think I'm going to let you hide in your barracks instead of having a warm meal, you're sorely mistaken. In you get!"

"She was always the match maker among our friends," Rugrat muttered to Erik as they got into the entry hall.

"Should've listened to her about my exes." Erik grinned.

"What are you two muttering about?" Momma said, Storbon entering behind her.

"Nothing. Hey, put the spoon away!" Rugrat yelped as it passed his defense and smacked him on the shoulder. She walked past and back toward the kitchen. "And you can tell me what you were supposed to over dinner!"

"Yes, Momma," Rugrat, George and Erik chorused, walking up the stairs.

"Bathroom in the back left!" Erik yelled back down to Storbon. "Thanks!"

Rugrat was down first, following the smell of dinner wafting up from the kitchen. Delilah and Momma were talking with wine in hand as the food finished cooking. Storbon had been set to work, pulling out cutlery for the table.

"Look like a couple of newly weds and the mother-in-law!" Rugrat joked.

Delilah blushed and glanced over to Storbon, their gaze catching, then looking away quickly.

"Who's a housewife, you incumbent emperor?" Momma brandished her spoon. "Help Storbon get that table set!"

Rugrat laughed, ducking, and running for cover. "I'm going, I'm going!"

His grin widened at seeing Delilah's face flush as she hid behind her wine and pulled her hair behind her ear. Storbon was just as flustered, focusing on the spoons. They grabbed what they needed and headed back through the swing doors to the dining table.

"So, you seeing any girls?" Rugrat asked.

"Uh, no, not really right now. Work, you know?" Storbon shrugged.

"You're young, fit, and good looking. I'm sure there are girls interested in you out there, *somewhere.*"

"Thank you," Storbon said dryly.

Rugrat laughed and elbowed him. "Well, it's not a bad idea to go on a few dates. Never know what it could lead to."

"What about you?" Storbon asked, eagerly diverting attention.

"Ah, well…" Rugrat paused, thinking of Racquel for a brief second. Then it was gone. A door had closed on that future. "Nope, no one I'm interested in. Got to focus on the Ninth Realm now." Rugrat forced his tone to lighten, putting on a smile.

Erik and George came down shortly after, helping with setting the table with plates and silverware.

Delilah and Momma pulled out food, setting it down on the table.

Rugrat caught Delilah and Storbon glancing at one another again. He raised an eyebrow to his mother. She wore a bemused expression that told him all he needed to know.

"Momma, Delilah, you shouldn't have. You two are so busy already,"

Erik said as they all sat down.

"You two did dinner the last four nights. Delilah was here going over work and was happy to help. Thank you, dear. These two eat enough that I scare the butchers."

"It's quite all right. I'm happy to help. It's rather lonely at home now." Delilah smiled.

Most of her family had their own homes or have moved out to the farms that were populating the realm.

"That must be tough on your own," Storbon said.

Delilah accepted a bowl of vegetables from Erik. "It's not that bad. 8ith all the administration changes, I have free time, and I eat out a lot."

"You deserve your free time." Erik said. "You've been worked to the bone with everything happening. Alva has gone through a lot of changes, and you've been at the heart of it all,"

"Yes, it's not what I expected when I took the job, but needs must as they say."

Erik opened his mouth to say more but decided to eat instead.

"Thank you, Delilah, for all you've done for Alva," Rugrat said.

"I've enjoyed it." She smiled. "Alva has become a home to so many people and created stability across the lower realms."

"Just need to set you up with the right girl or guy to take care of you," Momma said.

"Uhh, guy would be preferable." Delilah blushed.

Momma smirked and drank from her wine.

*Momma.* Rugrat mentally shook his head, hiding his grin, looking over his drink at Storbon and Delilah.

Momma put down her wine. "Now, enough of torturing my boss. What were you three delinquents talking about before I caught you?"

George ducked his head and worked on his newly acquired use of a knife and fork.

"An opportunity of sorts," Erik said.

"You going to get to the point or walk in circles?" She raised an eyebrow, looking between them.

"I want to train in Alva!" George threw in, like a drowning wolf.

"And we are thinking of going to the Ninth Realm to train in Avegaaren, the academy for the Tenth Imperium," Rugrat said.

"We've reached the limit of what Alva and our new allies can teach us. Lee doesn't have anything more for us, at least. It might take a long time, according to Egbert, before we can reach the knowledge base of Avegaaren. Also, it's a school, so a place for training. Not somewhere we would face danger, and we would have constant contact with the lower realms, too."

Momma nodded and listened while Delilah simply rolled her eyes.

"You two are bullheaded, sometimes more than I would like." Momma's voice dipped, and Rugrat was unable to meet her eyes. He remembered how they had overlooked her love as being overbearing protectiveness. *But she'll always be my Momma.*

"You two are grown adults. Other than your positions, there isn't much for you to do here anymore. We don't have many public events you need to attend since I was voted in as mayor, so you're off the hook for the time being."

Delilah cleared her throat. "Aditya is secure in his position and has close relations with the military, and we'll have elections for every town and city over the next couple of years. Information has always been our weakness. If you can learn more, it'll help our people immensely."

Momma sighed through her teeth. "Make sure you have fun now, you hear? And don't forget to send me messages!" She wagged a finger in his direction.

"Of course, Momma," Rugrat nodded and smiled. Momma knew him best, and he knew she was putting up an easy-going front.

Erik rescued him, turning to lighter subjects like Alva's recent expansions, new dining places and rumors, eating through dinner and dessert in short order.

Delilah started to clear the table.

"There's no need to do that, dear," Momma said.

"No worries. I'm happy to do it." She smiled. Momma sighed, but let her continue.

Delilah hurried out, putting the first load into the sink. Ever since that time in the hangar, she had been unable to look at Storbon without thinking of him in more than a professional way. Maybe that wasn't a bad thing. She hadn't even thought of having a relationship since she left home to travel to the city with the promise of becoming an alchemist. He was around the same age, and he had matured into a reliable man. He held himself tall, often hiding away that impish grin under his serious cover.

She let out a groan at her mind's wavering thoughts.

"That good, huh?" Storbon's voice made her nearly jump out of her skin as the door swung.

"Sorry, uhh, yeah, Momma's cooking is always good." She turned, composing her features, and looked at him as he put in his piled dishes, smelling freshly cleaned from his shower, his upper buttons undone, showing hints of tattoos underneath. She couldn't help but wonder what tattoos he had now.

"I can do these, you know. You had a full day and then made all of this. You're super woman. I, uh," He cleared his throat, rubbing the back of his head awkwardly. "Well, you're so impressive."

Delilah smiled as the hardened leader of a special team being brought to his knees by an awkward moment in Momma's kitchen.

"Who knows? Maybe Rugrat was right. I think I'd be a cute little housewife too. Three, no, four kids running around?" She winked.

Storbon choked and coughed, turning into laughter as she bit her lip and moved to the sink. *Why did I have to say that?* Despite her thoughts, she had a hard time forcing down her smile and keep the slight blush from her cheeks.

"Guess I deserved that," Storbon muttered, smiling as he passed her plates.

They talked about the new theatre that was being set up, the revival of music in Alva and the spread of food across the ten realms.

"After tasting the Sky Reaching Restaurant's food, people can't go back to the taste of chalky potions and pills," Storbon said, pausing with a plate half submerged. "Not that I'm saying potions aren't good…"

"Trust me, I will be the first to eat real food instead of taking pills and concoctions all the time to fill my stomach and keep me awake. There are some trying to flavor them. But high-level food already has buffs. Just runs out so quickly. You know that food is one of our largest sellers to the higher realms?"

"Didn't know that. I thought it might be concoctions and formations, seeing as we can pump them out," Storbon said.

"Tools are our second biggest. They're simple, but still need a crafter, making them really expensive. With assembly lines, we're faster, and cheaper."

Delilah closed her hand around Storbon's as he passed her a plate. "Oh, uhh…"

"Umm, here." Storbon turned the plate, and she grabbed the open part.

They grew silent before Storbon laughed. "Well, thank you for everything you've done."

"You know you don't have to say that every time. I would've quit a long time ago if I didn't like it."

"You have a tough job, being the council leader of Alva. Erik is lucky to have a student as great as you."

Delilah hid her wince as she fought her shoulders slumping and the sinking feeling in her gut. She had heard this kind of compliment hundreds of times before, but it hurt more hearing it come from Storbon.

She pulled on a smile. "I was lucky that he took me as a real student. Feels a long time ago now."

"That it does. You've really grown into it."

"You have too. Guess we've had to."

Storbon nodded, the clink of dishes and silverware filling the kitchen.

Delilah played dozens of things to say through her head, focusing her eyes on the dishes as much as she wanted to snatch glances at Storbon.

# 2

# Paying Old Debts

E rik watched the vertical train lock into its platforms leading up into the sky. "Welcome to the Water floor," the train operator said as it slowed down, coming to stop at the station with a hiss of steam.

The doors opened, releasing the passengers. They wandered into the town. The sounds of voices, the smell of food, and joy of laughter filled the air.

Erik and Rugrat hunched in their coats, two members of the military among dozens heading home, waiting for the arriving passengers to clear the train.

"Boarding for Alva floor."

The gates opened and the waiting crowd boarded the vertical train.

"Friggin' cold. If I wanted to be cold, I would have lived in Alaska," Erik muttered.

"I dunno, kind of nice not having all that swamp humidity and heat, and no sand," Rugrat said as they grabbed onto handholds.

Whistles rang out as the last boarders hustled onto the train.

"All aboard!"

The doors closed, and the train shuddered before heading upward.

"Massive freaking elevator," Rugrat said as they cleared the tower-like station, gaining a clear view of the Water floor.

Mana lights shone off the largest floor, catching icebergs and the grand mountain in the middle of the landscape. A city had grown out of the mountain, with several fishing hamlets around the edge of the stony outcroppings surrounding the large lake.

Boats moved through the water and under the bridges that connected the stony and icy lands. Homes of rough timber stood against the chill of the floor, with walls around the growing districts of the town to protect against the cutting wind.

It was harsh but beautiful, like the fire floor, with growing fields for Water attribute plants, healing, and stamina potions.

The train quickly picked up speed.

"I haven't been able to shake what happened at Kushan." Erik looked out of the windows as they kept rising.

"I thought those Dragons were strong in the Violet Sky Realm. They were on another level in the Ten Realms."

"If not for those people from the higher realms, we would have died. It took three of their people to kill Aziri. We couldn't kill him with a fleet and dozens of our strongest fighters, and just when I thought we were finally strong enough to defend ourselves." Erik sucked in a breath through his nose and let it drain between his teeth.

"We're getting there with new weapons and the new fleet. Once our people can use the dungeon cores and the warships without our help, we can go to the Ninth Realm in search of answers."

Erik ran his tongue along the inside of his teeth. "Tell me honestly. When you sensed them, did you sense they were stronger than us in cultivation?"

"Well, yeah, *but* they weren't that much stronger than us. Their gear was really strong, though our gear is as well."

"Which means we're missing something. If we can figure that out, then Alva won't have to worry about her security anymore."

Light broke the darkness again.

The Wood floor was covered in trees of all kinds arranged into coordinated sections. Birds moved among the treetops with their masters upon their backs, inspecting and checking the trees.

Each home on the Wood floor was a tree itself, magically grown and tended into form, peeking over their fellow trees. One could only note the towns by the raised trees and increased birds around them.

Erik clicked his tongue. "Problem is our lack of dungeon core controllers."

"We can use the Sha commanders that came with Edmond." Rugrat leaned against the pole behind him.

"If we do that, our warships will be controlled by the Sha. We want to integrate the two forces and break the Sha out of their old way of thinking. We've already got people saying that the Sha bought their position in Alva."

Rugrat grimaced. "Gah, like, well, dungeon cores are expensive. It's not like we could just take them from them. That'd be stealing."

"I know that; you know that. But people see them getting high positions and we get dungeon cores in return. It's hard to tell them that we're not being bought out. If we then go and turn our advanced warships over to them..." Erik turned his head to the side and slowly raised his shoulders. "Doesn't look all that good. We need to bring them into Alva's military, train them with our people, make them Alvans, not Sha buying their positions. Not only would people look at it badly, but it could also create a rift in our military."

Light flooded in as they entered the Earth floor. There were fields of crops everywhere. Growing floors, stacked one upon another, rose from the ground with towers along their edges, houses for the farmers, with a robust train system to transport their goods.

Erik cast a spell on his eyes, seeing Edmond's mansion in the distance, complete with its gardens. The home had been lifted from his warship, which now stood guard over Alva's gate, and supplanted here.

Lakes and rivers wove between farms of stacked greenhouses. Barges plied the waterways, docking at the base of the tower homes.

"Frickin' politics." Rugrat looked like he wanted to spit.

"Agreed, but we have treaties and alliances across the realms. Everything we now do is political."

"And why we're getting tapped to command the warships?"

"For now." Erik shrugged. "Few more weeks and we'll have people trained up for it. We knew how to use dungeon cores and basic knowledge of Ten Realm's airships and Earth planes. It has been a jump for the crews, but breaking down operations instead of having just one person controlling the ship, they've been quick to learn."

"I'm not complaining. It ain't all that bad, but I'll be happy to hand it over to someone else and go back to kicking ass on water and the ground instead of hanging my ass out in the wind."

Erik rolled his eyes. "You have such a way with words."

"I know, right?" Rugrat waggled his eyebrows. Still grinning, he looked out of the window as light streamed in from the Metal floor. It shone faintly under the mana light. Big mines lay open upon the ground. Formations lay engraved across different areas, infusing mana into the metals to increase their grade for harvesting. Large smelters toiled constantly to create iron.

Spindly, regal homes spiralled up the main pillars that connected the different floors and supported them, intermixed with blocky iron homes.

Machinery being worked on, made, or operating was everywhere, feeding the Alvan smithing machine.

They rose through the city and into the compressed stone floor that separated it from the floor above.

"Arriving at Tanaka Station," the train driver informed them. People shuffled to the doors.

Whistles called out, and the train shuddered, rising to a station and locking in place.

Erik and Rugrat moved with the press of people. They spread out, heading for stairs, exiting the station, or finding connections. Erik followed a familiar route, signs for the inter-city-floor express lines.

"Come on." He picked up his pace, seeing their train waiting at its platform. A cargo carriage was being loaded with crates. They jumped onto the train, finding seats.

"Time marches on." Erik snorted.

"What you mean?"

"Mean how we have a train system across all of Alva, like New York or London or something." Erik tilted his chin to their fellow riders. "Look, they're already used to it. Just a normality now."

A whistle blew out, people picking up their pace to make it to the train.

The doors closed, and the train rocked as it moved away from the platform.

No one was scared or confused by the jolting anymore. A father was trying to corral his two youngest into their seats.

"Been six months since we made it back from the Violet Sky Realm."

"Momma got elected as Mayor, we took out every base that the Black Phoenix Clan operated out of, and eliminated any remaining groups that attacked Vuzgal or Alva," Rugrat said.

"But we haven't tracked down their main fleet—yet." Erik ground his jaw. "*Eternus*, the ship that attacked us at Vuzgal, is still out there. Until we take out that ship and the fleet, it'll hang over our heads."

The train slowed to a stop with a jolt. The doors opened.

They stepped off, taking the stairs up to the city floor. Alva city spread around them.

Erik walked briskly down the sidewalk, weaving between merchants, workers, and the people of Alva. The living floor buzzed with an energy that he had only felt in some of the largest cities on Earth. People smiled and nodded, but kept on their path, determination in every step.

"You know we could just teleport down there?" Rugrat muttered as they slowed for a carriage and moved on with the press of people after it.

"Need to get my steps in, and we teleport all the time. When do we actually get to *see* Alva?" Erik kept his voice low as they wove through people. With some different clothing and a little stealth spell, no one paid the two emperors any more attention than any other person on the sidewalk.

"Drive the truck, not the body."

"It's walking, not like we're going on a ruck march." Erik rolled his eyes as the road ahead opened.

He slowed upon reaching the large main road that cut through Alva, all the way to Alva's gate—wide open to the First Realm. It had come to replace the tunnel bored through the hidden nation's mountain.

The Sha ship hulls had been transformed and landed along the main road outside, a testament to Alva's power and a warning to their would-be enemies. The ship's cores had been removed for Delfina and the air-force's newest project.

Statues lined the median in the road, wearing clothes from all walks of life. They each captured the determination of Alvans, stepping forward toward the tunnel entrance.

Erik saw the Alvans that had risen from the destruction of the outer mountain wall, rising to meet the sects that attacked their home. Gardeners, alchemists, teachers, medics, soldiers, mothers, fathers, brothers, and sisters. It was not their duty, but they stood and rose to defend Alva, to defend their home.

Erik cleared his throat, tightening with memories, the noise gruff to his ears. He glanced around, checking if anyone had noticed him pausing. Pulling his shoulders back, he stepped forward, his footsteps regaining their speed.

"Doesn't feel like the same city it did on that day," Rugrat said.

Erik rubbed his chest, phantom pain. "Alva certainly knows how to make a statement."

Rugrat snorted. "You can say that again. Though getting turned into dungeon core shrapnel catchers wasn't too fun." His voice dipped. "But we learned a lot from it."

Erik caught his eyes, sharing a look that connected the two of them deeper than many blood brothers.

He patted Rugrat's shoulder and nodded. "Fuck, we've been through a lot together."

"Known you too damn long."

They chuckled. Erik shook his head and turned to the main road, and the carriages entering and exiting the gates. Towers reached up to the ceiling, while skylights cut through the mountain above to let in sunlight between the crystalline web of the mana storage formation.

He looked around at the buildings that had been replaced or repaired, the rubble and debris long-since cleared, and the roads smoothed from the impacts and craters that had been there before.

"Erik, it's Elan. We've just received a report from our operators in the field. We found the Black Phoenix Clan's fleet. I contacted Brigadier General Kanoa, Admiral Dujardin, and Commander Glosil. They're on their way, as well as our agent on the ground."

Erik and Rugrat looked at one another, then looked up.

"Egbert!"

Light surrounded them.

Erik, Rugrat, Major General Kanoa of the combat wings, Commander Glosil of Alva's military, Admiral Dujardin of the Air fleets, and Director Elan of Alva's Intelligence Department blinked the light out of their eyes.

Aureus, one of Elan's intelligence officers, and Earthers, appeared in the meeting room. "Sir." He nodded to Elan, raising an eyebrow in question.

"At ease. Treat this as your de-briefing."

"Yes, sir." Aureus gathered himself quickly as the others took their seats. "Approximately three days ago, me and my partner Agent Sage were following up on a lead in the Seventh Realm—a group purchasing supplies in bulk and picking them up from a smaller materials trader. It seemed normal, but several traders were selling a small but steady stream of goods. We noticed a pattern. Every two days, a group would gather supplies from several traders and disappear out into the volcanic wastes of Kriva. They were different groups each time, but it was constant and the materials, when added together, were a lot." Aureus coughed and pulled out a water bottle, drinking from it.

"We called in the support of some other agents and watched the traders that had done deals with the group before. The group showed up yesterday, and they were actively trying to hide their appearances. Too hard for it to be normal and they were on alert, using several detection and stealth spells. We followed them out into the wastes. They were using trap and alarm spells that made it impossible to follow them without being detected.

"We swept the area instead, looking for signs of ships. The area is filled with fire, earth, and water attributed mana." Aureus shook his head. "We couldn't find any traces, but Sage came up with the idea to talk to people at the local mission hall. While the wastes are inhospitable, there are several areas where people might be able to stay comfortably. Three of them are large enough to house several ships." Aureus looked at the men in the room and tried to hide his grin as he pulled out an observation formation and placed it on the table.

The runes glowed, revealing a picture of a lake with a small island off to one side with several warships docked nose first.

"One cruiser, five destroyers, seven frigates and fifteen corvettes, each of the Black Phoenix Clan design. This is the Yori Caldera, deep in the Kriva range." Aureus tapped the formation and it changed to show a topographical map.

"Mountains create a rugged landscape around the caldera as the mana in the area creates a chaotic fog through the range. Corvettes patrol the caldera and there were several forces on flying mounts patrolling further afield and holding position in observation posts."

"What's a caldera?" Rugrat asked.

"A volcano that erupted so fast and hard that the top of it collapsed into its magma chamber, leaving a sizable crater," Kanoa said. "Growing up on an Archipelago made from volcanoes, you learn a thing or two." He shrugged.

"Where are your partner and the other agents?"

"They've taken up positions around the caldera as best as possible and created a network of sound transmission devices to communicate with our people in Kriva city. The Black Phoenix Clan ships remain inside the caldera."

Erik leaned forward on the desk. "I'll be the first to say that you and your people have done some damn good work. Now we just need to kick these bastards out of the air." He shifted his gaze to the leaders of the army, navy, and air force.

"It's a sizable force. If we want to cut them off, we'll have to field our own fleet," Edmond said.

"The agents that are on the ground, they know how to do a call-in for fire?" Kanoa asked.

Aureus stood at parade rest. "Yes, sir."

"Good, then we can pound them from a distance. If I were them, I would have spies watching every totem around the range. As soon as we show up, they're going to know we're there."

"We can teleport into the area, then accelerate at best speed for the caldera, deploy the air wings for long range bombing, and put our rail cannons to use, hitting the ships that are docked within the caldera at range before they even see us." Edmond said, mirroring Kanoa's thoughts.

"Right." Glosil's brows pinched together. "How long until you're ready to move? Every minute our agents are watching them is a minute that they could find them."

"Forty minutes. All ships are loaded with munitions." Edmond grimaced, his eyes sliding to Erik and Rugrat. "Though we have another problem."

"Captains," Erik said.

"We're training people to control the dungeon cores, but right now, well, there's about forty undergoing training. The ex-Sha captains were trained to fight with the old ship design, with broadsides and sails, not wings, turrets and missiles. The Alvan captains are just learning how to use the dungeon cores."

"Do you have a solution?"

"Erik and Rugrat have the ability to do both. I suggest we have them as our cruiser captains, then we can have the chief designer Delfina, Egbert, formations masters Qin Silaz and Julilah and myself manning our destroyers. The frigates are easier, being missile boats, and smaller, so they're much more manageable. I would suggest sending the corvettes in with the fighters and bombers to add to their punch. They're the fastest warships we have."

Glosil looked over at Erik and Rugrat.

"Just tell us where you need us."

"If the airships a-rockin' don't come a-knockin'!" Rugrat grinned.

"Admiral Edmond, I will leave this under your command. Kanoa, support him as required. Aureus, you will go with the fleet to act as our liaison with your agents on the ground." Glosil rose amongst the nods.

"We have work to be done. All leave is now cancelled. Let's be done with the Black Phoenix Clan once and for all."

The others rose from their seats.

"Yes, sir," Kanoa and Edmond acknowledged, saluting and turning to one another.

"Looks like we're invading the Seventh Realm. Change of pace," Rugrat said as he followed Erik to the door.

Erik walked onto the bridge of the cruiser *Eagle,* which was lightly bobbing on its iceberg dock around the water floor's airship docks. He took in the arrow-shaped room. To the left side were communications and sensors, at the front was flight control, and to the right weapons. Back from the pits was a raised command platform and his target, mirroring the flat arrow design of the room.

"Officer on deck!" Harrod's voice boomed through the area. The bridge crew rose from their seats in the pits, coming to attention and turning to the starboard door Erik had walked in through.

He returned Harrod's salute from the command platform and continued on his path.

"At ease. From now on, command your stations no matter if there is a new officer on the deck or not," Erik said as everyone returned to their seats. Harrod joined him at the command platform.

Erik lowered his voice. "You're looking rather clean."

"Stores told me I would have to start paying for my uniforms if I kept using them in my off hours experiments. Delfina secured me some coveralls." Harrod grinned. "Brilliant things. They're fire resistant and they have some formations added in for greater protection."

Harrod was one of Edmond's earliest friends and the chief innovator for the Sha clans. Since joining with Alva, he'd found a place working alongside Taran, Qin, Delfina, and Julilah. While he was a great innovator, there was a reason his body tempering was one of the highest in Alva. He'd been boiled, burned, and beaten up every way physically and magically that a man could. He was a mountain of a man, even larger than Rugrat.

"How are we looking?" Erik glanced to the pits, watching people new to their positions just a few short months ago, now running like a well-oiled machine.

"All stores are in place and ready. I had the crews run checks on all systems. Greens across the board. We're ready to depart."

"Good, we just finished four days of testing. Now we get the real thing to check they remember everything." Erik raised his voice, sure it would be heard by the crew, and passed on faster than he could send out a broadcast.

He moved closer to Harrod so others wouldn't hear him. "What's the feel of the crew themselves?"

"Eager. They've been training for this for months. We've had live fire drills, but this is the first time with a real target." Harrod's voice dipped lower, losing some of that eager edge. "They want to get some payback for Vuzgal and the attack on Alva."

"Do you think it'll be a problem? I want them focused on their tasks, not on revenge."

"No, there are enough veterans among them to give them an iron spine and show them how to act. They're channeling that eagerness as professionals. Everything I've thrown at them, they've completed faster and to a higher standard than in training."

Erik raised an eyebrow. "I feel like you might adjust their training in the future."

"Of course, Captain." Harrod grinned.

"How is the rest of the fleet looking?"

Harrod raised his voice. "Comms, status on the rest of the fleet."

A young woman turned her seat around. "The cruiser *Reliant*, destroyers *Vuzgal*, the *Tan Xue, Guerre a Mort, Independence, Stalwart*, frigates *Boomtown, Spear, Trident, Golden Opportunity, Javelin, Loyalty and Dart* all report full readiness, awaiting final crew to return. All corvettes are fully crewed and ready to deploy."

"Contact Admiral Dujardin aboard *Reliant* and inform him we're ready as well," Erik said.

"Yes, sir." She rotated back to her station, reviewing information coming in through her communications personnel.

Erik's gaze ran across the main screens that took up all three walls. To the left, there was a map of the ship broken into compartments. The ship was shaped like a lambda wing with one forward ten centimeter wide, ten meter long three rail cannon turret and two more raised and back, repeated on the underside. Missile hatches lay under the armor of the craft, while rocket nozzles lay in alcoves under and behind the warship, with large air scoops built into the frame. Each section was dotted in multiples around the massive warship: engineering, turret operators… Missile reloaders was labeled green.

A glance to the middle screen showed a live view from the front of the warship, as if they were looking out of the nose instead of safely entombed at the center of the vessel. The *Eagle* bobbed on the massive, flattened iceberg she called a landing pad. Other completed ships lie around her. The destroyers, laid out in the same manner as the cruisers, but smaller. The frigates festooned with missile hatches and corvettes with their bomb doors, lighter turrets, and hard mounted railguns in their wings.

The right-most screen showed a map of the area around the cruiser. The fleet in their berths and the docks where they had been built were filled with ships in different stages of completion, from nearly finished corvettes to the battleship behemoths.

"Admiral Dujardin requests we get in the air as soon as possible and to use the King's Hill Totem," the communications officer called out.

Erik rested his hand on the dungeon core built into the armrest of his seat. Formations as big as a dinner plate to the size of a small car rotated and turned into position, power flowing through them as the ship's systems were brought to full readiness.

He activated a formation to carry his voice across the ship. "All personnel brace for lift and teleportation." He cut the formation. "Helm, make it so."

All around *Eagle,* Alva's fleet engaged their flight formations, creating waves and throwing up water spray.

"Aye-aye, sir."

Tattoos in the metal skin glowed as the *Eagle* the formations and thrusters pushing its landing pad downwards, creating a divot in the water as it rose vertically.

Erik breathed deep, feeling the power thrumming through the decking, running through the ship like blood through the body. His own mana channels resonated with its power, willing him to bend it to his will.

Ships disappeared all around them as the monstrosity of weapons, armor and wings that was the *Eagle* retracted its landing gear.

"Teleporting." Egbert's voice rang through the ship.

Light surrounded the ship. King's Hill stretched under the cruiser as the light dissipated, the Alva fleet now all in position.

Erik's sound transmission device chirped. "All captains, this is Admiral Dujardin. Make weapons ready. Teleportation in three minutes. Once we're through the totem, go for rocket acceleration on heading two-seven-zero. Admiral Dujardin out."

Each section carried out their tasks with drilled proficiency.

Erik knew that the next time they carried out their tasks, they could be in combat. He glanced over King's Hill. It had grown ever larger, with wood buildings being replaced with magically extruded stone. Its roads widened to support the increased commerce from across the realms. Gathering formations built into towers glowed, focusing and increasing the mana density closer to the heart of the Beast Mountain Range.

He couldn't see the edge of the Beast Mountain Range, or the farmlands beyond. All part of the Alvan nation.

"Teleporting in ten seconds," Helm called out.

"All hands brace, brace, brace." Communications rang through the hull.

The First Realm disappeared, and the twenty-four-warship strong fleet appeared in the Seventh Realm, above Kriva City.

"Turning on heading two-seven-zero." Eagle pivoted with the rest of the fleet in a careful dance.

Aerial wings in their Sparrows shot out from the warships, turning away on their heading. The corvettes, much more agile than the larger ships, moved to support them.

"We are being contacted by the Kriva City officials," communications said.

"They're scrambling warships and aiming weapons," sensors said beside her.

Erik noticed the city turrets turning and their barrels elevating.

"Good thing we're not sticking around long. Weapons, how are we looking for firing solutions?"

"We're out of range still, sir. Turrets are shifting to pre-planned altitudes and latitudes," Weapons said.

Erik nodded. "Understood."

"Accelerating." Helm's word kicked as formations turned and power routed through different sections of the ship. Fuel was injected into the rocket engines, creating a cone of force.

"And... we're flying." The helm's sense of wonder made Erik try to hide his grin.

"I read the math, but damn, hearing that they would stay aloft just going forward, I didn't think it was possible," Harrod whispered.

"Maintain our position in the formation. Helm, time till we are in weapons range?" Erik called out.

"One minute for missiles, eight for guns, Captain!"

"Very well. I want the turrets to fire from the bow backward. Offset their timing so we know what they're hitting."

"Aye-aye, Captain."

Erik settled into his chair, eyes darting between the different views on the walls. The dungeon core under his hand thrummed with power, mana gathering formations and air scoops working together as they piled on the speed.

*Eagle* and *Reliant* were in the middle of the formation, the *Eagle* forward of *Reliant*. The frigates around them interspersed with the destroyers. The corvettes and all their Sparrow wings were broken into five formations with three corvettes at their center, using their smaller mass and greater speeds to surge ahead, gaining distance with every second. He fought to keep his hand from balling into a fist, eyes flicking to the area's map on the wall.

He turned to Harrod. "How are we looking?"

"Everything is going smoothly. Teams are working well together, like an oiled gear, as you say."

"Thirty seconds until we're in range," weapons called out.

There was a slowness to the air, a weight between his shoulders as muscles bunched, ready for the pounce, the attack. He ran through plans and thoughts and actions even while knowing that there would only be time to act and react. He'd done it tens, maybe hundreds of times before. He wished that he didn't know that they were about to get into a fight. He hated the fucking wait.

"All ships, fire one salvo missile on my mark." Dujardin's voice rolled across the bridge.

*Here we go.* Erik's stomach dropped as calmness spread. It was time to roll the dice.

"Mark."

Hatches along the underside of the wings and on the back of the main fuselage opened with the flare of formation-enhanced rockets, covering the warships in plumes of smoke, leaving streaks across the sky as each warship created a swarm of missiles along their target path.

"All ships, fire missiles as you finish loading. Captains, you have fire control. Dujardin out."

"Weapons, time to reload?"

"Two minutes until complete."

"Good work, weapons. Fire once we're fully reloaded." Erik watched the streaking lines across the map, racing between fleets, crossing the nearly two hundred kilometers in between. The minutes slid by.

"We're connected to an observation orb!" sensors said.

Every eye snapped to the close-up view of the caldera. Warships were in various states of powering up and rising from the lake and island below.

The ships with faster reload times released their second salvo. The cruisers were nearly last.

"Second salvo away! Thirty seconds for first salvo impact," weapons said.

It took every ounce of self control to not learn forward and bounce his knee before lights bloomed on the screen.

"Impacts!"

Missiles dipped into the caldera, rushing to meet the Black Phoenix Warships. A corvette circling the caldera was turned into a spray of metal and wood. Other missiles sought out the larger warships, hitting a destroyer and taking out a part of its bow before barriers were interposed, their spherical shapes lighting up with impacts.

Attack spells shot out to meet the missiles, destroying some as barriers began to fail, secondaries taking over on the larger ships. Corvettes without backup barriers were torn apart by missile after missile tearing into them.

*There you go, you bastards.* Erik worked his jaw as ships reloaded and fired, offsetting their missile to create a constant screen arriving at the caldera.

Corvettes used their speed to get away from the attacks while the larger ships tried to coordinate their fire as their barriers buckled and weakened.

A frigate's final barrier popped and collapsed. Missiles hit the ship, and it dipped under the attacks, pushed back in the air. It stabilized before a new flight of missiles arrived. They must have struck a mana magazine as the ship went up in a cascade of explosions, chunks of the ship raining down into the waters below.

"Bring turrets to bear onto target. Let me know once we're in range."

"Aye-aye sir." Weapons said.

The super-heavy turrets rotated onto the target, gaining elevation.

"We're in range, Captain!"

"Thank you, weapons. Rolling barrage from the forward turret. Fire!"

*Eagle* shuddered. Her decking rumbled as her spine and belly's forward turrets fired, the formations lighting up her barrel. A light stain burned into his retina. Formations and rocket engines fired in concert, arresting the recoil of the cannons and keeping the warship stable.

Erik's body cultivation kept him standing from the forces imparted through the ship.

Heart pounding in his ears and through his chest like a wild stallion, the side-by-side dual three-rail cannon turrets fired, riding the wave of force the formations and rockets kicked in to cancel them out again, jostling the crew as if on a subway train coming into the station.

Smoke flew over the warship, blown clear as the first turret's barrels were lowered and began the process of reloading.

"One minute to splash."

"Well, hell, weapons! I'm excited to see what kind of impression you make on our recipients."

"Me too, sir. Me too." The weapons officer laughed out loud. A few others choked down their own laughter.

He *heard* the *Reliant's* guns firing, even entombed inside several reinforced decks.

Guns and missile tubes were reloaded, firing in controlled concert. Erik caught Harrod frowning, pursing his lips at the images on the main screen. He seemed distracted.

Erik moved closer, lowering his voice. "Something wrong?"

"No sir, it's just… odd. Whenever we fought the Black Phoenix Clan, we were always able to see them using different spells and spyglasses, but they could see us, too. It's always been close quarters and a terrifying battle. Now, I can *see* them through this orb, but we're tens of kilometers away, and it's taking minutes for our attacks to land instead of seeing it in seconds."

"Modern warfare just means we can hit them from further away. Though they're getting smart to us already."

The BPC ships were throwing out massive spells and working together to cover one another from the salvos.

The cruiser's shells smashed through the Black Phoenix barriers like they were soap bubbles. A destroyer staggered under three shell hits, breaking the ship into two sections. It crashed against the side of the caldera and rolled into the waters below.

An unlucky corvette met one of the cruiser's shells and was thrown through the air, crashing into the waters below.

It would have been beautiful if not for the deadliness of it all. The flash of spells and mana cannons met shells and missiles, the forces throwing the water into chaos, coloring shields and smashing into ships.

Wood and stone, mana cannons, entire sections of warships crashed into the waters that filled the caldera, sending up white plumes. Ships, unable to remain aloft, plunged into the blue depths.

"BPC Fleet One is all airborne. They're accelerating away from the caldera."

"Thank you, sensors. I expect the admiral will have a course adjust for us shortly. Harrod, do you have an update for me?"

Harrod cleared his throat. "Enemy ships have taken significant damage, except for their corvettes, of which they have only lost five. All others are fully operational. Scratch two frigates and three destroyers. Their cruiser has taken several hits, but it is still operational."

"Understood."

"Captain, communication from the admiral. He wishes for the fleet to intercept with BPC One."

"Thank you, comms. Helm, make it so."

Erik watched the observation orb feed as several ships' salvos hit the running fleet. This was where they would end the fight with the Black Phoenix

Clan, and in such a way that they would never again be a threat to Alva.

"Forward corvette and fighter screen has made contact with BPC One. We have a visual."

The observation orb screen changed to a vantage point over the *Eagle*.

Smoke puffed around the Alvan corvettes, firing their smaller turrets and missiles. In short range, the BPC ships had little room or time to dodge.

"BPC One's corvettes are breaking away from the fleet to attack our forward force."

The corvettes and air wings broke apart and dove, the enemy ships attacking where they had been moments before, fighting to try to bring them back onto target.

The Sparrows came down nearly vertically with the sun above them, blinding BPC mages, trying to hit them. The Sparrows sliced through the barriers, releasing their bombs.

Corvettes bloomed as the Sparrow's bombs struck, tearing apart decking, staggering, and breaking corvettes, sending them tumbling below.

Sparrows leveled off, their speed carrying them out of battle as they circled around.

The Alvan corvettes left the remains of the BPC corvettes little room to recover, coming in on a gliding path past the formation. Their underside cannons peppered the enemy ships, tearing through barriers and holing hulls.

Missiles impacted, breaking the back of the BPC screen as corvettes followed their fellows to the ground below.

Few of the Alvan corvettes showed signs of damage. Some had blackened marks on their hull, or a breach in various places. The dungeon core would repair it. It was as one-sided of a fight as Erik had ever seen. He watched, hollow and detached from the destruction. Destroying the Black Phoenix Clan didn't give him satisfaction. It was something that had to be done.

"All right, I think that they should be able to see the futility of fighting on." Erik let out a breath through his nose and raised his voice. "Comms, put me on broadcast."

"Yes, Captain, you are live." The bridge grew silent.

"This is Emperor Erik West, of the Alvan Empire." *God that still feels weird.* "Power down your cannons, drive formations, and lower your mana barriers. There is no need to die today. One way or another, our fight will end this day. Surrender and you will be reunited with the others of your clan that we have captured already. Do not, and we will be forced to destroy your remaining ships and hunt you down."

He pressed the transmit button, cutting him off.

Several of the Black Phoenix ships opened, revealing the Phoenix breath cannons that ran the length of their ships.

They fired. Corvettes scrambled, evading the worst hits, barriers coloring as they moved too fast for the BPC ships to follow.

Erik sighed. "Very well. Weapons, target that cruiser."

Phoenix Cannons fired on the *Eagle,* causing it to shudder under the impacts that traced lines along their barriers as helm brought them out of the Phoenix Cannons' sights.

"Good work on those evasive maneuvers, helm. Saving me a few mana stones."

"We're here to save, sir."

Erik barely held back his grin as a few snorts broke free. The helmsman stiffened in realization.

"Steadying," helm said in his most professional voice.

"Firing," weapons called out. *Eagle's* turrets returned fire. Its barriers started to crumble, two shells punching into the ship's skin, causing it to lurch.

"Good hits on the BPC Cruiser! Mages are attacking," weapons called out.

Spell formations spread across the forward section of *Eagle* as other Alvan turrets punched holes in the cruiser.

His earpiece chirped. "All captains, slow to glide speed," Dujardin ordered.

The spell formations across *Eagle* discharged, chaotic lances of light twisted through the sky, drilling and tearing apart the cruiser's outer skin, warping it and diving deep inside as explosions rippled through the ship.

*Reliant's* turrets punched holes through the ship.

"Sweet hell," Harrod said.

Sky was visible through the cruiser. Formations shuddered barely keeping the ship airborne.

"Full salvo," weapons said.

Every gun on the *Eagle* fired as one, making Erik sway.

The shells tore the cruiser into several sections. Explosions rippled through different parts as they crashed into the mountains below.

"Changing targets," weapons called out.

The destroyer and frigate screen that had been bitterly fighting it out with the BPC ships, three with barriers down and minor hull damage, paused as a silence fell over the battle-space.

"They're surrendering!" Sensors about near jumped from his seat. "They're powering down and landing!"

BPC ships barriers flickered out of existence as the ships descended for the mountain range. They'd barely gotten out of the caldera.

# 3
# Avegaaren Academy of the Ninth Realm

Rugrat checked the bag for the second time.

Erik opened his door. They both had their own apartments, but chose to stay at Momma's house still. "What are you grinning about? You ready?"

"Excited to get on the road. Just finishing up with this bag. I'll be down in a minute."

"All right, ya slow bastard." Erik smiled, leaving the door open.

"You think that Storbon and Delilah...?" Rugrat's words holding him there.

"Hell if I know. They're interested in one another, around the same age, so why the hell not?" Erik shrugged in the doorway as Rugrat did up the last strap.

"Should we do anything?"

"Pfft, we'll screw things up more than we'll help. Now hurry up!" Erik headed down the stairs.

"I think that might have been the most expensive trip I have ever taken," Erik muttered to Rugrat as their guide raised one of the celestial mana stones they'd given them in payment and disappeared in another flash of light.

Erik took a moment to examine the defenses around the totem. It appeared to be a welcoming courtyard garden. Firing slits and formations had been carved into the walls, enhancing it visually, instead of it looking like the utilitarian formations stamped into some of the Alvan creations.

The effort that had gone into the make a defensive work look like a garden must've been monumental.

"Yeah, just burning the mana stones."

"Something on your mind?" Erik asked. "Anything wrong?"

"No, no, don't worry about it. Just got to get my head clear, y'know?"

"Sure. Well, you need anything, I'm here, dude."

"I know." Rugrat nodded and gave a forced smile.

Erik patted him on the shoulder, and they headed towards the ornate metal weaved gates. "Think we should ask who their crafter is? They've weaved working formations into the defenses like an art form."

"Blending beauty and destruction together. Reminds me of some of the buildings in Kushan and the Under City."

"Doesn't look like Alva, so Elven?"

"In parts. The structure looks Gnomish, from what I've seen."

They walked up to the statues waiting at the entrance. A human guard stood, stretching in his booth.

"All the statues are golems as well." Rugrat muttered. "Place is a death trap."

Erik heard the appreciation in his voice.

"Are you looking to head to the cities, academy trials, or just looking for tutoring?" the guard called out as they approached.

"We're looking to enter the academy."

"You've been to the Third Realm?"

"We have." *A long time ago now.*

"Ninth Realm is just like that. There's no fighting here unless it's sanctioned. Treat the whole realm as one big city and you'll be just fine. Just remember the advice your Association gave you. Once you're through the gates, you'll see a blue, purple, and yellow line on the ground. The purple line will take you to registration. Blue is for the city, and yellow is for the Mission Hall."

"Thanks," Erik said.

The guard nodded and went back to his seat. "Good luck!"

Erik and Rugrat walked through the totem defenses and found themselves looking at the clouds beyond. The lines on the road led to the other four corners of the floating island.

"Well, this is new." Erik tried to peek over the side, clouds hanging low over head. "A floating totem island."

"A new realm, new things to discover."

They followed the purple line to a doorway entwined with runes. Around it were clouds, but through it, Erik could see a large open area with other glowing doorways.

"Huh, must be an active teleportation portal connected to one destination, powered all the time," Rugrat said and walked through. He turned around on the other side of the doorway, still speaking, but Erik couldn't hear him.

Erik stepped through. "What was that? Couldn't hear you."

"I was right," Rugrat smiled as they surveyed the spacious hall made of obsidian. Floating gems filled the room with a soft light. Portals ringed the walls near them, people stepped through and moved to join a line before booths before twin open doors.

"Registration?" Erik shrugged.

A family hugged their daughter before she stepped to a booth. They moved off to another portal, leaving the hall.

Formations and runes ran through the wall the main doorway was inset into. Four statues, Human, Gnome, Elven, and Demi-Human, stood beyond the booths and towered between them and the door, judging those that passed between them.

"Golems?"

"Golems," Rugrat agreed.

"Big fucking stone robot."

They joined the line after several minutes of walking. There were just a few dozen people ahead of them. The majority were human, but there was one Elf, seven Demi-humans with different heritages, and two *gnomes*.

Erik tried not to stare, but he couldn't help himself. The gnomes were shorter than most people, their working clothes covered in various magical tools. Like most things known and unseen, Erik got used to it after he'd taken a good look.

Families and groups passed on their last words of support, heading through portals to get seats to watch their admission fight and cheer them on.

Erik caught people looking at them, talking to one another, speculating on something.

They got closer to the booth, those ahead and behind losing their entourage.

"They're wondering what Association you're from and why you don't have any supporters," a girl behind them said with a nervous smile.

"Oh." Erik smiled and nodded.

"You look like a smith, and you look like an alchemist, but... Hmm... Blue Lotus?"

"Guess we're elders there," Erik said.

"Heh, I almost forgot. Been a while since I used that emblem." Rugrat held his chin. "Don't trust them after Vuzgal much, though."

Erik grunted, fighting the urge to spit.

The girl looked at them, perplexed. Erik hoped that not being from an Association wouldn't be a problem.

"What about you? Which Association are you from?" Erik asked.

"The Fighter's Association, of course." She smiled. "Forty-three years of training. Been a tough road."

*Forty-three?* She looked like she was in her early twenties.

She laughed, mistaking their expressions. "I know I'm rather young, but there are some true prodigies, like Rekha Bhettan, the Imperium head's only Disciple. I hear that she can take on missions in the Tenth Realm already with her party. She's just thirty years old! Wild."

"Yeah." Erik smiled, not wanting to say anything to draw attention.

Several people joined the line behind them as they continued to move forward. Soon, it was the girl's turn.

"Good luck," Erik said as she was called up.

"Thanks, see you in there!"

Erik and Rugrat were called up next, each going to a separate booth.

An elderly grandpa looking man sat at the booth opposite Erik. "Association symbol?"

"I'm not part of an association," Erik said.

The older man frowned and raised an eyebrow. "Identification? Something to say who you are?"

"Uhh, I have this." Erik pulled out the four-star emblem that Eli'keen had given him.

The man stared at it.

*Crap.* "Uhh, I have this honorary Blue Lotus emblem too, not sure if that helps. Oh, and I've got an expert alchemist emblem. My teacher is a Master level alchemist from the Alchemist Association, but I'm not part of the association myself."

The man's eyebrows pinched together as he looked through the different emblems. He opened his mouth.

Erik cringe inwardly and held up his hand. "Wait. Wait, I have an invitation too. It came with the hero emblems. Uhh, what was that Elf's name? Eli'keen gave it to me." Erik searched through his storage rings.

The man raised a disdainful eyebrow.

"Where are you?" Erik fished around some more. Just as the man made to speak, he found the letter. "There it is."

The man stared at Erik as he took the letter. He looked at it lazily and paled upon seeing the imprinted seal.

Erik winced again, expecting an angry outburst. He looked away as the man opened and read the letter.

"Eli'keen. *The* Eli'keen? Deputy Head Eli'keen?" The man's voice was a bare whisper. He raised his head, patting away the sweat. "I-I, uhh, I am sorry. Yes, that is all quite all right." His sound transmission device went off with a burst of light. "Sorry about that." He cut it off, but it went off again. His eyes darted to his device, then to Erik. "I, uhh…"

"Take it if you want to," Erik said. *The team and this guy know of Eli'keen? Maybe Zen Hei wasn't over-exaggerating. Just who is he? Deputy head of what?*

The man talked on his sound transmission device, smiling and turning away as he got more irate. He turned his mouth into the microphone part of the device before putting it away and patting his brow.

"Don't worry. Your identities have been verified. Would you like to pick a student in the top one thousand to compete with?" the man said, indicating to a formation that showed different names and numbers.

"Uhh, who is the lowest ranked student in the school?" He didn't know what the standard of the students was, but with only ten thousand students who had to have passed the Eighth Realm. They weren't going to be weak.

"Rank ten thousand?" The man looked perplexed before schooling his features. "Are you sure? Once you're admitted, you can only fight ten people per week, and they have to be within fifty ranks of your own position. The higher your ranking, the greater the access to higher grade resources."

"Will I get less time with teachers or in the library?"

"No, but you could miss out on star grade level pills and concoctions," the man pressed.

Erik needed training, resources he could go to Alva for. He didn't know much about the school internally and didn't want to gain interest from others from day one.

"I'll fight number ten thousand, then please."

The man frowned and went back to turning formations on his booth's console. "Very well. Your opponent will be notified. Please take teleportation formation five."

"Thank you."

Erik met with Rugrat as they walked through the statues and toward the doors beyond that had teleportation formations with numbers above them.

"Your registration person give you a hard time?" Rugrat asked.

"Not really. That letter seemed to do the trick though."

"Ah, yeah, mine was thinking I was an imposter or something, muttering about how there was no way. Then called someone, and they went white as a sheet and processed everything. I'm fighting number nine thousand nine hundred and ninety-nine."

"I hope they're not as strong as the people we met at Kushan."

"Well, if we lose, we just need to wait a couple of months before we can challenge the registration again. If we get in, though, we can finally learn about what makes officers tick with their higher education."

"We're going to learn how to beat people up. I don't know how much higher education will be involved." Erik snorted.

"You got a point there. Don't think many places of *higher education* would let me in with my grades," Rugrat said.

"See you in there." Erik bumped fists with Rugrat and waved him off, heading to his own teleportation formation.

Erik stepped onto his pad. It activated and he appeared in a simple corridor. Doors lined both sides. A Demi-Human read from his clipboard in front of the teleportation formation.

The Demi-Human looked to have a Fu Manchu that dropped to his chest, but they were tentacles, and his eyes were indigo with star-like pupils. "Your challenger has accepted the fight. They will arrive in three hours to fight you. Head down the corridor to waiting room three. There's some equipment on the left if you want to prepare for the fight. Once the red light goes on, be ready to head up to the arena. Green light and the door will open. Got it?" He looked up.

"Yeah."

The Demi-Human nodded and looked back at the clipboard.

Erik read the numbers on the doors, passing the Demi-Human, whose skin shimmered like scales in the dim light.

The corridor was utilitarian. Sand covered the ground, and there were signs of where blades or fists had hit the walls. Promptly repaired, but the lighter colored materials remained.

The door to room three was open. Inside there was a meditation chamber, an open area for stretching, as well as a cultivation room, a couch, and a bed.

There was even a small garden in the corner with a water feature.

"Best damn waiting room I've been in. Still, hurry up and wait, though." Erik moved to the open area and started stretching to burn through the time.

Erik finished his last stretch as the room was bathed in red light. The door opposite the one he had entered through pulsed.

A section of the wall opened and a metal formation as big as a side plate pushed out.

"Please don the protective formation. It will measure your current defenses and protect you against lethal attacks from your opponent. All attacks are permitted within the arena. Please hold out your weapons and armor to be checked."

Erik pulled out his helmet and put it on his head. His vision expanded, dulling the bright light, and piercing through shadows.

He pulled out his rail rifle, tapping the toe of his boot against the ground.

"Have you selected your weapons and armor for the fight? Additional weapons and items will not be permitted into the arena."

"I have the gear I want to use."

"Very well."

He felt his skin prickle as a scan ran over him.

"Please apply the formation. You can adhere it to your chest or back."

"New toys." Erik grabbed the formation and put it on his back.

He stored his rifle away. *I'll pull it out as a last resort.* He wanted to test out just how strong the bottom ranker of Avegaaren was.

The light around the room turned green, and the door slid into the wall, revealing a ramp upwards.

"Feels like some gladiator movie." Erik grinned, shaking his body, and twisting to wake himself up. "Let's do this."

He jogged up the ramp, coming into the arena. The size of it struck him first. It was a kilometer wide, a full circle, and the ground was made of rough stone.

There was not one person in the thousands of surrounding stands.

Opposite Erik, a man teleported in through a formation. He had gold and red tattoo lines that ran down his forehead, around his eyes, and down his chin. He wore a casters robe without any head protection, making his scowl clear to Erik as he walked across the arena.

Stone rose around him, crushed sand-fine as the air distorted with heat.

Erik advanced warily towards him, circulating his mana and elements.

"Begin!" a voice called.

Erik jumped to his side out of instinct. Glass blades tore a line through where he had been standing, exploding, and releasing a fierce heat. Twin whips of shards, like a spine, tore through the floor.

He drew on his elements, his body changing as he rushed forward.

"Stay still, you rat. I don't have time to waste on Association fighters," the man spat.

Erik was hit from behind as the whip that had crashed into the ground reformed and struck him like a train.

His fire resistance saved him. He hit the ground and rolled and punched out with his fists, empowering his body, and smashing the shards of flame and sand. He destroyed those in his path, more filling the space in seconds.

His opponent compressed glass and stone together to form spears, turning around and shooting towards Erik.

He rolled to the side, feeling the spears slam into where he had been. The air crackled with mana. Erik extended the ground beneath his feet, throwing himself upward as he jumped, flinging himself to the side.

He compressed the mana around his body, cutting through the air. Blue flames shot from his hands and legs to increase speed.

A forest of spikes appeared around the pillar he had thrown himself up with.

The man removed his hands from behind his back. "You might have some skill. Let me test out some of what your school has so kindly taught me. Thank you for the dust." The ground cracked and exploded, turning into an expanding dust field so thick as to make it impossible to see through and five meters tall.

"Oh, fuck."

Glass shards shot out of the dust field like diamond rain, deadly and in the wrong direction.

Erik rolled, using his legs and arms like a sky diver. A plan formed in his mind. He didn't look forward as he sent out a blast of lightning, tearing apart glass shards and clearing a hole in the dust field. He threw himself to the side as glass appendages, like scorpion tails, lashed out at him.

Shards hit Erik in the side, the force of the blow causing them to explode and throw him sideways. Scorpion tails lashed out at him.

The dust cleared a path between Erik and the man above, who raised his hands. Erik sensed the mana streaking towards the mage, crushing another spell construct. He waited for his opening and reached out with the Earth Element, resonating with it.

The mage yelled. Erik threw himself to the side and *pulled* on the Earth element, breaking the mage's connection, throwing dust and glass everywhere. Erik cast silence on himself, disappearing among the cloud.

He moved erratically as meteors cut through the cloud, hitting where he had been.

"What? Where are you!"

Erik saw the world in a makeup of elements and mana. No cloud could obscure his vision.

He weaved through the smoke, coming in at an angle as the mage trying to take control over the dust and glass cloud.

*There*! Erik burst out of the dust, just meters from the man, whose smirk turned into a look of surprise. Channelling a meteor mid-cast, he tried to stop the casting. Erik drew in mana and elements through his body, illuminating him in yellow, red, and silver. He focused on his fist as he smashed it into the man's barrier. It went from clear to yellow, bronze, and then black as the man shot away, using spells to arrest his movement. Buzzers went off, ending the fight.

"What, no, that's—"

"Please step upon one of the teleportation formations," the same voice from inside the waiting room commanded them. A sound dampening field cutting off Erik's opponent.

The caster rushed forward, gathering a spell. A spider shaped golem shot out of the ground. Wrapping around the caster and forcibly cancelling his spell.

The caster's face paled with the spell backlash.

"Please step upon one of the nearby teleportation formations," the waiting room voice repeated.

*Must be a robot, or some Ten Realms version of it.*

Erik walked toward the nearest formation, drinking a stamina potion. The destruction around the arena was fading. A ripple ran through the ground and evidence of the fight disappeared entirely.

Erik clicked his tongue. "Going to need to do better." *What kind of freaks are there in Avegaaren if that was the weakest of them?*

The formation's light covered him as he started replaying the fight in his mind.

"You'll be back sooner than you think. Be like a vacation from this place," Kujo Hikokie said, trying to comfort his brother as they walked through the formation plaza.

Ujisuke sighed. "Easy for you to say. I have to wait four months before I can apply for another admission fight."

"You had him. Your spells and blade technique were on point. It was that weapon he used. Never seen anything like it before. At least you'll know how to deal with it in the future."

"The weapons and the arrow had their own formations, and they were layered with spells."

Ujisuke was several years younger than Hikokie, but he had made it into Avegaaren already, a prodigy of the Kujo family.

"Look, I'll keep an eye out for you. You have plenty to train on, and you won't even need to go to classes. I'm jealous," Hikokie said.

"Are you ready to depart?" a Proctor asked.

"Come on. Now you have someone to beat in the future. Make sure you train well," Hikokie said, hoping to calm his brother and not get him in trouble with the Proctor.

It took all Ujisuke's power of will to just sigh. "Look after yourself, brother. See you in four months."

Hikokie patted him on the shoulder as the Proctor guided him to the formation. They disappeared in light and Hikokie turned his eyes back to the two men, the one that had defeated his brother and the other that had defeated the glass mage.

He'd arrogantly declared that his sect was better than the Imperium. Like all the sects' rabble, he had lost his position as fast as he gained it.

Different groups in the realms sent people to Avegaaren to better themselves, but they were also hoping to take their teachings and pass it on to the rest of their people to create a power that could compete with the Associations.

They didn't care for the Ten Realms, just their own greed.

The glass mage had barely gotten into the academy, even with all of his sect's resources, and being the most promising fighter of the younger generation.

Hikokie looked at the two new students talking together and heading deeper into the academy. He pressed down his anger at the sight of the one that had defeated his brother. They didn't wear clan or sect symbols, or any association medallions or markers, either.

*I wonder where these two came from.*

# 4
## Trainer?

Erik shook his head. "These fights are on another level up here."

"Yeah, I wouldn't have won if not for my rifle. That kid was like a damn blender!"

Erik laughed, looking up at a signpost and pausing as Rugrat kept walking. "Looks like there's a fighting training area down this road."

"Don't want to check out our new accommodations?" Rugrat asked.

"Probably just some apartments. We just got here. Shouldn't we check out the place some?" Erik turned his head.

"I was expecting more than a 'welcome to Avegaaren' and then teleporting away. Like a map of the place, or how to sign up for classes, if there even are classes, and training places. That would've been nice."

At the end of the downtrodden street stood a square building with a sign hanging from it that read: combat training. It looked like poured concrete, with no doors in sight and leading down into darkness, like an elevator shaft. "I think we've taken a wrong turn. This place hasn't been cared for in some time."

Rugrat pressed a formation. It lit up and lights appeared in the descending tunnel as a rush of air rose out of the tunnel. A dented elevator came to a halt.

"I'm getting some serious missile silo vibes about this," Erik said.

"You too? Sweet. Let's go check it out." Rugrat grinned, raising his eyebrows comically.

"All right, but if this thing breaks, it's on you." They stepped onto the elevator and Rugrat turned another formation. It glowed. The elevator dropped. Erik grabbed onto a railing that came free as it arrested itself. His feet back on the ground, the elevator started to descend smoothly.

"Just needs some grease is all," Rugrat said, not even turning to see Erik's glare.

"Some grease? This is supposed to be the best school in all the Ten Realms, and their elevator is falling apart."

Rugrat sighed. "Hard to find the right help nowadays."

The elevator ground against something for several seconds before it clunked and kept going.

"I officially name this the shit chute. If you don't shit yourself making it down to the bottom, must be some kind of iron-blooded mother fucker."

"Guess that didn't come with your own metal blood tempering."

"Smartass."

Rugrat chuckled at his joke. The elevator reached its destination several minutes later, the doors opening most of the way.

"What the — Who's there?" A human man said, slurping around a mouthful of food.

Erik and Rugrat walked through a small corridor and into a reception area. It was immaculately cleaned and cared for. The reception took up the back wall, with sealed doors to the left and seats to the right and back of the room.

The man groaned and put down the noodles. "Who sent you?"

"Uh, is this the combat training area?" Erik asked.

"Oh? Uhh, so no one sent you?" His eyes narrowed.

"Nope," Rugrat said.

"Your elevator could use some work." Erik pointed back at the corridor.

"Elevator?" The man looked around, frowning, before shrugging. "Not sure what you mean. Anyway, you said that you were looking to train?"

"Yeah, we just joined the Academy. We want to work on our combat skills, if that's possible?"

"Certainly is. Uhh, head to training room one and two. The teleportation formation will take you to the training area. Oh, and wear one of those." Holding his noodle bowl in one hand, he leaned down behind the counter, taking out two emblems. He blew on them, coughing from the dust, and tossed them to Erik and Rugrat.

"Put that on. Safety measure. Hit those and you'll be teleported out of the dungeon."

"Thanks. What's your name?"

"Xun Liang at your service."

"Good meeting you, Xun Liang," Erik said.

Rugrat dipped his head as well.

"You will be teleported into a combat test so we can best understand your strengths and weaknesses. See where you need to develop and what is already developed. What are your names?"

"Erik West, and this here is Rugrat."

"Jimmy Rodriguez on any forms, though."

"Well, it is nice to meet you both. Have fun training!" He smiled and grabbed his chopsticks, waving them toward one of the two doors in the lobby, going back to eating and watching something on a seer stone.

"Thanks."

Erik and Rugrat walked past the empty desk. The door opened to reveal a corridor filled with formations.

"You know, I think they might have gone a little overkill with the formations," Erik muttered.

"You got the white spots in your eyes, too?"

"I think they're burned in by now. Though I might trust it more than that elevator. Say we try this out for a round or two and then head back up? Maybe we can get something out of this, and I'm interested to see how we do in this combat test." Erik rolled his shoulders and shifted around to loosen up his muscles.

"Sure thing."

Erik arrived in a wooded area with a fog that made it harder to see more than ten meters in any direction. The forest was alive with the calls and noises of wild beasts. Erik looked up but couldn't see through the foliage.

A roar preceded the humanoid creature that rushed out from the trees to greet Erik. It almost looked like a Behir, with horns sticking out of its humanoid head and body, but with markings that showed it was no human, like the black-silver teeth and claws that extended from his fingers.

"Fun." Erik dodged the creature's swipe. The wind imbued attack cut through the tree behind Erik and left eddies in the fog that drifted back together. Erik drew upon the elements and punched at the attacker.

The creature jumped away, then used a tree to propel itself at Erik.

Erik jumped forward with his punch, discharging it uselessly into where the creature had been, barely shifting the fog.

An attack hit him in the side and slammed him into a tree, ruffling some of its leaves. The tree was as tough as iron. *He cut through this?*

Erik faced the creature again, keeping the tree at his back. The creature roared, tearing mana from the world, and pouring it into his attack. The sonic attack hit Erik, his heels digging furrows into the ground as he hit the tree behind him, dislodging leaves and branches.

He used a blast of mana through his foot. The creature turned away from the mana bullet.

Erik stepped forward as the creature used the rotation to bring its claws at Erik.

The claws left bloody wounds on Erik's side and arm as he was launched to the side. He hit the ground and rolled, grinding his teeth as he turned around in the roots and vegetation to keep the creature in his sight. His wounds were already healing, but at a visibly painful pace.

The creature didn't wait. It charged forward. Erik drew upon the elements and punched out, missing the creature, and smashing through the tree as the creature jumped to another tree. It was getting faster. Erik's attacks were always a second or two behind.

The creature scraped off part of the tree it was jumping from and accelerated.

Erik drew his elements into his body, grunting from the wooden shards stuck in his arm. The creature lashed out with its claws.

Erik fought with his left hand as the shrapnel was expelled from his body.

The creature seemed to glide across the ground. Erik couldn't keep up with the speed, and his Expert grade clothes offered little protection. The creature's claws were cutting into his skin.

He got his right arm back into the fight. Throwing up stone spikes, he unleashed lightning, aiming for where the creature was heading. The lightning connected, sending the creature spinning and crashing into a tree.

*Gotcha.*

Erik wiped the blood from his face and moved closer to the creature. As a tombstone appeared, so did two new familiar howls.

"Ah shit." Erik turned to face where the noise came from.

"I thought I heard voices?" Weebla, an older gnome, yawned, pulling her comfy sweater around her. She wore fingerless gloves, and her hood was worn up and over her head.

"Some new people wandered in."

"You going to do anything but eat and watch the arena fights and combat rooms? Don't you have other things to do?"

"A mind rested is a mind ready to deal with life's problems."

"Rested? You sure you do *any* work with your new job? You come and hide in here most of the time. Are those my noodles?"

"I made enough for two and added more to them!" Xun Liang quickly pulled out another bowl, ladling in broth and making sure to give her plenty of meat and noodles.

"Hmmphf, good thing my cultivation is broken, or I'd kick your ass across the room!" The old gnome grumbled and accepted the bowl, sitting down next to him.

Xun Liang opened his mouth, sighed, and shook his head. Weebla ate from the bowl, watching the fights.

"They're pretty bad." He tilted his chin at the two views.

"You sent them into the training area? Already?" She stared at him. "Where is the layabout Xun Liang and who are you?"

"Hey, I do work from time to time!"

"Pfft."

*Crazy old gnome.*

"Ow!" He held his ear as she grabbed her chopsticks.

"You know what you did."

"Damn mind reader."

"Don't need to read minds to know what's going on in that empty space between your eyes. So, these two, why do they interest you?"

"Just joined the academy, don't know anything or else they wouldn't come here. Not Association anyway and they're *strong*. That one, Mana heart, and an Iron tempered body. That one there has Earth-level tempering and has opened his Five aperture heart."

"Plenty that jump ahead in their cultivations."

"Opened their fifteenth mana gate, tempered in all the elements up to their current stage, and not only that, tempered *fully*."

Weebla sat up. "Legendary resistances?"

"I'm not sure. Need to test them out. But look at them." Xun Liang waved his free hand. "*Aish,* they might be strong but they're like a child with a club, don't know how to use it. Mana wasted all over the place, enhancing his *entire* body. And this one is only using three or four different spells. Reliant on range only."

"There has to be more than their cultivations to interest you."

"They were nice."

Weebla raised an eyebrow.

"I'm just an attendant for a run-down training facility. Hey!" He raised a finger against Weebla's curling fist, ready for her lightning-fast pinching attack. "Through that and just arriving, being that strong, and not from the Associations, I thought they were amicable."

"There are nice people out there, you know, Xun Liang."

"Most of the strong people in the realm aren't. They've stepped over so many to reach their current position. Death and coldness lay behind them."

"These two have clearly fought before."

"But…" Xun Liang let out a breath in a rush of frustration as Erik was hit with a blast of wind. "Come on, can you not see that attack? Dodge it! *Ughh.*"

"Seems like they need a teacher to train them."

"Yeah, though it'll be a lot of work to teach them out of whatever wrong habits they've gained. Ugh, are they blocks of stone or people? There's no movement to them, none of the flow. At least Rugrat has movement techniques. Erik fights like a brawler. Does he even know how to fight with his fists? Just seems like he's taking the hits." Xun Liang scooping more noodles up and into his mouth as he looked at Weebla's smile. "Nhmhmm."

He shook his head vehemently, chewing rapidly to try to clear his mouth. She continued on, not giving him time to respond. "These bones are too old to teach nowadays. They'll need a good teacher." She smiled and ate from her bowl.

Xun Liang slumped, slowing his chewing, giving her a half-hearted glare. Damn those tasty noodles! Maybe he should eat in smaller bites.

He leaned forward, thinning his eyes in thought as he munched slower, watching every move Erik and Rugrat made. His eyes captured it all, eating by rote habit rather than conscious thought.

Xun Liang was waiting for them, standing between the teleportation formations, when they appeared in the teleportation room. Erik coughed, then groaned, picking himself up and looking over to the other sad sack in the room.

"You look how I feel," Erik said.

"One sexy beast?" Rugrat coughed and rolled over.

"Fuck." Erik groaned to standing. "Wasn't sure if that emblem was ever going to activate."

"Tha—" Erik spotted Xun Liang as he opened his mouth.

"Eh!" Xun Liang raised a finger, stopping Erik as he looked away. "What in the *hell* was all that? You two have the mana and you have the elements, but damn! You could compete with the strongest in the academy with those if you knew how to use them. Damn, you're about near useless."

Erik opened his mouth, but Xun Liang rolled on.

"You have no or little experience in the arts of hand-to-hand fighting, but you resort to it constantly. Rugrat, ugh, going to have to clean the blood out again. You've taken on the role of a ranged fighter, but your spells are a mish mash. Are you trying to slow your opponent or hurt them? Why do you insist on such powerful spells when smaller ones would help you? You have fought through life and death, but have little in the way of proper training, or you've had training in something else and haven't developed the skills you need for the Ten Realms yet. Oh, and let us *not* talk about mana and element usage!"

He slapped his forehead, looking at Erik. "Using *all* the elements in your body *all* the time... Use one element at a time, understand them. They are a part of your body. Don't just use it like, I don't know, a club maybe, but then that has a purpose, and you're throwing it around like fresh water in an ocean. That sounds pretty good. Should record that."

"Xun Liang," Erik said.

"Right, training. You two, *dodge!*"

The teleportation formations flashed, and they disappeared. He walked out back to his seat.

"You going to get the tea going?" Weebla asked, looking over her glasses. She wore a blanket in the office behind the reception counter that looked markedly homely.

"Ah, right, I'm on it." Xun Liang busied himself with the tea, watching the duo from the corner of his eye. Their moves were direct, killing moves, each delivered to end instead of wound. Their actions were simple—too simple. He could read them, but they had been trained on an instinctual level.

That kind of dedication was hard to find in young students, or in those that had been geniuses in their sects. *Give me the inept ones anytime, the ones who have to fight for every inch.* It wasn't about genius, but hard work.

A smile spread, their expressions betraying the cursing and murderous intent behind their eyes.

"Might be better to tell them more than to just dodge next time. Shouldn't be long now."

He had just sat down with his tea. Groaning, he stood and walked and walked to the teleportation formations as Erik appeared and ran down the hall.

Rugrat rolled out of the teleportation, a wound running down his arm, knitting together as he took off at a run as well.

Xun Liang twisted mana and element, grabbing them both and tossing him back into the center of the teleportation formation. "Dodge all the attacks you're faced with. Don't try to attack."

"We're dying out there," Rugrat yelled.

"Oh, come on. It's only flesh wounds." The white light of the teleportation formations cut off their curses as they were teleported back in. Xun Liang huffed; his tea floated into his hand.

"It's cold now," His shoulders slumped. *Maybe I should put the chair and viewing formation in front of the teleports?*

The chair, table, and viewing formation floated over as he sat down into the chair, the others arranging around him as he sipped his tea, watching the viewing formation.

"Oh, watch out. Gonna need a new tree now. Why are you... huh? That's an interesting way to use air."

Xun Liang clucked his tongue, crossing his legs as he watched.

Erik and Rugrat mixed their fighting together with dodging. The Telarri continued to come for them. As they ran, more would join the chase and the longer they took with their attacks, the more Telarri would arrive.

"Haven't even combined yet. What are you?" Xun Liang pressed his face to his hands, exhaling loudly before pushing his hands to his eyes. "Please tell me they're not."

He watched longer.

"No, yup, they are. Like some damn instant fire formation."

They teleported back, Rugrat ahead of Erik.

"What the hell are you doing with your domains?" he said, ignoring their groans. "Use your domain as if it's your nose or ears. Always active, always perceiving the world around you. You treat it like a light going on and off, using it only when you remember about it. Your domain is a sense above your other senses, one that detects the elements, the other that senses mana. Last more than twenty minutes without attacking the Telarri and I'll let you out."

He threw out two bags. Powder exploded over the duo, recovering their wounds and stamina before they teleported away.

"Twenty minutes? You're growing soft!" Weebla yelled from her room.

"Who said they were too old to teach?"

"I'm spry enough to tan your hide!"

Xun Liang mimicked her voice without daring to say it out loud and continued watching the duo.

"And stop mimicking me or I'll put *you* through a round of training!"

Xun Liang shuddered, watching his students.

*They look angry now.* He smiled as Rugrat used distance from the Telarri. Erik tried to dodge the first Telarri and was hit several times, leaving bloody wounds as he lashed out in pain or rage.

Still, he was tending to move himself *out* of the way of attacks now, instead of trying to take the Telarri on.

*Might be the pain, but pain can teach.*

"Erik, you're not a punching bag. Move more. Rugrat, I see that rifle one more time and I am liable to break it!"

They barely had time to recover as they disappeared again.

And so it went several times.

He made sure they were ready and sent them back in. They didn't even try to run anymore. A quick pointer here and there each time.

"Hmm, maybe they are workable."

"Reminds me of training you," Weebla said next to him.

Xun Liang ducked his head, turning to face her slowly. "Wear a bell or something!"

She smiled and walked back to her room. "You stubborn lot think you know everything when you come up here. Sometimes you just need to get thrown into a few trials to keep you on your toes. Get them to try to prove you wrong."

Erik had been punched, scratched, and wounded a dozen different ways. He rolled over with a groan, blood spilling on the teleportation formation as he raised himself to seating, the wounds closing. With a hiss, he grabbed his arm, which was bent at an unnatural angle, and moved it into place with a whimper. A flash of fusing spell and he stretched out his fingers, his strength returning as the pain receded.

He withdrew a stamina potion, chugging it down.

"Well, that was suitably gross." Xun Linag's face was pulled back into a series of wrinkles. They disappeared with a shake of his head as he held his hands behind his back. "Erik, dodging is more than just moving out of the way of an attack. You need to read what's coming for you. Focus on your domain. Rugrat, ughh, the trees are your friend. Why are you so focused on making a clear line of sight between you and the enemy? Domain! Stop turning around so damn much and maybe your ankles would stop spraining, hmm? Again!"

Erik arrived in the forest, again landing on his feet. At least he'd started to get that. Falling on his ass or in some other unorganized heap had gotten old. His eyes scanned for threats, wincing as Xun Liang's words rang through his head. He used his domain like a pulse, but there was so much information even in that short burst.

It was all so confusing, not replacing but adding a layer of complication he wasn't sure what to do with. Maintaining it constantly would just overwhelm him!

It wasn't like he was out of his body when he used his domain. His senses were everywhere, flipping his entire perspective. He had always been an observer, one point looking out upon the world. Now he was a big sphere, sensing everything inside and outside, through the air, the trees, the ground. He only knew where his body was by the mere fact it was leaking elements and mana all over the place.

He dismissed Xun Liang's orders, using the pulse instead to find his quarry before he could get ambushed. That was getting old fast.

*There you are.*

Erik jumped to the side as a Telarri appeared. Trees bent around it as the ground rippled with roots, snapping out at Erik. He pulsed his domain again, jumping out of the path of the attack as he enhanced his body with elements, touching the ground.

There was a sudden rush of air as a bush near his feet hardened and lashed out.

Erik burned the bush with the fire elements in his leg while ducking under the tree limb aimed at his head.

A root shot out of the ground for his neck. He side stepped, using a pulse of his domain to see the Telarri, and used a fire spell on its side. Spinning away, he landed on his feet and ran, his mind swimming as his domain showed the crater where he had been standing while his vision tried to organize what he was seeing with the domain's flood. He barely caught the Telarri rushing him.

Roots and limbs wrapped around the creature, using them as a second set of limbs. *Like Aziri and his water tentacles.*

In close, Erik reduced the area his domain stretched out to but pinged it constantly. Sometimes he saw the roots coming through the ground or the tree moving behind him. Sometimes he didn't try to compensate and increased the frequency of the pulses without losing his footing or where the hell he was.

He pressed down on his frustration, for every attack he dodged, two more slipped through his defense.

He increased the frequency of pulses, but he kept getting hit. What he was doing just wasn't working; it happened time and time again. He'd teleport in, get torn up by the Telarri until he returned to the training hall, where Xun Liang would glare at him, as if expecting better, and he'd be teleported back in, repeating the cycle.

*Damn you, Xun Liang!* He gritted his teeth, cursing the man who did nothing but sit on his ass and send them back into the fights as if he was some god given trainer.

His information was useless. Erik had disregarded most of it. It would only get him sent out quicker.

*Fine. I'll do what he says, right down to the letter to show him just how wrong he is. Then I can get on with my own damn training.*

He recounted everything that Xun Liang had said, his short snippets of information between bouts of pain, and started to follow it.

Several minutes later he lay battered and bruised on the teleportation pad, but he felt that he was at the edge of something, that things were starting to congeal.

Rugrat was already waiting for him.

"Shave off your motions, Erik. Use the space around you. Eventually, you will be able to twist and turn out of the way of the attacks. For now, try to read the elements, the mana, and your enemy's body language for their attacks. Eventually, you will not just see the body, you will understand the movement of their mana, the elements, reading their true intent. A spell, a punch, a kick, a feint, enhanced with fire, or water, or earth."

"Okay."

"Ah good, you aren't mute." Xun Liang smiled, and the forest appeared around Erik again.

And so it went on. Erik turned into a sponge, trying to forget everything he knew and accept Xun Liang's information. He had rare moments where things *flowed,* and he was so focused on what he had done right that he would mess up the next thing that happened.

"Baby steps forget the bad habits. Learn the new ones. You don't need to do it all in one go, just by degrees," Xun Liang said.

Erik and Rugrat were battered and bruised, but they drank in his words now, even as their bodies repaired.

"Erik, work on your hips. Your hips move and your body will move. It gives you the greatest motion. You're used to always advancing. When dodging, you must learn to give ground before you learn how to advance."

Erik was fighting a Telarri with the metal element. The chaotic forks of lightning numbed his limbs and made his muscles twitch as they passed him. He kept his fists tight to his chest as he moved backward, using domain pulses constantly, spreading out from himself as he stepped backward between roots and stones, finding sturdy footing by information turned instinctive.

Erik jumped backward as iron nails tore through the ground before him.

The Telarri's lightning retracted, and it shot forward, its speed jumping upwards.

Erik drew on his elements, increasing his perception, defense, and speed.

*The hell?*

Erik's momentary shock allowed the Telarri to hit him twice before he adapted to the new speed.

He shifted to accept non-lethal wounds that would still hurt but wouldn't restrict his mobility while using his domain in combination with organic scan to see what was happening in the body of the Telarri.

The lightning flowed through the creature's body, activating its limbs faster than it could on its own.

Erik forced his perception, his domain, and his scans together to try to predict what the creature would do next. He was accurate one time in five as he continued to take hits, the numbing effect running through his limbs, reaching deeper into his body.

Erik yelled as the white transportation light surrounded him.

"Lightning Telarri are among the most annoying." He squatted down across from Erik. "What were you trying to do with those rapid, directed pulses?"

Erik shuddered with the leftovers from the lightning, jerking suddenly as he pushed himself up into seated as the lightning was transmitted to his bones and drawn into his elemental core.

Erik let out a heavy breath through his nose. "I was scanning him. Could see how his muscles are reacting sometimes, depends if they are protecting against it or how strong they are."

"Oh," Xun Liang tapped his finger on his chin. "Rather interesting."

Rugrat appeared on his pad, bleeding and battered, but in one piece.

An old lady walked into the room. She looked like she was attending a wool wear convention in the arctic circle. Thick but small glasses hung on the end of her nose. Her hair escaping the cap was blue, purple, yellow and pink, fading into a regal silver. One side of her head was braided, while the other hung straight down.

Twin pointed ears poked out on either side of her toque as she puffed on a pipe that let out green smoke.

"You two still here? Liang," she growled.

"I was running tests."

"Been seven days. You've been running tests on them two lads. You keep them in here any longer and they'll turn into battle idiots like you," she grumbled. "What you two staring at? Never seen a gnome before?"

"You're really a gnome?" Erik asked.

"Do you often see diminutive sized people with pointed ears outside? And don't say I'm some Elven dwarf. It's offensive to me and to Elves."

"Uhh…" Erik looked at Rugrat, who just shrugged.

She snorted out smoke, a grin around her pipe.

"Odd duo, you are. You might be right, Xun Liang. They could be good. Now tell them why you've been stuffing them into the training rooms time and time again before sending them to their classes. It's been a week already!"

She turned and left a trail of smoke behind.

Xun Liang cleared his throat, drawing their attention. "So, first I wanted to see how you fight. *That* was revealing. Then I needed to see how stubborn you were, and if you were teachable, and well, at the end, I wanted to see how adaptable you were when you were actually listening. First, whoever taught you to use your elements and mana did a good job. Whoever taught you to fight…" Xun Liang widened his eyes and shook his head.

"That hurt to see. That rifle you were using Rugrat, I'm guessing it's the type of weapon you're both familiar with. Erik has transitioned away from it more than you have, using his fists and his body to fight, kind of. You both need to learn what to do when you're in a close confrontation with an enemy and then at a distance, since you have those weapons. I trust you are good at distance so we will work on close range situations first. You're both as stubborn as hell, and while there are things you think you know, you are willing to learn." His hand stopped Erik. "I know there are undoubtedly things that you do know, but it is my job as your trainer to teach you the things you *don't* know.

You've both started to listen to what I'm saying, probably because it was the only thing that wouldn't hurt as much. The most interesting aspect about you special cookies, you're determined bastards."

Xun Lian grinned. "You took wounds, but you were moving your bodies to take wounds that wouldn't impair your movements or stop you committing to a dodge if you weren't attacked, and you're as heartless to yourselves in training as you are to whoever you're fighting. You push yourself to do whatever you want to learn one hundred percent, force yourself to learn as you go along. Means that to start it is hard as hell, but then you learn faster."

Xun Liang stood and stretched. "All right, I'll be your combat trainer."

"Why would we go with you?" Rugrat asked.

"You don't want all of that to be for nothing, do you?" Xun Liang draping an arm over Rugrat's shoulders. "And I think I can teach you a thing or two." He patted Rugrat with a grin and stepped away, looking at them both, standing next to the door out of the formation filled corridor.

"Erik West and Jimmy Rodriguez, you two are rather interesting. I looked into your background. Alchemy, smithing, healing, Earth tactics with firearms. While it has allowed you to scrape by in the different realms. In the Seventh Realm, you needed to be careful as there are many that can overpower you in technique. You've been learning from Lee Perrin. I would guess on the manipulation of elements, a fine teacher by accounts, but like you, he looks at the elements as an external tool. Let me ask you, when you're using your cauldron or your hammer, do you think of them as tools or do you use them as extensions with only random conscious thought? Can you anticipate what happens as you work with them?"

He looked at them both.

"I didn't really think about it, but I control the flames," Erik said.

"Yes, you control it, but are you focusing on controlling the flames, or is it just happening because you have become so used to the process?"

He smiled and looked at Rugrat.

"What are you getting at?"

"I want to teach you how to fight the Ten Realms way, not the Earther way. To use your domain like an extra sense, to fuse mana and elements into everything that you do to the point it is a muscle you don't notice you're using it when you breathe. Now you're thinking about your breathing and taking conscious control. You breathe when you're fighting, don't you? Lots going on there. What if you were to use your mana and element domains? Now, take two days. Go do your classes. See what the academy has to offer. Go and test out what you have learned so far. If you want to learn more, then come back in two days. If you're not interested, don't come back."

He tossed Erik a map.

"What's this?"

"Academy map."

"Will the training...?"

"Hurt like this? Yes, but the more you bleed here, the longer you'll survive out there." Xun Liang's smile faded. "Aren't you already getting used to taking wounds now that would have been life threatening before your tempering? Since you started your assessment, do you think that you could take more wounds than before and keep going?"

Erik opened his mouth and closed it.

"Pain lets us know that we are alive, but you can get used to it, build up a tolerance and understanding over time."

"So, our training is going to suck."

"Yes, but then it is easier to get rid of those bad habits and give you new ones."

He turned and left the room.

Erik and Rugrat looked at one another.

"I guess we should go see our accommodations now," Rugrat said.

"Yeah, I need a proper shower and some real sleep." Erik took out his map, pressing the map to his as he stepped off the formation. He passed the map to Rugrat for him to do the same.

They walked out into the reception. The gnomish lady was knitting with iron threads while rocking in a reception chair.

"He might be a tough trainer, but you won't find another one better than him in the Ninth." She pursed her lips. "Well, maybe not one so determined. Won't be easy now. Best to think carefully. You can't quit halfway."

"Thank you...?" Erik asked.

"Weebla. Name's Weebla. Now, take care, you two, and make sure that you take time to learn more than just how to fight."

Erik and Rugrat bowed their heads and went to the elevator. The gates opened, revealing a gap between the elevator and the top of the gate.

"Does that look like a... footprint?" Rugrat looked up. Erik looked with him, seeing light from above.

"That looked like a hole in... You don't think that he just jumps on top of the elevator and flies out the top of the shaft?"

"It looks human sized."

"He strikes me like the kind of person that would do such a thing."

They got onto the elevator and Erik pressed the button.

They leaned against the walls of the elevator as it groaned upwards.

"You know, he might be insane," Rugrat started.

"But you can't deny that we started to learn by the end of it," Erik said.

"If he can teach us to fight?"

"He was leaking even less mana and elements than Lee. His control must be on another level, and then him appearing beside you, he's got some skills," Erik rubbed his face.

Rugrat groaned, hitting his head against the side of the elevator lightly.

"Why do we always find the weirdos?" Erik agreed.

Storbon was about ready to march on the Avegaaren administration buildings when his sound transmission crackled to life. "They've been spotted heading this way."

He checked the ping on the map and ran out of the courtyard, through the outer buildings, the stables, and to the outer wall that was equal parts decoration and defense.

Special team members spotted the duo and moved around them with looks of concern. Erik and Rugrat's carriers were torn and frayed, the plates pitted and scarred while their clothes were dulled from cleaning spells. Their shirts and pants had turned into t-shirts and shorts.

"Storbon, whatever it is, can it wait until I take a bath and get some sleep?" Erik asked.

Storbon seemed to hold his breath, looking them over and nodded. "It can wait."

"Good. Now, you know where the hell our accommodations are?"

"Uhh, this is it." He indicated to the compound behind him.

"Which room?"

"Umm, all of it. This is your residence. Rugrat's is about a kilometer away and is similar in style."

"All right. Well, I'm going to take a shower. Only danger there is that I'll fall asleep standing up."

"I think I'll crash."

"Sure, dunno if I have a couch for you somewhere," Erik muttered, the two sounding almost drunk from their fatigue as they wandered in.

"Fancier than some of the hotels I've stayed in."

"Dude, it's fancier than any hotel we've been in. Remember our hoochie hotel in Panama?"

"Ah, that was a beaut. Had a pool, too."

"Yeah, only cause Simmons' hooch was busted."

They wandered into the accommodations as Storbon's team sealed the gates and he radioed Yang Zan and his team watching Rugrat's residence.

"We've got them here. They're going to crash. Look like they got mauled by bears."

"Maybe they found the bar around here?"

"You know we're in a school?"

"You know that there are old fogies like five hundred years old wandering around here as students, right?"

"Trying to find your long lost great-great-grandfather?"

"Hell, no, but wouldn't mind meeting a perfectly normal twenty-year-old lady interested in rugged men that smell like gunpowder and dust."

Storbon snorted and rolled his eyes. "Don't think that would be any normal lady, and I doubt that anyone that young is gonna make it into the Academy."

"Hey, a man can have dreams!"

# 5
## Day One of Class

The next morning, after Erik and Rugrat splayed out for a few hours of rest, they were eating from their storage rings, telling Storbon about their entry test and their training. Scribe formations recorded everything.

"Here are your schedules." Storbon passed them both a box.

They opened them.

"Another emblem. Shit, should start a collection for these," Erik muttered, pinning it to his shirt. He checked the papers.

"We said that we were your retainers to get those and get posted outside your classes. You have one that everyone gets, a history of the Ten Realms. The rest are up to you to pick. Classes here are like our Expert classes in Alva."

"So, we can go into whatever class we want, listen to them, ask questions and use the facilities, just develop on what we have already?"

"Pretty much. There are basic courses on different subjects, but they're just golems going over the information. Be faster to go to Alva and learn it, I'd think."

"Four hours until we have history." Erik checked the time against the schedule. "Library?"

"I think I'm going to go to the lecture on smithing in twenty minutes." Rugrat finished off his toast and washed it down with coffee.

"All right, see you in history then."

The Special Team members were allowed to hang around their quarters and were free to leave, but they weren't allowed to go anywhere inside the academy, which left the city surrounding the academy for them to discover and wander.

They left Rugrat to enter the smithing lecture hall by himself. It was smaller than he expected, with only a handful of people in a room that could fit around a hundred.

Rugrat took out a pad of paper and a pencil, sitting and waiting.

Others glanced over, stealing glances at the school emblem hooked to his shirt, then making remarks to their friends or looking away, uninterested in talking to him.

The lecturer walked out onto the stage, a young man with a smudge of soot on his cheek, his skin tanned by fire.

"For those of you that don't know me, I am Master Wolff. Pleased to meet you. I am a Star Level smith, and this lecture will be about going from Expert to Master smith." He stretched and leaned on the pulpit.

"When you go from Expert to Master, it's like answering your why question. At one point, you are a Seventh Realmer, and the next you can enter the Ninth. One moment you are an Expert smith. Then you make something and become a Master. You can copy something another master has made, but this will not increase your overall rank. You need to make something that is original to you. It doesn't mean it has to be original in the Realms."

He moved to the board and wrote "Life, Work, and Enjoyment", circling them to make a Venn-diagram. At the intersection, he wrote "master works".

"Life." He tapped on the board. "Your life experiences, your roots. These are the things that have changed you, molded you, made you who you are. Work, well that's what you're going to do. In this case, smithing. Everything that you have learned in your profession, from teachers, on your own, everything. Enjoyment. If you do not enjoy your work, if you do not enjoy your life, then it will be hard to do either. You will not be motivated to do more."

He underlined "master works".

"To make a master-work, you must have a combination of all three. An enjoyment in what you are doing to go further into the subject and dive into the depths of knowledge. The more you enjoy it, the greater you will be inspired, and the more you will learn and retain. Your work, well, to break rules, you must know what the rules are first. You must have developed techniques to the point where you can manipulate them to your needs. Life, what you have done, what you will do in the future, that changes everything. Go back to your roots. You like to draw? Then draw out the sword you are working on. Look, you have combined the work, the sword, with your life interest in drawing, and enjoy it."

He threw the chalk into his storage ring and looked around the room.

"When you find out why you fight, you gain a greater control over yourself. If you find out what you enjoy, why you smith, and why who you are makes you want to smith, then you gain control over these areas."

A student raised their hand.

"Question?"

"So, the answer is inside us?"

"Nearly all the answers to the important questions are. That said, these three can be out of balance. If they are, then figuring out the foundation they are laid upon will make it easier to see where you are lacking."

No one else raised their hand, and he cleared his throat. "An exercise to think about and look into… Examine how you smith. Examine how you fight. See how you can combine the two. See the connections within yourself. Follow them and test them."

Rugrat raised his hand. "What if you don't fight?"

"Well, then you wouldn't be here. This is a realm for fighters." The teacher lowered an eyebrow before another person raised a hand. "Yes?"

"What about techniques? If we were able to make items with a different technique, could that get us to a master work?"

"Possibly. Many develop their techniques in a moment of epiphany, but it's what you make with that technique, the merging of ideas, imagination, and reality that creates a master work. It is your life and work smashing together."

Rugrat listened to the other questions. *Do they really care about fighters so much that they're not willing to let crafters into the Ninth Realm? What kind of broken system is that?*

Students bowed and moved out of the way of David Mueller as he nodded to other teachers and students he knew.

With new students entering the academy, it made classes chaotic. Mueller was assigned to general history, the only class that everyone could take without costing them points. His job was to teach the younger generations the truth about the Ten Realms and the purpose of the Imperium and its supporting associations.

And two of his newest students hadn't shown up in over a week. *Emperors from a First Realm sect.* Mueller's wrinkles deepened into a frown. The Sects were annoying at the best of times, a liability and a blade in the dark at the worst in his opinion.

He walked through a common area, hearing a group of friends laughing, heads together, taking in the day's sun with a collection of books around them.

The corner of his mouth lifted, thinking of easier times. *Seems a lifetime ago I was one of them with Mercius and Namia.*

His throat tightened as the smile faded. He swallowed. There wouldn't be another time he would hear Namia make one of her bawdy jokes or Mercius pulling him along, running from the latest trouble he'd gotten himself into, laughing all the way.

*Forty years.*

"Some marriages don't last that long." He slowed down, looking at a familiar classroom door.

A part of him wished he could go back in time, walking through that door, nervous, excited, and determined, the third son of the Mueller family, fourth generation Fighters Association. He'd thought back to when he had just made it through his first fight and going to his own history class. He'd found a seat next to Mercius, who introduced himself, even though the next day they might be opponents. His first friend at the academy introduced him to Namia in their formations class.

They had retained their positions, reaching into the top two thousand of their generation and passing out after their five years of training.

His smile grew bitter as his stomach twisted. Mercius's and Namia's faces frozen in shock, fear and pain. The blood, like a stain upon his memory. David pressed his hand to his stomach, a wound long healed, yet he still felt it, even now.

He cleared his mind, trying to calm and clear his thoughts. He forced his feet to move, walking down the hallway.

The classroom was no different from the other lecture halls, but this one was full instead of the few that would attend other classes. A quick scan of the room with his domain told him that nearly everyone was there.

Two men walked into the classroom. Unlike the others who wore their association affiliation alongside their school emblem, these two only had a school emblem.

*Two from the sects come to try to get what they can out of us.*

"Nice of you to join us… Erik West and Jimmy Rodriguez, I assume?"

"I go with Rugrat instead of Jimmy, sir."

"I am here to teach history, not figure out your name, Mister Rodriguez. Please take your seats."

Three more entered the room behind them, filling up the classroom.

"Okay, we *were* talking about the third Incursion. Once the Ten Realms were unified and secured, the Devourers needed to change their tactics. Depending on their strength, they could create tears into the Ten Realms to send their Sworn over vast distances. The stronger they were, the further away they could create the tears. The unification made this impossible, leaving only the Tenth Realm within their reach.

"Can someone tell me what advantages the Elves and Gnomes had at this time against the Devourers? Remember, the Humans had only just joined the Ten Realms?" He glanced around the room, trying to make his target less obvious. "Erik?"

The man shrugged. "No idea."

"Have you not looked into the history of the Ten Realms?"

"Thought that was what this class was for."

David glowered at him, turning his gaze to a lady in the front. "Miss Jung?"

"There are several. The Devourers compete against one another as much as they competed against the Realms to become stronger, while the Imperium could focus on training and building. We had the home advantage, and formations to move people across the Realms at a moment's notice. The mana in the Tenth Realm is so dense that it adversely affects the Devourers, who only have a limited amount of mana, reducing their overall power."

"Unless they can get used to it," David interjected, waving for her to continue.

"To get from the Tenth Realm to the Ninth Realm requires a lot of elemental power. If they move to the Ninth Realm, we can cut off their rear at the Tenth Realm and whittle down their numbers over time."

"Very good, Miss Jung. Because of this, there have been no incursions into the Ninth Realm. In the Third Incursion, a group of Devourers worked together to enter the Tenth Realm, and it proved the effectiveness of the Tenth

Realm unification and routed their attack. They are smart beasts and can, and will, adapt. In the Fourth Incursion, they attacked our preparation stations, clearing out several with mana-based systems. The Devourers require mana to teleport into the Ten Realms. In the Fifth Incursion, they attacked the preparation stations again and used mana stones to gain entry to the Seventh Realm."

"What is the importance of the Fifth Incursion on the Ten Realms? Mister Rodriguez."

"Dunno."

"Well, I would hope that for someone who hasn't shown up to his classes, that they would have at least some basic knowledge." The other students smirked while David picked out an Association student. "Mister Khan?"

"The Fifth Incursion reached from the Seventh Realm down into the Fifth Realm before it was stopped. To suppress it, an agreement was reached between the Humans, Elves and Gnomes, ending the Ten Realms' Rising Wars and creating the Imperium and Associations. The Eighth Realm became a testing ground, the Ninth an academy. All preparation stations were decommissioned and closed off and the three races united against their common foe."

"Correct. It was the last Incursion to make it lower than the Tenth Realm in seven hundred and thirty-eight years. The Associations were developed to reach into the lowest realms and assist in the growth of all people within the Ten Realms. We must all know why the Devourers fight us." He pointed at Erik, turning it into a question.

"The Devourer we fought wasn't too focused on telling us about his motivations. It was just looking to kill us all and consume mana. Thing was strong as hell once it made it to the Seventh Realm."

"Doubtful," David said dismissively. Causing a rise of sniggers in the class and glares shot at Erik and Rugrat. "Probably only a high-level demi-human. Even Ravagers are hard to find past the Ninth Realm."

"Dunno. People from the academy did say he was a Devourer, right?" Rugrat mused aloud.

"Yes, yes, they did. Apparently, graduates don't know as much about it as their teachers, though. Must be saying demi-humans are Devourers for credit."

"If you are trying to insult my academy—" David raised an eyebrow. *The lower realm sect members know nothing but strength, lying through their teeth, full of words without merit.* Devourers had only been spotted in the Tenth Realm and then rarely, with Ravagers being the main attackers.

These two had to be lying and had gone so far as to bring his academy into it. David turned away from them to quell his frustration.

"Devourers, for those who *don't* know, are creatures from the shattered realm that have complete mastery over a single element. As they gain control over more elements, they will increase the number of stars associated with them. A two-star Devourer, for example, controls two elements. They do not have mana. Instead, the reason that they come to the Ten Realms and want nothing more than to eat us is because they want to consume our mana. This calms down their elements and gives them much greater control. Unlike those that pass through the Ten Realms, they do not have elemental and mana cultivation processes implanted into their bodies."

He removed the pressure from Erik and Rugrat, hiding his frown. They looked unaffected.

"It is the duty of the Imperium to keep the Ten Realms safe from the Devourers and Ravagers of the Shattered realms. Unlike the sects, clans, and others that look to use the Ten Realms for their own gain, our actions allow others to do as they want and live comfortable lives."

He scanned the room, seeing everyone but Erik and Rugrat sitting taller. Some of the other students were sending them dark looks.

"What about attacking the Shattered Realms?" Miss Jung asked.

"Numbers. There are few from the lower realms that are willing to put their selfish ways to the side and join the Imperium's cause."

David ignored Erik's snort.

"There are many Shattered realms connected to the Tenth Realm. We would need to clear out all of those planets before we could push on. The Ravagers and Devourers, if they have the opportunity, will charge through any opening into the Ten Realms, and not all the people of the Ten Realms are prepared to do the same to secure the safety of the Realms."

Erik was almost relieved when he and Rugrat walked to their combat classes.

"I don't think that the teachers like us much."

"We're not from the Associations. They probably think we're taking up space for their precious people from the younger generation."

"Xun Liang seems different, at least."

"Well, I could tell you that for free." Rugrat snorted.

"Does something look different?" Erik looked at the broken building and the elevator parts scattered across the area.

They ran towards the gap where the elevator had been, drawing their weapons and pulling on their helmets. They jumped down the hole, crashing into the ground and rushed into the reception.

"Are you *trying* to make me choke on my food?" Xun Liang complained.

"Chew with your mouth closed." Weebla rocked in her chair, moving her thread out of the way.

"The elevator and the building?" Erik asked.

"I went to raid-uhh *gather* some food from the cafeteria and when I was leaving, there was a great big metal thing in the shaft. You're saying that was an elevator? Huh, well, yeah, might need some people to fix it. Those things move so *slow* though." Xun Liang waved his hand.

"Will you stop breaking things in my training room?" Weebla sighed.

"Sorry about that." Xun Liang bowed toward her and jerked his head toward the teleportation pads. "Got to take these two for their training now."

Erik took a half-step forward, remembering all that he had gone through the last time.

"I'm glad to see you both!" Xun Liang said.

Erik felt him grab the back of their armor, pushing them forward through the doors whether they wanted to or not.

"I can walk by myself!" Rugrat complained.

"Best to help you along!"

They all stepped onto a formation and appeared in a training square. There were golems against one wall, and a door that led to an arena as big as the one Erik and Rugrat had competed in to join Avegaaren.

"All right. While sending you off to the training areas all the time is fun, it is limited. You need to learn how to fight. Don't worry, the Telarri will become a fun way to test out your skills. Erik, Rugrat." He indicated to two squares of the four in the room.

Erik and Rugrat walked to the different training squares.

"I think it would be best to train three days with fighting, then another doing any other courses that you've signed up for. I am a master cook and formation master. Weebla is a master smith and tailor; are there any crafts you are interested in?

"I'm a healer and an alchemist," Erik said.

"Strange combination for someone from the lower realms. I applaud you for your forward thinking."

65

Erik remembered David Mueller, but there was no condescension in Xun Liang's voice as he looked at Rugrat.

"Just smithing for me."

"Very well. There are many teachers of both here. What levels have you reached, if you don't mind my prying?"

"Expert," Erik said.

"Same."

"In which one?" Xun Liang asked Erik.

"Both."

"Well, then you are two oddities. This should be very interesting. I am excited to get started! Okay, to get started, whatever you were doing before, forget it. While you're with me, unless I say so, you are not to use your rifles. You should always wear your armor, though. Try to forget everything you've learned. Not actively; that's impossible, but always press upon what you're trying to learn, as you did the last time we were together."

Erik and Rugrat checked their gear.

"Good! We'll start with movement techniques. You have some rudimentary ones, but it's time we expanded on that." With a clap of his hands, two humanoid golems animated and moved toward the sparring squares.

"All right, first I'm going to teach the two of you how to dodge properly. You two are jumping around all over the place and it's just a mess. Try to limit your movements. Move to the side when there's a strong attack coming for you. Move, but try to not fall to the ground. Begin!"

"What?" Erik was punched in the helmet. He hit the ground and rolled up.

"What did I just say? Center off with your opponent. Rugrat, don't look at him sideways."

Erik and Rugrat proceeded to get their ass beat over several hours while Xun Liang gave them advice in real time, reading a book as he did so.

"All right, we'll end here today." Xun Liang was reading a book as he gave them advice.

"Are you even focusing on us?" Rugrat asked.

"Unlike you two airheads, I can use my domain all the time and see everything that is happening inside it without pulsing. Something that I noticed that the two of you *weren't* doing. Don't worry; I'll get you to do it next time." He threw two tokens and flipped the page in his book.

Erik and Rugrat caught the tokens. Erik grunted as he stood upright.

"These tokens will allow you access back into the training area. I'll see you at five a.m. tomorrow. Have fun with your study day. Toodles." He fluttered his fingers.

"How long will it take us to get better? Aren't you supposed to be showing us forms or something on how to dodge?" Erik asked.

Xun Liang looked up from his book.

"That is what the golems will teach you. There are hundreds of ways to dodge and attack. First, the golems are going to teach you how much it sucks to be hit. You are already adjusting well."

Rugrat grunted into his hand.

"All the attacks coming from the golem you should be able to redirect, then dodge. With real opponents, it is better to dodge than redirect because any contact with your enemy they can hit you with a spell or deliver elements right into your body. Your first goal is to remain on your feet and not get hit."

"And the second?" Erik asked.

"Will come with time. You two are the type to hear the final goal and start working toward that from the beginning instead of taking all the steps along the way. Now, go to your other classes. You will be able to use any formation in the academy to reach the training area here. And Rugrat, I talked to Weebla. She will be happy to teach or guide you in the way of smithing for a lesson. If you can work together, then she might teach you more."

Erik and Rugrat used the teleportation formations and headed to their accommodations. Meeting the Special Team members, they were debriefed again. Armed with a list from Alva and Egbert, they headed to the library to learn.

Erik and Rugrat's time at Avegaaren had started.

# 6

# Development

Xun Liang strolled through the training area. Erik was facing three golems while Rugrat faced two. They kept getting hit from time to time, but they were at least dodging half of the incoming attacks.

Neither used spells nor released their elements. They could only rely on their bodies. They were forced to use their domains to keep track of all the moving golems to anticipate their attacks.

"Remember, you do not need to turn and face your attacker every time. Use your motion, if possible!" Xun Liang growled, but internally, he was pleased with their development. Over the last two months, they had some of the basics down.

*Still reliant on full elemental enhancement, though.*

"Hold," Xun Liang said. The golems slowed to a stop while Erik and Rugrat slowed down. The golems stepped back, creating a triangle around them.

"You are pushing the elements into your body, enhancing it, but you are not utilizing them to the best effect. Let the mana and elements flow through you like blood or air. Assimilate the elements—which you have already mastered—and integrate them. You're drawing them all into your body. Sure, it enhances you, but do you need *every* element?

"Cultivating your elements so quickly means you haven't had time to work with them in detail, to learn and understand them. Your homework is to study them and to use only one element at a time to enhance your body. Instead of just enhancing, I want you to let it run through you, use the element's abilities with your own."

He started pacing and whistled. The golems glowed, activating once again. Erik's golems conjured flames, earth, and metal, and charged at him. Rugrat had one with fire and the other with earth.

"Dammit," Erik grunted as a fiery fist hit him in the shoulder, sending him spinning as the golems moved to rain attacks down on him.

He threw himself back on his feet, dodging blocks of earth kicked up from the ground.

Delilah sat at Alva's council table, turning her eyes to Storbon, the latest addition to the staff to join the room, standing behind commander Glosil.

"Erik and Rugrat have been working with a combat trainer since they arrived in Avegaaren. They spend most of their time training," Storbon said. "They have two days off every three that they spend attending lectures and going to the libraries. They're not allowed to remove the books from the library, so they read them and make notes that are delivered to our own library."

"So, have we learned more about this mysterious Tenth Imperium?" Blaze asked.

"They're the governing body of the Associations, originally the nation created by the Elves and the Gnomes when they made the Ten Realms. They now have many humans in their ranks. The Academy is supposed to be open to anyone, but from Erik and Rugrat's experience with the teachers and staff, they tolerate them, but it is very much an Association facility. The Ninth Realm serves as the academy for *only* fighters. If one does not fight, then they will not get to the Ninth Realm. Most of the administration related to the Association is run from the Seventh Realm, but the Academy clearly controls the Association."

"It seems there's an ongoing conflict in the Tenth Realm, if our information is correct," Elan interjected. "It seems to be at a steady state with the Imperium's Avegaaren graduates going to the Tenth Realm to fight back the Ravagers and Devourers and close these tears. This isn't verified because we don't have anyone in the Tenth Realm."

"So, getting into the Ninth Realm, you can be level seventy if you pass the trial the first time. If you don't, then you need to be level eighty. You have to answer the Why quest, which is only unlocked going to the Eighth, and to join the academy you should be an Association fighter?" Blaze asked.

"Don't forget, it costs a Celestial mana stone to get up there if you don't make it in the first trial."

"Can we go to the Eighth Realm, do the test, and get into the Ninth that way, a second time?" Blaze asked.

Delilah looked at the others.

"Haven't tested that out," Glosil said.

"Worth it if we can save a few mana stones!" Delilah said, getting grins around the table. "So, the information we are getting back, how useful is it, Egbert?"

"I gave them a list of questions that we are running into down here that are hindering us. They have found some answers and noted down everything they learned to get there. From what I have read, I think it will help out those in the Academy immensely. It has also led me to see a flaw in our current training and cultivation." He looked over to Jia Feng, but continued, "Right now, everyone is training to increase their cultivation as fast as possible. This means that they have little time to understand what they've gained before they start increasing their cultivation again. I propose that we have a program where people learn about the elements they've just cultivated and the changes that happen to them as they increase level and mana cultivation."

Jia Feng bit her lip in thought.

"I can see how that might be a problem. I agree, having classes on the different stages of cultivation would be greatly beneficial to our people."

"Anything else, Egbert?"

"Not at this time. I am compiling the information and passing it off to anyone that requests it or who I think would benefit from it."

Delilah nodded and turned to Momma Rodriguez and Aditya. "Anything new on your side of things?"

"The Empire still stands. The rolling elections through the various towns and cities has created a stir, but people have gotten into it. We reduced the number of officials in most places, focusing on defenses, access to houses, clean water, healthcare, and the academy. The whole First Realm would run to do what we asked them. We have non-aggression pacts with nearly every nation, allowing for the widespread creation of Sky Reaching Restaurants, academies, and healing houses. There may be issues in the future with nations and kingdoms fighting one another to gain a position closer to us."

"Used to be a time that nations avoided the Beast Mountain Range." Delilah smiled.

"Good work, Momma!"

"Alva continues her development. We have increased the dungeon core's reach and their speed of growth with new formations. This should mean we can create more dungeon cores for other projects." She looked at Glosil.

"That sounds good, then. Commander Glosil?"

"We have several ship building programs underway. The resources of the Sha contingent and spoils of the Willful Institute's corvette shipyard accelerated things. After Kushan, most of the Sha warships have gone to ground and are undergoing their upgrades and alterations. Edmond Dujardin has been named Admiral of the fleet, with Esther as his second in command. The first Crow companies have finished their training and are running exercises with airship crews to gel them together under Chonglu. All our forces from Kushan have returned. They're still undergoing repair efforts; their crafters were hit hard in the attacks."

"We have become the head of one of the largest alliances in the Ten Realms. We must maintain our position and power now more than ever. People are hoping and watching for us to fail. We must move slowly and steadily forward together." Delilah took in the faces around the table.

At the end of the meeting, Storbon waited for the rest of the council to clear.

Delilah could feel he wanted to talk to her. She hadn't been nearly as nervous in a meeting that decided the direction of millions.

He stepped up, opening his mouth and closing it.

"Would you like to get dinner with me, a date?" He coughed.

Delilah's heart did a double take.

"Uhh."

"It's no worry if you're busy or you don't want to. I just…" Storbon's words failed him as the venerated Special team leader looked at the desk awkwardly.

Delilah smiled. "I'd like that."

Her heart jumped again, seeing the smile on his face.

Another two months passed in what felt like a painful blink of an eye.

Erik panted, shifting between the four golems that surrounded him as they backed up. He let out a relieved sigh and fell to a knee.

Xun Liang squatted, a toothpick between his teeth. He took it out and pointed at Erik. "So, you know the body pretty well, right?"

"I'd say so."

"Then, are you blind or just being dumb? I told you to flow the elements through your body, not enhance them in sequence."

Erik grunted; it was a familiar topic. "I'm doing what you said."

"No, you're doing what someone else taught you."

Erik thought to Lee Perrin and about the elements running through his body.

"Thought so." Xun Liang sighed. He tapped the toothpick against his teeth. "That could work. Come with me."

Xun Liang stood. Erik got up, moving warily through the inactive golems, ready for them to try to hit him in the back. Only when he got out of the training square did he relax. Rugrat was getting beaten in his own space.

*Sorry, dude!*

He hurried after Xun Liang.

"I think my wording might have been wrong. Stop trying to force the element through your body. Use the properties of the element to create a reaction in your body. What if you increase the heat in your body? What if you increase the healing ability of your body, or the speed your muscles clench?" He waved Erik onto the teleportation formation.

"First of all, stop trying to control every little thing the element does. Let it run a little wild, see what happens. Then start to increase your control. Learn the rules and then break them! Watch the Telarri. What's happening when they use their elements? Think of the elements' affects, primary and secondary, and any diverging affects. With power over the elements, you can control the world. With power over mana, you can create another one."

Erik appeared in the godforsaken forest to an old and familiar roar.

"Goddamn forest."

Erik snapped around to face the Telarri. It came at him with lightning. He focused his senses on the creature, casting organic scan.

He dodged the crackling punch, lightning shooting out from the creature's hand.

Erik took the hits, using the earth element and healing spells to keep him in the fight. Between the fast and furious blows, Erik saw something incredible.

*It's channelling lightning from its elemental core, through the nerves, resonating with the bones!*

Erik felt as if someone dumped cold water on him, hissing at the kick that hit him in the leg as he batted a fist to the side, deflecting the blow, another already coming for him.

The creature's attacks sped up as Erik guided lightning through his own body, his movements slower than the Telarri's still.

*Stop trying to control.*

Erik gritted his teeth and released the lightning element down his right arm. It struck out quickly, but it was unguided.

*Use the nerves.*

Erik directed the lightning into the nerves. He snapped out a punch that cracked through the air. The blast pushed the Telarri to the side. It looked at him in confusion for a second, then yowled again and attacked once more.

Erik fired out his fists. They were like cannons, and he had to turn his body to aim his fists into the Telarri.

He was beaten up, black and blue with lightning all over, when he returned to the teleportation formation.

Erik moved his fists without the lightning and then used the lightning element through his nerves. He said nothing to the watching Xun Liang, working on what he had learned, trying to infuse it into his mind, his body.

He saw the impulses, tiny as they were, travelling through his body with every movement.

"Everything is just a puppet string away. The string is the nerves, and the pull is electrical impulses. Muscles and everything add force on top of that small impulse."

He felt he was just on the edge of something when he returned to the forest. Another metal element Telarri attacked him as Erik released lightning down his different nerve clusters, testing what happened.

He became the puppet master of his own body as he tried out the different combinations.

He appeared on the teleportation formation again, chugging a healing potion.

Each fight he developed, finding new nuances, tracing through his nerve system, through his muscles and body.

He threw his healing potion away, his mind focusing on the nuances of what he'd just experienced, the information filling his mind and the nugget that was just out of reach.

Time and time again, he appeared on the formation pad with just one word on his lips. "Again!"

He didn't see Xun Liang's smile as light surrounded him, chasing the epiphany so close at hand.

A whistle called the golems away from Rugrat. He coughed and pulled up his helmet, spitting on the floor. He couldn't help but think this training was more suited to Erik with the close-range combat. *Still nice to not get hit.* He focused on Xun Liang, who took out his toothpick.

"Rugrat, next I want you to dodge without touching the ground."

"Without touching the ground?"

"You have incredible control over mana, and you've infused your smithing into your spells to some degree already. Like Erik, you have preconceptions about what is right from Earth. You have the ability to fly as free as a bird, but you keep yourself grounded. When you move through the sky, you create panels of condensed mana to step onto. What if the mana was to move you directly? If you didn't have to run across the sky, you could move without wasted effort."

"The power from the mana launching me forward and then pushing off of it makes me faster than flying mages."

"Yes, but most flying mages are just using mana. They're not using fire elements, and they usually have the mana push against them instead of it pushing against you. And why are you flying with the force at the bottom of your feet? Your front and back have a larger surface area and you won't be looking up all the time.

"What is mana?" Xun Liang asked.

"It's a force we can manipulate to a much greater degree than elements and is an enhancing catalyst and form for elements."

"Well, thank you for the lecture, professor." Xun Liang shot a mana bolt at a target. It went off with a large bang. Then he released mana from the mana gate in his wrist and it came out in a rush, blowing up dust and shaking the target. "Mana is energy—energy that we store within our bodies, and through our will, we can contort and guide.

"Passing the Eighth Realm trial granted you greater access to that will—greater access to your body. Energy, when it interacts with matter, creates a reaction. Energy can react nicely or not nicely. The elements and mana are all different energy sources, but they can fuse and enhance one another, or, in the case of elements, they can also weaken and subsume one another. Mana is your ally and your tool, but it is not your friend. Not until you can control it as if it is your finger."

Xun Liang took in Rugrat's puzzled look and smiled. "Take a few minutes and no more touching the ground!"

There was a flash from the teleportation room and a yell of frustration.

"What did you think would happen when you sent an impulse through your *entire spine?*" Xun Liang chided. Erik's complaint was cut off with white light.

Rugrat thought about the mana bolt and the rush of mana from Xun Liang's mana gate. He directed mana through the mana gate in his right hand. He felt his mana going down, but also the force from it being released.

He fired a bolt of mana at the target as well, using his domain to see everything. He fired another, and then another, watching the target and then focusing on the path of the mana through the air as it pushed the mana around the bolt away. It reminded him of a diver jumping into a pool.

A whistle caught him off guard as he solidified mana under his feet.

"The barrier will keep you inside the sparring area, so don't fly too hard or fast!" Xun Liang moved to an easel, pulling out a brush and paint.

Rugrat dodged the golems, but the mana blocks under his feet changed his height and he misjudged their attacks.

One golem jumped in the air, attacking him. Others followed.

*Crap.*

He tried using the mana to push and pull him through his domain, attempting to move with just mana and dodge four flying golems.

"Ow. Ow! Stop it, will you?" Rugrat said, getting hit out of the sky like a broken rocket engine in a pinball machine, skidding into the ground. The golems retreated as he healed.

"Figured out what the golems are doing yet?" Xun Liang asked. Flares of reds, yellows, blues, and greens adorned his canvas.

The golems attacked before he could answer. Rugrat's frustration fueled his anger. In turn, anger fueled his mind to beat these damn Golems and wipe the smile from Xun Liang's face.

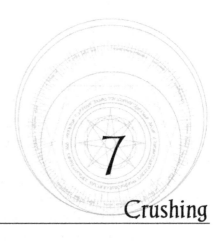

# 7
## Crushing

R  ekha's spell crashed into the sole remaining sect fighter, sending him
        crashing through several adjoining inner house walls.

        Sam followed behind Rekha, his eyebrow raised as if to ask if her
force was necessary. His elven features served to heighten the imperious nature
of the expression.

She flew through the hole in the walls. Cayleigh was waiting for them,
her twin short axes ready. Her domain pressed Sect Leader Anwar Hassan into
the pile of rocks that was all that remained of the wall.

He coughed, his face bloodied and cut as he looked to his family huddled
in the corner, his wife standing in front of a half-dozen children. "The Alvan
Alliance will not let this go, no matter who you are. You and your people can
only survive if you leave now," he growled, regaining the fire in his eyes, even
with Cayleigh a moment away from taking his head from his shoulders. His
guards were already defeated.

Rekha snorted, her hazel eyes dancing with the colors within.

"An alliance of sects? I'd be surprised if it lasts a year. You sects and clans
and nations care for nothing but what you can take from one another, and you
took something dear to us, Anwar. There is no one above the Imperium."

Anwar paled.

"W-wait."

"Ah, it seems you've remembered something. Is that right, Anwar?" She stopped in front of him, still behind the Gnomish Cayleigh and her hair of red, yellow, and silver. Cayleigh shifted her blades, keeping Anwar down by an implied threat.

"Look, this is all a misunder—"

"Anwar, we're beyond that. Because of your actions, the attack on the supply convoy going through your allied nation's lands resulted in twenty members of the Crafter's Association being killed," Rekha growled.

"We didn't mean—"

"For something to happen. Oh, Anwar, why do you attack the very people that are fighting for your future? Why are you playing your stupid little games?" Her yell made the room shake. The children hiding behind their mother cried and ducked their heads.

Rekha exhaled, bringing her anger in check. "The Alvan Alliance may or may not care about you, but the Imperium looks after its own." She threw down a scroll next to him.

He flinched as if it were a viper.

"Open it and sign it. You will be stripped of all your property; all assets will be transferred to the Imperium. Your trading sect will become a vassal of the Imperium and you will give up the people that attacked the convoy."

"This will make us no more than slaves!"

"You made your choice. Now, you must live with it. At least with this, your children have a future."

"A future within the Associations."

"Do you wish for them to have a future without a father?"

Anwar gritted his teeth.

"Anwar, just do it," his wife hissed.

He shot her a look, but his expression faltered. He opened the contract and wiped the blood on his hand on the contract.

"Very good."

Rekha grabbed the scroll out of the air and turned, leaving through the door.

"You Bhattan bitch!" Anwar hissed.

"Rekha," Cayleigh warned in a low voice.

Rekha looked back to Anwar. "You are a vindictive little man. I hope you're apt at cleaning toilets. Seems about the only use for someone with a mouth as useless as yours. And what Bhattan clan are you talking about? I can't seem to remember one." Her smile carried an edge as her domain leaked out.

Anwar shuddered as a wet patch appeared on his robes.

"Ah, such a fine example to show your children. The Imperium will be a better teacher than you could ever be."

Rekha left the room, Sam and Cayleigh trailing behind.

They were halfway out of the building when Cayleigh sighed. "Seems like everyone has lost their minds these last couple months. Challenging us at every turn."

"Most of it has to do with the Alvan alliance. It reaches through all the realms, tying people together. People are starting to think they can do anything they want under the protection of someone else," Sam muttered.

"Waste of time," Rekha agreed. "This alliance will fall apart with time, but the Associations will persevere as they always have. Wish they'd send someone else to deal with all this. There are plenty of tears in the Ninth Realm that need sealing."

"Even the mighty Rekha is arguing against Imperium orders?" Cayleigh said in a mock surprised voice.

"We go where we're sent, but let's get out of here before anyone else thinks to give us more tasks in the lower realms. Huh?"

"The sooner we can get out of here, the better. I sense that the local Association's guards have reached the sect entrance."

"Only about forty minutes late," Cayleigh said.

Rekha smiled. "They're getting better."

They reached an open courtyard and launched into the sky, leaving a dust plume behind.

"I feel properly shiatsued," Erik said as they walked out of the teleportation formation close to their homes.

"Supposed to be three days, not three weeks." Rugrat held his neck and rolled his head.

"Yeah, but I think it was worth it." He looked at Rugrat's feet. They were moving an inch above the ground.

"I didn't notice. You know it doesn't even draw on your internal mana, just some minor concentration." Rugrat floated next to Erik without moving his feet.

"That's—can you just walk normally? You're like a mall cop on one of them scooter things."

"Who you calling a mall cop?" Rugrat muttered as they reached Erik's accommodation. An official wearing an Avegaaren badge standing outside the gate walked up to them. He stopped in front of them and looked them over.

"I was wondering if you would show up. It's been four months since you joined the academy, and after three months, you are supposed to fight at least two people per month. Whoever wins takes the rank of the person that lost, and they take the rank of the person that won, so if someone who was one hundred beats someone ranked ninety, the ninety becomes rank one hundred and the one hundred becomes ninety. The higher your rank, the more resources you gain access to — materials, concoctions, teachers, books. You have to challenge two people per month, you can only challenge people a higher rank than you. You can accept up to ten challenges per month and you can challenge up to five people. Once the challenge is made, you must agree upon a day to fight. There are several pre-selected time and day slots. Do you understand?"

Erik and Rugrat nodded.

"Very good. Use your emblems on a challenger pedestal. There, you can see who challenges you and you can pick who you want to challenge. You can only challenge someone one hundred ranks above you. A Proctor such as myself will come to gather you if you are not in the arena at the allotted time. If you cannot be found, then you will automatically lose." He looked at them both.

"Understood." Erik and Rugrat nodded.

"Have a good day."

The man launched himself into the air and shot away.

"Well, he was a bag of smiles."

"At least he was neutral, which is more than I can say about some people in here."

They headed into their accommodations. The Special Team members were training, using information Erik and Rugrat had provided.

They found the challenger pedestal in the central courtyard of Erik's home. It was angled with a recess for their medallions on one side. Once slotted in, it showed a list of every student they could challenge in the school. Some were blacked out and couldn't be challenged anymore, but most glowed a soft blue. Clicking on them, they could send a challenge. There was a list of also all the people that had challenged them.

"Huh, that... I think that's the guy I fought to get in here," Rugrat pointed at a name.

"Kujo Ujisuke?"

"Yeah, he's one of the people I'll have to fight."

"That gonna be cool?"

"I dunno. I barely won against him using my rifle, and he knows about it now. Could have a defense for it. He's probably been training for this."

"Yeah." Erik chewed on his lip. He had barely made it into the academy as well. It was only the arrogance of his opponent that had allowed him to get the blow he needed to enter the school.

*I don't want to miss out on Xun Liang's lessons.* They were hard, damn hard, but in just four months, he was faster than ever before. He was still using his domain in a pulse-like way, but his coordination had never been better. The growth was rapid, and there was so much more to learn. But being the lowest rank in the academy was working against him.

Others trying to get in might think the same as he had when challenging the entry trial. Take out the weakest person first.

"Well, best to get it over with. Our first match is in a few hours."

The light in the waiting room turned to green and the door unlocked. Rugrat let out a heavy breath. Not even the tinkling water feature had done anything to reduce his stress. They had spent the time before the match in the library studying for answers to different questions from Alva. If they were expelled, they wanted to get as much from Avegaaren as possible.

Rugrat stepped out into the arena, studying Kujo Ujisuke. His armor was pared down on the legs, chest, arms and head, leaving his limbs free to move.

Rugrat shifted his carrier around with his shoulders. He tensed his hands around his armored gloves, his rifle in his storage ring. He wanted to use his skills for as long as possible before resorting to the rifle.

*I hope I've learned enough.*

At least he knew the two main elements that Ujisuke used: fire and water to create wind. Special tattoos were on his shaved head, the red and blue elements dancing in his deep brown, almost black eyes.

Ujisuke held the end of his sword in a draw stance.

Rugrat focused on him, stretching out his domain to cover the arena, getting a feel for it before he reduced the area it covered to just him and Ujisuke.

"Begin!" The proctor's voice rang through as Ujisuke forced Flame and Water elements into his scabbard, creating an explosion of steam that he poured mana into. It wreathed his blade as he shot forward with flame mana at his back in time with his step, crossing a hundred meters in the blink of an eye. His blade exploded free of his scabbard, the superheated water turned steam imbued with mana and directed by the slash turned into a wind blade.

Rugrat grabbed onto the mana around him and shot to the side and forward, casting a chain spell.

Ujisuke took a second step, his blade covered in Water and Fire elements, creating steam that gave form to superheated air blades.

He sliced out three times as he took two steps.

Rugrat jumped into the sky. Mana latched onto him as he shot forward and dropped. Instead of casting a complicated chain spell, he created mana-formed chains that shot out at Ujisuke.

Ujisuke cut through the chains and leapt into the sky. His blades chased Rugrat.

*What the hell do I cast now?* The chain spells needed to be on the ground because it was so heavy. He could make larger chains to reach higher, but he needed an immediate solution.

Ujisuke shot across the space between them, his sword slashing out, creating a silvery afterimage.

Rugrat reached out, compressing swirling bowling balls of air. They flew like moths to a flame from every direction around Ujisuke. He tried to dodge the first. It exploded, buffeting him. Several of his blades fell apart as Rugrat used mana bolts. They broke some as he was forced to dodge others.

*I need something that will work at range. Gun? No, bullets. Fire.*

Rugrat turned in mid air, dodging a blade coming for his side. He bent backward and dropped several feet. Flame *erupted* around him without touching him, flickering blue and white tongues at the edge of his aura.

He yelled, drawing that heat closer and tighter, a bare flicker around him as he touched the ground. Using mana and flame under his feet, he shot into the sky at a different angle.

Several blades hit the ground, causing the stone to crack, the heat turning the scars shiny.

Ujisuke's attacks redoubled, raining down on Rugrat as he was pushed back.

Rugrat used mana bolts, working to shape the mana and the fire element.

*Keep it simple, stupid!*

He created a hollow bullet of mana and injected flames into the hole at the bottom. The mana bullet shot off, hitting near Ujisuke, creating an exploding fireball.

Rugrat encapsulated flame in mana, then scooped up flames with a hollowed mana bolt.

The tempo changed as Ujisuke was the one being thrown back.

He dropped to the ground. Stone darts shot out from the ground at Rugrat, striking his fire bullets as his sword attacks came slower, but their speed shot upwards.

Rugrat called up mana chains and cast spells into the ground. He had little time to do so and used several smaller spells instead of larger ones that Ujisuke would cut off.

He formed an artillery shell of flame behind his back. He was no longer scared as he had pinned Ujisuke in place, and was able to dodge him and see what he was doing from every position.

Rugrat took a hit from Ujisuke to get within twenty meters. The shell rotated into place. Ujisuke's eyes widened as Rugrat released the shell.

Ujisuke yelled, his blade releasing a blade of fire and a blade of water. The two crashed into one another, creating a hair-thin blade of air that hit the mana shell. The mana tore apart the air spell. The fire contained within was diverted, but went off in an explosion.

Rugrat wasn't idle. The ground churned with the sheer number of spells as he created several more shells.

A klaxon sounded.

"Jimmy Rodriguez announced winner of the competition," the Proctor said.

Rugrat watched Ujisuke, who had been thrown back several meters, getting to his feet.

*His blade at the end. That was dangerous as hell.*

He breathed a sigh of relief and nodded to Ujisuke, who seemed confused but nodded back.

Rugrat turned and left the arena, frowning at a proctor that was waiting before the teleportation pad.

"There are several people who wish to challenge you to enter Avegaaren. Would you be interested in fighting them?"

"Oh, really? Yeah, sure, I feel like I'm at the edge of something here, the interaction of elements."

"When would you like to fight them?"

"Sooner the better, right?"

He missed the proctor's look. He was too busy thinking about the interactions of elements, like the interactions of materials in the forge.

"Very well. I will notify them right away. Please rest in your waiting room."

"Sure." Rugrat changed direction and walked toward the waiting room doorway, stuck in his own thoughts.

"I thought you said that there was no way Ujisuke could lose against him? What was that?" Their father berated Hikokie under his breath outside of the arena.

"He and the other one don't attend any of the classes. How can they have learned anything? They haven't gained the interest of any of the teachers. They're outsiders. They must have been hiding their abilities."

His father's growl died in his throat as Ujisuke appeared.

"Ujisuke, that was a great fight. Your split blade is coming along so quickly!" he praised.

Ujisuke had a faraway look on his face as he approached his family.

"You'll get him next time," Hikokie said, getting a glare from over Ujisuke's shoulder.

"I don't think I will fight him next time; he has improved in the time since I last saw him. His movements were more refined. He could dodge and didn't rely on his rifle. It gave him time to counterattack me."

"He must have been holding back when he fought you before," Hikokie's mother said.

"I don't think so. There was something different about him. I think it would be better to fight the third ranker rather than him or his friend. I learned a lot from our fight. I'd like to return home to study it."

"Of course. Of course." His father patted him on the back, indicating to his wife to start walking back to the teleportation formation.

A sound cancelling formation formed around Hikokie and his father.

"I do not want this to become a stumbling block for your brother. Find out everything you can about these two."

"What are you thinking of doing, Father?"

"I am not planning to do anything. You said that they were from the lower realms and not from the Associations? Well, what power are they from? What are their aims? Are they here to learn or to crush others and take our information?"

Hikokie's eyes brightened as he frowned with his father. Protecting the Imperium was essential. "I will look into it, Father."

He nodded and closed the spell, moving to follow Ujisuke and his mother.

Hikokie sighed. He hoped his brother would be able to make it forward from this setback, too. A stronger member of the family meant greater security in the Imperium.

"Why are you two late?" Xun Liang complained as Erik and Rugrat appeared in the training room. Weebla had moved down into the training room, turning one of the sparring areas into a comfortable seating area with a kitchen against one wall.

"You live here?" Erik asked.

"No dodging the question."

"We had a number of challengers that were trying to take our positions, so we defended them," Rugrat said sardonically. "Apparently, that sort of thing is common knowledge and if you don't show up for your challenges, you can be kicked out."

"Oh, huh, I forgot about that." Xun Liang chuckled.

"Because everyone gave up trying to beat you." Weebla raised an eyebrow and faced Erik and Rugrat. "Sorry about that, boys. I keep thinking that he will, you know, remember things, or not be an idiot *once* in a while."

Xun Liang made a *pah* noise, opening and closing his mouth, but unable to form his words.

"Shall we get started?" Erik said, eager.

"Usually, I have to drag you into the sparring areas," Xun Liang said, holding up a finger, keeping them on the teleportation pads.

"Well, we had a chance to test out what we've learned, and if we have a month before our next round of fights, we have a long way to go," Erik said.

"Okay then, next is going to be your domains. You're getting better with dodging, but to dodge, you need to know where the attack is coming from. So, use only your domains. Erik, keep working on using your elements through your body in short bursts. Rugrat, work on chaining your spells together. If you cast one spell and overlay another on top, you will get a stronger effect. Should cut down on your casting time. Also, if one spell is destroyed, it still leaves elements and mana behind. Why don't you use that with your pure magic ideas?"

Xun Liang, the devil himself, threw out formations that stuck to Erik's and Rugrat's necks. Erik pulled at it, but it had fused with his skin. He could cut it out, but stopped himself.

The formation activated, and the lights went out.

"What?" Erik created a flame in his hand, but he couldn't see it or sense it.

"That's a sense blocker. You won't be able to see anything. You can only use your domain to see around you. So, I'd say get used to it!"

Erik used his domain, feeling the room around him. It was like when he was a child, relying on the light coming from the television downstairs through the crack under his door to see with.

"About time you learned how to use that domain of yours properly. Dodge, evade; don't attack the Telarri. You want to show that I'm wrong? Show me what I'm teaching you is wrong."

Light wrapped around him. The sounds of the forest disappeared, but he still scrambled to his feet.

*That bastard.* He turned around, centering himself in the domain. It fed him information on the mana and elements around him.

He stretched it out across the ground, pushing it into the ground. He was confused about the sphere of information coming in and had a hard time focusing on where he was in relation to everything else, tripping over as he thought himself at the edge of his sphere instead of the middle of it.

"I can sense mana," Erik paused. He was talking but heard nothing.

"Well, that's freaky. Okay, I can sense mana and the elements." Erik looked at the disturbances of mana at the center of the sphere, finding himself. He was like a sputtering candle, releasing and drawing in mana through his gates. His body lit up with elemental power.

"Okay." Erik felt another presence charging through his sphere before he was hit in the back with a claw of air, sending him spinning. He lost all sense of where he was in his domain.

Erik started running through what Xun Liang had been telling him and Rugrat.

*Sense the elements, the mana around you. While someone can hide what they are doing internally, the external world has many signs.*

Erik felt another surge of water and fire turning into a superheated claw of air. He jumped and rolled, hitting a tree, but the claw missed him.

*On your feet. Know your footing by your feet, not your eyes.* Erik adjusted to the ground, confused at how easily he started moving once he stopped over thinking things.

A kick, *close.*

He leaned back, hitting the creature in the knee instead of dodging. He'd misjudged his location as he grabbed the creature's leg and spun with it, throwing them.

Erik's existence was mana and elements, sprinkled with the fear of injury.

He forgot how many times he was sent out of the training area and shoved back in, battered, bruised and determined.

"What did you learn without your senses?" Xun Liang asked as the formations on their necks were pulled away and the world came into almost painful focus.

"Keep your eyes closed," Rugrat grimaced.

"If you don't need to see someone to attack them, you can hide behind a dozen trees," Erik said.

"Both valuable. Now make sure to use your senses to sense everything around you."

Erik would have turned a circle before. Now, he pushed out his domain to sense his prey. Instead of overwhelming as it had been, it had become familiar, understandable.

A Telarri approached.

"Let's tango, mother fucker."

Erik ran behind a tree as it released a sonic blast from its mouth. He ran away, keeping trees between him and the Telarri. It jumped from tree to tree. Unable to get a clear line of sight, it slashed through a tree in a rage.

Erik didn't look down. He scanned with his domain

*Come on, pull it together.* Erik wanted to smack himself in the head. It was like learning how to dance, except his whole body and movement had too many old and bad habits. He had to force them out and replace them.

He channelled elements and mana through his body, making it easier to see through his domain and react faster and stronger as he dodged to the side. Claws hacked into a tree as he tried to not fall over from the leap.

He tried to send lightning through his body, but it didn't respond. He drew on mana, nothing. Earth, nothing. Flame. He swatted wildly with a fist of fire.

The Telarri hit him in the side, spinning him around and slashing at his back.

Erik was disorientated as he tried to run.

He lasted for several dozen minutes, running blind through the fog with a screaming, clawing, and kicking Telarri getting more inventive every minute. Two more jumped out from the ground, stabbing stone spears at his face. He fell on the teleportation pad, the light draining from his surroundings as he panted on the formation.

"Domains stretch out in all directions. About time you two idiots started paying more attention to what's happening under your feet. Again," Xun Liang said, sickly sweet. Erik could see his smile as he appeared in the forest again.

*This is going to be a long three days.* He circulated his fire element, the only thing he could rely on.

# 8
## Gatekeepers

K ujo Hikokie's face pinched together as he raised his hand over the door, pausing a moment before he knocked.

"Come in."

Kujo Hikokie stepped into the room and bowed to Professor Mueller.

"Hello, Kujo. How can I help you?" Mueller asked.

"Professor, I hope you don't take my words as rude. My younger brother Ujisuke was in your history class, and he spoke highly of you. I wanted to ask you some questions, if that would be okay with you?" Hikokie bowed deeper.

"Very well. I will allow your questions." Mueller put down his pen.

"There are two students in your class. West and Rodriguez. They do not come from any of the Associations. How many of your classes have they attended?"

"Those two." Mueller sighed and sat back in his chair, rolling the question around. "I guess if you ask anyone in my class, they will tell you the same thing. They've only attended one of my classes. Why are you interested? Please tell me you're not looking to take revenge for your brother." Mueller's voice hardened.

"I cannot say that I am not motivated by my brother, but I am also a member of the Fighter's Association and I wish to protect the Imperium with everything I can."

"Tell me how this is not motivated by your brother and why you are asking me questions?"

Hikokie stood up straight. "Last month, they fought my brother and ten other applicants that wanted to join the academy in the same day—both of them. They defeated them all and retained their position. They were much stronger than they were when they arrived."

"Avegaaren is a school to make people stronger."

"Yes, but professor, they have no registered teacher or master. In fact, other than going to lectures and the library, there is no record of them doing anything else. They don't show up to anything for three days at a time and their accommodations have their own guards who, incidentally, travel to and from the First Realm. I believe they are using the academy to gain information and have become gatekeepers."

"Calling someone a gatekeeper is a serious claim, not trying to advance and focusing on keeping out new talent from the academy." Mueller leaned forward.

"This is the information I have found," Hikokie presented an information scroll.

Mueller opened it. It burned away, light streaming between his brows, pinching together harder with each passing second.

He patted away the ash remains of the scroll, his face drawn together.

"And last week they defeated another ten applicants in the same day. Three months in a row now. What will you do even if they are gatekeepers?" Mueller asked.

"I will ask for a special dispensation to have them retested to see where they rank and clear them from the bottom ranks, so people that deserve to join the academy are given the chance to do so."

Mueller studied Hikokie, making him lower his head. "A retesting. I will put forward your recommendation. You will fight both of them to see just how strong they are, and the depths of their ability."

Rekha listened to her sound transmission messages, leaning up against the wall of the smithy, ignoring the probing eyes as men and women walked past.

"You it's easier to deal with all the glares when you're wearing your helmet and not covered in gore," Sam said, sitting on a barrel next to her.

Rekha was proud of her looks, but at the same time she wished that others, like Cayleigh and Sam did, would look past her beauty. "As long as they leave us alone, I'll be happy."

"Unless they propose a marriage." Sam raised an eyebrow.

"They want to marry, they can marry the ground."

"About ten feet down?" Sam smiled.

Rekha smiled. "I think I could embed them fifteen, at least."

The door to the smithy opened as Cayleigh walked out. "Mom says hi. Shall we get going?" She wiped sweat from her brow.

"Warm in there?" Sam jumped off the barrel and they walked through the stores that lined the street. They were simple affairs, but each held at least a master level crafter.

"Even with my fire resistance, it leaves me sweating. Mom's got legendary resistance. She barely feels a thing, even with a block of celestial iron in her hand." Cayleigh grinned.

"Elemental freaks."

"Mana dumbass." The two of them smiled at one another before Cayleigh pulled him down to kiss him on the cheek.

"Lovebirds," Rekha muttered.

"Ah, you never know. Maybe one of the gentlemen or ladies ogling you might be a match," Cayleigh said.

Rekha groaned as they approached a teleportation pad to head home.

They appeared at a palatial estate. The entire building was set up in a formation, condensing mana and elements and focusing them into training rooms across the area.

"Feels good to be back," Sam said as they walked up the stairs, finding an older human lady wearing a maid's outfit.

"Madam Li."

"It is good to see you, little Rekha."

"She is a ball of destruction. Should have seen what she did to some guy's walls. Surprised the place was still standing when we left." Cayleigh grinned as they continued their climb.

"Sam, Cayleigh, will you two be staying over?"

"Yup!" Cayleigh grinned.

"Any of that divine moruasi wine?" Sam smiled.

"Certainly. Sam, your rooms have been cleaned and are waiting for you."

"Thank you, Madam Li," Rekha said.

"It is my duty. Now, shall we get all of you out of that armor? Dinner will be at six tonight; that's in two hours. The west garden is rather lovely right now. Refreshments will be laid out there for you."

Servants appeared, guiding Sam and Cayleigh away. Rekha watched them go, talking amicably with the servants they had made friends with.

"I wonder if we shouldn't give their residences to another. They spend most of their time here," Madam Li said.

"I don't know what I would do with all this by myself," Rekha said as she followed Madam Li. Madam Li waved her hand and a doorway in front of them shimmered, showing a different room beyond.

They passed through the doorway, teleported across the palace.

"Anything happen while I was gone?"

"Your master went missing again."

"Makes sense." The corners of her mouth lifted in a rare, soft expression.

"He is the Head of the Imperium and he's as bad as you for disappearing all the time."

"I just had the right role model."

Madam Li's snort seemed to disagree as they passed through another doorway. "There are also two people from the lower realms that are making a stir."

"Which Association?"

"None. They're from an empire."

"Oh?" Rekha raised an eyebrow as they passed through another doorway. The doors to her room opened. It was large enough to fit a modest home. Light drifted through the thin curtains that danced with the light breeze passing through the room. A small waterfall trickled into a bath big enough for a dozen adults, letting off a light steam, overlooking the southern gardens, carefully and perfectly molded.

A modest bed, a training area, closet, and desk filled out the rest of the room.

Attendants moved to Rekha as she raised her arms. A burst of specific mana and force of will unlocked her armor. Their deft fingers went to work on the armor, shedding the kilograms.

"Which empire?"

"An empire in the First Realm."

"First Realm?" Rekha turned, startling the attendants. "Sorry."

"They are from the Alvan Empire. From their names, they might be the emperors of the empire."

"Alvan? Not the same with the Alvan Alliance?" Rekha's face hardened.

"I believe it is one and the same."

"I doubt they are here for anything good."

"There are rumors that they are acting as gatekeepers. They spend most of their time in the library now that they have been shunned from the lectures. Otherwise, they do whatever for days at a time."

"Trying to get as much information to get stronger to secure their control over their alliance, probably."

"They have been here for nine months and defeated all the people that have challenged them. People are now challenging those ahead of them in the ranking and making it in. A man ranked in the eight thousand has issued a challenge and requested a retest. I believe Academy Head Serkin will give it."

"It is a stain for someone so highly ranked to have to fight them."

Rekha shed the last of her armor.

They started working on her under clothes, stained with dirt and sweat, as one worked on her hair, teasing out the knots.

"How were your missions?"

"The lower realms are getting lively because of this Alvan Alliance. There are a number of tears in the Ninth we dealt with. Small incursions, but a lot of them." Rekha frowned.

"You think that there is more to them?"

"Who knows what Devourers and the Ravagers are thinking? While the tears are all over, not one Devourer went through and once we attacked. Several Ravagers fled, returning to the Shattered Realms."

"Even a year ago they would fight, no matter what."

"They have changed their behavior from what happened in the past." Rekha agreed.

In nine months, Erik and Rugrat's growth was monstrous. Xun Liang and Weebla watched them as they practiced in the training dungeon.

Their movements, which had been jerky and unsure before, were now graceful, born of new instinct. Attacks came in from every direction as they sweated to counter it all.

Fire increased the strength they were able to use in a moment. Earth allowed them to heal and recover from their fatigue, keeping them in peak condition. Mana was another limb to move them as they needed, turning it into a dance of blurs and cracks as blows tore through the air.

Rugrat shifted mana, turning it from shields into weapons and restrictions, controlling the flow of the fight. It seemed alive under his control.

Erik's fists cracked out; lightning no longer danced on his skin as his knuckles hardened at the last second before impact. He struck a golem, taking out a knee joint, twisting, striking a shoulder joint. His attacks were quick and destructive, each aimed at a key weakness of his enemy, disabling them before their bodies could recover.

"They have a greater control over elements and mana now. Restricting them worked well," Weebla said.

"They needed time to learn their elements and mana. Having the threat of the Telarri only sped things up."

Erik and Rugrat were dodging and even counterattacking some of the attacks that rained down on them, each dealing with five Telarri at the same time with their eyes were closed.

"They have been working on whittling down their opponents instead of defeating them outright. See how Erik is targeting their bodies, hitting them at points that will create the most amount of damage over time? Rugrat is using spells all over the place and has integrated in the use of elements. Still, he is better suited for range, but he can at least defend himself in close. It's reversed with Erik."

Weebla turned her head to the side. "Someone has come to the training reception," she said.

"Ughh really? I was hoping for more time."

"I don't think he's here for you."

"Really? What for?"

"It's a proctor."

They frowned at one another. "I'll go and take a look."

Xun Liang stood up and went through the teleportation formation. The proctor was looking around the place and seemed confused.

"You—" The man's mouth opened and closed as he stared at Xun Liang. He wrung his hands together, not quite knowing what to do

"You're not looking for me, so who are you looking for? And none of that bowing crap."

"S-Sir, I'm looking for two men." He rushed over, clasping his fist. "They might be hiding nearby, intending to harm you!"

"What are their names?"

"Erik West and Jimmy Rodriguez, but he goes by Rugrat most of the time."

"Yes, and what of them?"

The man smacked his lips, his voice regaining its strength. "They are from the lower realms, sir, from the Alva Empire, and they are acting as gatekeepers."

"Gatekeepers. Oh, I guess that they *were* just fighting the people that were trying to take their positions." Xun Liang looked up at the ceiling and frowned. "I thought they would try to climb the ranks. I know it was all I thought about when I was younger. They're training demons, but hmm, yeah, they might just not care about the ranks. Their gear from Alva is already high tier."

Xun Liang rubbed the side of his head and sighed. "Ahh, these professional fighter types. I've not run into their kind before."

"Sir, do you know of them?"

"You're going to have to promise that you will not tell anyone that I am here or what I am going to tell you?" Xun Liang's words made the man drop to his knees.

"I will say nothing!"

"Good." His lighthearted tone returned. "Then what do you need with my two students?"

"S-Students?" The proctor looked up with wide eyes.

"Yes, they needed a bit of kicking around, but they're shaping up nicely. I guess they must not care about the rankings in the Academy. They are very low key and humble."

The blood was quickly draining from the man's face.

"So, what did you want?"

"I, uhh, there has been a challenge against them. A retest by another student and supported by their history teacher."

"That is not what I was expecting." Xun Liang sighed. "Why are things always so complicated? Fine, I will tell them. It should give them some more pressure to deal with, hmm. Maybe I should make it a goal of theirs to fight their way up the ranks? You said that he was at the eight thousand rank, right? Wait, is he fighting both of them or just one of them?"

"Both of them at the same time. It would be fairer that way."

"Well, how would the ranks be sorted out? Would they both take his rank?"

"We—"

"You didn't think that far because you don't think that they could defeat your fighter. I think you should put some thought into it." Xun Liang started to pace. "If they are to challenge people one hundred ranks higher than them with their five challenges, they can go up five hundred positions in a month. They might need to increase their cultivation some to compete with those in the higher ranks. Could get them into the team fights." Xun Liang sighed as he muttered. "Then Master is going to kick my ass for making them fight all the time. Need to leave them some time to learn from the library. Wait."

Xun Liang stopped. "Where are they from these two? You said Alva right?"

"Yes, they are its emperors."

"Didn't Alva create that alliance that is spreading throughout the lower realms?"

"Yes."

"Urgh, give me a minute. Eli'keen gave me some boring report." Xun Liang paced, looking at the ceiling, and tapped his chin. "They defeated an alliance of sects that attacked them and rebuffed attacks from a group in the Seventh Realm." He closed one eye and clucked his tongue. "Used that to take over cities, build up alliances, create trade. Are you *sure* that they're the leaders?"

"Yes, sir."

"Huh, must have some good assistants. Those two are idiots." Xun Liang snorted.

"It is said there is a council that runs things, but they are all elected, so it could not be them."

Xun Liang's eyes moved back and forth, pulling information together.

"Erik and Rugrat care about ability over all else. I could see them overlooking personal power for people's abilities in other places. But then having elected officials that control their empire? Everyone gains power by taking it in the realms." Xun Liang clapped his hands, startling the proctor. "Well, this is great. I've been reading about this Alva; they created a newfound peace in the lower realms. They're spreading information and teaching across the realms in a way the Associations haven't been able to in the centuries they have existed for. People have stopped fighting for what they can gain in peace over war. Huh, and they're still humble. Well, mouthy when I train them, and stubborn bastards, but good people." Xun Liang cleared his throat at his ramblings. "You okay? You look rather pale and sweaty?"

"It is nothing sir,"

"Okay. You're sure? Erik could take a look at you and get you healed in a moment. He's a good healer."

"Ah, I do need to pass on the challenge to them."

"You got the papers?"

"Yes, sir." The proctor pulled out the scroll. Xun Liang pulled it to his hand.

"I will pass this on to them and not a word of where I am."

"No, sir."

"Oh, and if you could pass me information on what's happening, that would be great. Save me sneaking around the campus and the cafeteria."

Xun Liang turned and headed back toward the teleportation formations.

"Guess I'll have to focus on their training together sooner now."

Erik barely heard the whistle, newly ingrained reactions driving him for several more seconds. He took out two more golems, restricting their movements, a destructive punch here, a kick there, almost living flame burning through a joint.

He breathed heavily, scanning around him, all senses and his domain working in combination. It felt like a lifetime since he had been this alive. He breathed, calming himself and flipping back the switch as he rolled out his shoulders, walking out of the sparring square.

"Was just starting to get into the groove."

Rugrat laughed. "Thought we'd be in there for a few more hours."

"Telarri time?" Erik raised an eyebrow, unable to hide the grin on his face. His fear had turned into respect. They were powerful beasts and smart. Each time he went in, he felt that he was fighting a new group, smarter than the last. Always a level higher than him in elemental and mana utilization.

*You don't get stronger fighting against weaker opponents.*

"I have a challenge for you." Xun Liang threw a scroll. Erik made to grab it, but Rugrat snatched it away with mana.

"Show off," Erik muttered.

"One must work on their mana when they must," Rugrat affecting a wise old accent.

"You know that is nothing like how he sounds." Erik rolled his eyes, resigning himself to work on his mana system more. Sitting and meditating for so long, drawing in mana, was so *boring* compared to directing the elements through his body and tempering it down to the cellular level.

"You sound more like a constipated teddy bear."

"Hey, I have a perfect Yoda impression!"

Erik snorted and shook his head.

"Guess we've been challenged. Both of us?" Rugrat tossed the scroll to Erik.

He scanned through the contents.

"Both of you at the same time by someone called Kujo Hikokie. It has been agreed to by your history teacher, Professor Mueller. They think that you are gatekeepers, staying at the lowest ranks to make it hard for people to enter the Academy," Xun Liang said.

"So, the rules apply to everyone but us?"

"Students usually challenge those that are higher than them to increase their rank. Why didn't you?" Weebla asked.

"What's the point? Getting more resources and the like? There are already people that don't like us and we're at the bottom of the pile. The higher our rank, the more interest we'll get. You think that people will be happy when we're taking *their* resources? Resources we don't need?" Erik realized what he had just said.

"I'm not saying the entire academy is like that. You two aren't."

"We know the reality of the academy. It's nearly all people from the Associations, or those trying to escape their past. They all have a great affinity for the academy, which can mean they're more zealous in their actions than is perhaps necessary."

Weebla looked at Xun Liang, who shrugged.

"Who cares what others think? This is the Avegaaren Academy. It's supposed to help the development of the people of the Ten Realms to fight those from the Shattered Realms. I was planning to develop your team fighting skills later, but this moves up the schedule some." He waved for them to follow.

"Your control over the elements has increased rapidly now that both of you are applying your knowledge. You both have a strong control over flames due to the use of your crafts. Erik, your utilization of the elements within your body has reached a level that I have not seen in many others, but you must decide. Do you want to use your mana to enhance or to affect the world around you? You both must pick out what you will focus on and go from there. You have been too general for too long. Rugrat, you must figure out if you want to use spells, or go with pure magic, as you call it. Your use of the elements and mana is impressive." He stopped in front of the teleportation pads as the duo stepped onto them. "What do you decide?"

"Right now?"

"Best to decide right now than in the middle of your fight. We have but fourteen days before your fight. We will need to develop your skills quickly. I had hoped we would have more time."

"I like forming the mana and elements together. It makes me more versatile, and I can use the elements and mana in my domain with the mana inside my body instead of relying on the mana and elements from my body to cast spells," Rugrat said.

"Master?" Xun Liang turned to Weebla, who had followed them.

"I will have more to teach you in the future, but, Rugrat, look at this." Weebla reached out. Threads of elements and mana gathered under her hands, forming a pale purple sword covered in runes of different colors. "As you use your mana in your smithing, forging metal, you can forge the elements and mana together." She smiled at Rugrat, who looked at the sword in wild wonder. "Much like the gunpowder you talked about, it is temperamental."

"Erik?" Xun Liang asked.

Erik wanted to cast great big spells and see the effects, but he had never really walked down that path. From the start, he had used his body. He had been on the front line.

"I want to use spells, but I know that the main way I fight is with my fists. So it would be best if I can use mana internally, though I have a lot of control over the fire element because of alchemy."

"Everyone walks their own path. There is no one path that is better than the other. They are all different by degrees. Very well. You know how you have been trying to control the elements? Stop thinking of your elements, your will, and your mana as different things. They are all part of you." Xun Liang blurred, snapping out attacks at an invisible enemy as he *danced*. Each movement looked light, but every kick and punch or head butt was a release of motion, *cracking* the air with force.

He lowered his defenses, allowing Erik to see the mana and elements that flowed within him, acting and reacting upon one another, the effect greater than the sum of their parts.

"Momentum is your friend; force is your product, and your body is the tool. Use it."

Erik bowed his head. Like Rugrat, he was quiet, trying to take in what he had seen.

"You two are closer than blood brothers might hope to be. You have been since you came here, and you will leave the same. It is time that you got to understand the other's position." Xun Liang stepped onto the teleportation pad and the trio entered the fog filled forest.

"Rugrat, you will be fighting the creatures up front. Erik, you will be in the rear."

"I want to use my mana internally. How can I fight in the rear?" Erik asked.

"You can heal at range, and you can throw, right? What if Rugrat is in danger? Best get ready. They're coming."

Telarri roared, jumping out at the invaders.

Rugrat rushed to meet them as Erik drew a spear from the ground, holding it in his hand as he exerted control on the mana around him. Erik rose to gain a better view of the fight and saw Xun Liang casually floating around. Rugrat engaged the first Telarri, weaving through their defense. Mana blades appeared, stabbing into the creature as he rushed to meet the next that invaded the area.

"Rugrat, slow down. YHou need to gather them up." Erik turned and threw a spear at a Telarri that came from another direction.

"All right," Rugrat said.

The Telarri dodged Erik's spear. Erik drew the fire element into his hand, raining down attacks on the creature. It had become smarter, dodging most, but Erik finally overwhelmed it.

"Erik!"

He turned around. Rugrat was dealing with four Telarri at the same time. Erik cursed himself for becoming so focused on his opponent.

Rugrat shifted to draw other Telarri towards him, his magic pissing off others and drawing them to him.

Erik tore off a branch of a nearby tree, infusing it with the Wood element and throwing it. It tore itself into swirling darts, cutting down a Telarri. A bolt of lightning leapt from his hand.

"Rugrat!"

Rugrat moved in a panic to dodge. The lightning barely missed him and hitting a Telarri.

Erik breathed again. He heard only the rustle of leaves before a Telarri dropped. He threw himself forward, narrowly missing the attack that tore through the ground below. He had no time to see as he flew through the air. The Telarri jumped through branches, hurling attacks at him.

"Remember that you are not in your old roles. Erik, survey the area, make judgement calls. Move Rugrat where he needs to be. Communicate with him. Anticipate his moves. Rugrat, stop trying to control the battlefield. Go where you're directed. Trust in Erik."

Xun Liang stood on a tree branch. A Telarri went through where he had been, appearing twenty meters away, floating down to another branch.

Erik fought off the creature and turned toward Rugrat.

"Rugrat, on your right. I have the earth one on your left!"

Erik released a fire arrow. Rugrat moved to his side as the fire arrow pierced through the earth Telarri.

Erik turned and drew up metal from the ground and cast lightning upon it, catching three Telarri running toward Rugrat's back.

"Back up!"

Rugrat jumped back, taking some hits as Erik condensed the lightning. It hit the beasts Rugrat had been fighting like a train, burning through them.

More Telarri roared in the forest.

"Rugrat, move to your left fifty meters!"

"Got it!"

Their timing was horrible. Their anticipation was worse. They failed several times over the next eight days, but they trusted in one another, and even while frustrated, they worked, revised, and became stronger together.

"They are worse than you are," Weebla said, watching Erik and Rugrat. They ate, discussing their latest fight, talking about what went well and what they needed to change.

"I was an exemplary student."

"Do you want me to get your school record? I don't think that there is a single professor that would call you an exemplary student. No, the thing is that you were was alone; you didn't have a team behind you. You were stronger than all the others and you didn't have peers. Those two, the way they fight, the way they work together, even in one another's roles, they've adapted in the space of a week."

"Trust," Xun Liang said, from a place much deeper and solemn. "They trust one another with their lives, and that is not some throwaway statement with them. It is a real statement that they feel down to their bones."

"You think that the academy is going to let this go?" Weebla couldn't hide her concern.

"I don't think they will," Xun Liang sighed. "For too long we've been up here at the top of the pile, looking down on the people in the lower realms as if they are somehow lesser because they do not fight in the Tenth Realm. Ironic that we want more people to fight beside us, but we alienate others."

"Do you think you'll need to step in?"

"Not yet, no. I don't want to take away from them." Xun Liang looked at Erik and Rugrat. "They are both strong, and they are not from any Association. If they can cause an upset in the academy, create a stir through the ranks, and show them that we need to work with those outside of the Associations it will be a start."

"You know their backgrounds," Weebla said.

"Yes, of course."

"They have the backing of the Alvan Alliance, and control the lower realms. The last time the lower realms had the power to contend with the higher realms, it caused the Rising Wars. They very nearly wiped out all the Elves and Gnomes, and it almost led to a genocide of the humans in the lower realms."

"Erik and Rugrat are not the kind of people that would pursue war for the sake of war."

"No, but their people are protective. If something were to happen to the two of them and the Associations were to blame… You know that in the agreements to allow the Associations into Alva that the Association is regarded as nothing more than any other merchant, no extras."

"I didn't, no." Xun Liang frowned.

"The Associations tried to get around this by enticing the other nations around the empire to host them. *All* of them refused. The Associations have little hold in the First and Second Realm. While those Realms hold millions of people, their population is more than five times that of the Fifth, Sixth and Seventh Realm combined. Alva is much closer to them than the Associations."

"Why is it that I don't feel angry or upset in the slightest, but think it makes sense?" Xun Liang said.

"Because in dealing with the sects and others of the Ten Realms, the Associations have become used to dealing with threats to their power. They are not used to allies." Weebla patted his arm. "They're waiting on you."

Xun Liang cleared his throat and stood. Erik and Rugrat took a drink of their water, clearing away their food into their storage rings.

"Okay, you two have just learned how hard it is for the other in their role and what they have to consider. You have just two days until your fight. Now you will be fighting in your original roles. Erik, you will be on the front line, and Rugrat, you will be acting as his support. Try not to to get too seriously hurt. Oh, and the Telarri might be a *bit* stronger this time. See you in two days."

He waved as the duo disappeared.

"When thinking about the elements, just considering them as just fire, metal, or earth is really only surface level. With metal, you can use lightning as a ranged attack. You can use the metal aspect to reinforce your shield. They are two sides of the same coin." Erik shovelled in more food, chewing enough to talk again.

"Lightning runs through our bodies. You use it to fire your nerves and that makes the rest of your body react. You speed up the transmission of those electrical impulses." Erik's hand appeared next to Han Wu's head, a breeze rushing past as tingles ran down his spine. "If you shoot current through someone, they're not going to have a good time and you can take them out of the fight. You hit that lightning into their muscles or their nerves, you can give them a lot of pain and you can mess up the signals running through their body. Fire, we think of flame, but it is also heat. If you can warm up your muscles, they are more supple, and you can react faster. You can also reduce the heat if your muscles heat up too much, draw that heat away. Flush through with earth element, remove the lactic acid, you can last for hours. You'll remain focused, no heat strain. At your peak for days, not hours or minutes. Just a shot here and there as well. Focused use will win over unfocused wastefulness every time."

Erik continued eating. "Now that impulse." He snapped his fingers. "That's the good stuff. That's what I want to get to."

Han Wu knew the look in Erik's eyes. Many would take it for wildness, chaos of the mind. It was drive. Erik had seen a path forward, a way of progress, and he was chasing it with every fiber of his being. Every discovery led to the next advance. In nine months, the way he moved, the way he fought, was completely different.

Han Wu looked over to Rugrat, who was busy forming mana into different solid items, talking on the principles of smithing, mana and elements and the combination of craft with fighting.

"All right, back in," Xun Liang said. He had allowed the Special Team to meet Erik and Rugrat at the teleportation pads to debrief them in between training.

The Special Teams moved off the pad as Erik and Rugrat quickly put away their food and drank down water.

"Erik, work on your coordination when you're using your elements. Rugrat, you need to work on disrupting your enemy. As you adapt and use the elements around you to cast your magic, the more or less of a given element around them, the weaker or stronger the attack the Telarri can hit you with."

"Disrupting the elements around them should weaken their attacks," Rugrat said, putting on his helmet, dampening his voice.

"See you later." Erik's body radiated heat, relaxing him, ready to fight as he disappeared.

Han Wu moved toward Weebla and Xun Liang and bowed. "Thank you."

"What for?" Xun Liang frowned.

Han Wu rose and laughed. "Those two are hard to work with, stubborn as the roots of a hundred-year-old tree. They're good people. They've been going through the motions for a long time, trying to learn as much as possible, but it's been too long since I saw them this alive. So, thank you for igniting their passion again and making them feel alive."

He bowed again, the Special Team joining in.

"What kind of teacher would I be if I didn't do this much?" Xun Liang said, waving them off, embarrassed.

Han Wu laughed.

"No matter if we are no longer to stay in the Academy, know if you ever need something then we would be happy to assist." Han Wu left it at that and headed out with the rest of the team members.

"Did you sense their cultivations?" Weebla asked as the last member shot up through the elevator shaft.

"All of them are around Erik and Rugrat's cultivation," Xun Liang said.

"How many nations in the lower realms would have dozens of others that are as strong as them as their guards? And their guards still respect them?"

Xun Liang tapped his hand in thought.

"I also hear that the Prime Student has returned with her team."

"That one is a terror." Xun Liang shook his head. "Those three are nothing but trouble."

Weebla snorted. "You can say that again. Did Erik and Rugrat pick a name for their team?"

"The Door Kickers."

"What does that mean?"

"Not sure. Some Earth thing probably."

# 9

## Door Kickers

David Mueller took his seat in the teacher's booth. Several professors had come to see the match, as had a few dozen students and people from Avegaaren City. The matches were open to anyone in the Ninth Realm to come and watch for free, allowing the academy to promote the talents of the students and for friends and family not in the academy to see their development and cheer them on.

"A nasty business, dealing with gatekeepers. You did well to notice it," Gars, an older teacher, said, shaking his white hair. "The nations from the lower realms have grown so bold as of late. It is time they remembered who keeps them safe. I hear these two are from that alliance?"

"Yes, they are supposed to be the emperors of the Alvan Alliance."

"Emperors." Gars let out an irritated growl. "If they were to meet the Head of the Imperium, they would be nothing but paper in the wind."

Mueller had only seen the Head fight twice before, each match only lasting a handful of exchanges before his opponent was unable to continue. He was a force to be reckoned with.

"They've kept themselves hidden from prying eyes, and use our libraries and lectures to gain information that they share with their guards and funnel into the lower realms."

"Despicable to think they can use our academy as their personal vault."

Gars angrily closed his robe.

"I hope that, after this, they will know their place and adhere to the rules of the Academy, become true students or head back to the lower realms."

"I'm not sure they have the ability to become true students. I have always found those that don't come from the Associations to be *lacking* in the right kind of fundamentals and foundational information."

Mueller wanted to agree, but he was supposed to remain neutral in these matters.

"It looks like it is about to start." Gars said.

Mueller and the other teachers moved to the front of the booth, some sitting, others drinking or eating from the snacks at the rear.

Kujo Hikokie walked out into the arena.

Erik and Rugrat arrived on their teleportation formation, bowing. They stood up straight and pulled on their helmets.

Two faceless warriors. Their clothes, boots and armor, while different, were worn, not the clean and polished rune-carved formations artistically integrated into his flame-red armor, styled in the Japanese samurais of his family.

A proctor stood between the two sides. He raised his arm, stopping them where they were.

The faceless emperors looked at one another, Rugrat the taller one and Erik the smaller one. They bumped fists and started to circulate their mana and elements.

"Begin!" The proctor shot into the sky and out of the way of the fight.

Erik cracked the ground beneath his feet, turning into a blur. Stone weapons tore free, attacking Hikokie in mid-air.

His sword shot free of his scabbard, escaping the first attacks with a burst of speed. The ground seemed to be coming apart underneath him as Rugrat's attacks sprouted around him.

Erik weaved through Rugrat's attacks, landing his own. Hikokie fell back under the attacks.

Erik's blows struck his weak points, slowing his reactions.

Erik drew power into his fist, going for a final blow. Hikokie dodged the attack and sliced at Erik. Erik detonated the mana gathered in his hand, pushing him out of the way. Hikokie stumbled as his blow passed through air, his side open as a dozen mana blades hiding among the stone struck.

Hikokie was trapped by the attacks as his barrier activated and he shot away.

Erik and Rugrat moved forward for the kill. The proctor stopped in front of them. "Erik and Jimmy win."

Rugrat stepped forward, but Erik put his hand on his chest.

"Fucking academy for the Associations." Rugrat took off his helmet and spat, looking up at the teacher booth, glaring at them.

"Proctor, what rank was he?" Erik asked.

"Seven thousand eight hundred and forty-seven."

"I'll fight whoever is seven thousand seven hundred and forty-seven."

"Jackass. Fine, I'll take on whoever is one below that," Rugrat said.

"I—" The proctor looked at Hikokie, who was being checked by medical staff, and glanced up to the teacher's box.

Another proctor landed in the arena and talked to him. He looked at the new arrival quizzically.

"Very well."

The new proctor tilted his head to Erik and Rugrat before departing.

"This might be a bigger problem than we thought," Gar said.

Mueller grunted, his eyes never leaving the duo as they left the arena.

Rekha finished reading the latest report, looking out over the sparring room.

"Who are you thinking about murdering now?" Sam tilted his last word playfully.

"Those two emperors. They defeated the challenger, then went on to rise five hundred positions in a week. Their fights were quick and efficient. They've been hiding their strength this entire time."

"So, they weren't gatekeepers." Cayleigh wiped away her sweat with the back of her hand and rested an axe on her shoulder.

"No, but I think they are trying to crush the academy and use us as a way to look stronger."

"All the resources they'll get access to alone can't compare to anything in the First Realm."

"You don't think they'll really get that far? They have some confidence getting from ten thousand to the top seven thousand, but the higher up in the ranks one goes, the larger the power difference," Sam said.

"They do control most of the lower realms," Rekha said.

"I heard they defeated a corvette warship and channelled a Sky grade dungeon core through their bodies." Cayleigh smiled, full of challenge.

"You just want to fight everyone," Sam said.

"And you like watching me." Cayleigh winked.

Sam pursed lips that stretched into a smile.

Rekha rolled her eyes.

"Can you two stop flirting all the time? My master told me to look after the Academy in his absence. This seems like something we should be paying attention to."

"We're the top-ranked team. There's not really anything we can do to them right now. If they make it this far up the totem pole, we can hammer them right back down." Cayleigh spun her axes.

"The teachers know what they're doing, and it would be nice to see another challenger. Been so long since someone has tried to fight us." Sam threw a dagger, sinking it up to the hilt in a target across the room.

"There is always someone stronger. We're a year from graduation, and we won't be dealing with tasks in the Ninth Realm anymore. We'll be on the front lines in the Tenth Realm," Rekha reminded him.

"All the more reason to have fun now," Cayleigh said.

"So, what's next?" Rugrat asked.

"Next, Rugrat, you need to work on your smithing, and you should temper yourself at the same time. Erik, you should use the resources you gained to increase your mana cultivation. I have a feeling you might need the extra power."

"Can I sell the resources?" Erik asked.

"Why would you do that? They are some of the strongest master level pills and concoctions in the Ten Realms." Xun Liang frowned.

"Well, they're the strongest of Avegaaren, but it will take a few months to refine them. I should only need a few weeks, maybe, of Alva's training to increase my cultivation."

"The resources are yours to deal with. Would you need to go back to Alva to work on your cultivation?" Weebla asked.

"No, I could have it setup here. It might go faster that way."

"All right, for the next month, I want you to cultivate and work on your craft. See how you can use what you've learned in fighting, in smithing, alchemy, and healing. Take missions from the Mission Hall," Xun Liang said.

"We'll have new challengers next month," Erik said.

"Then challenge the person one position higher than you. Maintain where you are. Do five fights and you won't need to deal with others. If you're able to complete more missions in the Mission Hall, then the overall number of people you need to fight decreases. In the higher ranks, you have a certain number of missions you have to complete every month to hold your position," Weebla said.

Xun Liang finished up his orders. Weebla talked to Rugrat about smithing and agreed to give him some more private lessons.

Erik and Rugrat were set to their tasks. Xun Liang served Weebla tea as they sat down to the side of the training area.

"Do you think you'll need to do something?" Weebla asked.

"About time we stirred things up here. The Academy is too stuck in its ways and Alva and the people in their alliance will reach into the Ninth Realm sooner rather than later." Xun Liang shook his head. "No, I think it might have been too long since the Academy had a tournament."

"A tournament? Are you sure?"

"Avegaaren was built to bind humans, Elves, and Gnomes together. Now we need it to break the divisions between the sects, clans, and Associations."

"That's rather ambitious."

"There is something happening in the higher realms. You know it too. The Devourers are playing it safe. So many tears have opened, but none of them have come through. The Devourer in the Seventh Realm was the first one we've seen in nearly a century and a half."

"Do you think Akran has something planned?"

"He's the strongest Devourer I've seen in several centuries. There are few that are willing to attack him, and he has fifteen Devourers sworn to him and thousands of Ravagers. He made it to the top of the Shattered Realms aggressively. Since he's gained power, attacks have decreased against the realms."

"He was waging a war to command more of the Shattered Realms."

"He consolidated gains, but I'm more worried about the Devourers he brought to his side without fighting. Creatures from the Shattered Realms look to gain from any agreement. They must think they have a lot to gain to have so many allied with him."

# 10

## Cultivation and Crafting

E rik sat in front of his rumbling cauldron. Beasts of metal and earth joined the beasts of flame, working together to concoct a pill.

Smaller beasts of water had entered the cauldron as well. He had taken Delilah's theories on elemental alchemy and combined it with his own command of the elements. With his will and increasing control over the elements as the level of his elemental core had increased, all he'd needed was Xun Liang's kick in the right direction to combine the things he hadn't been thinking of before.

They moved together, altering the different ingredients, preparing to combine them before his cauldron shook and rumbled. The fire and metal beasts crashed into one another, creating a rolling destruction that ended in black smoke rising from the top of the sealed cauldron.

Erik coughed and waved away the smoke.

"Well, that didn't work." He laughed and cleaned up the cauldron, storing it away now he had used up the last of his ingredients.

He stretched, cracking his back, using heat to loosen his muscles and body. The earth element made him alert as he ran a low thrill of lightning through his spine, waking up his entire body, bringing him to peak readiness.

He took a quick glance at his notifications.

| **Skill: Alchemy** |
| --- |
| *Level: 112 (Master)* |
| Able to identify 3 effects of the ingredient. |
| Ingredients are 10% more potent. |
| When creating concoctions, mana regeneration increases by 40% |

| **588,785,913,157,831/1,168,160,000,000,000,000,000 EXP till you reach Level 105** |
| --- |

The Special Team member recording what he had been doing and assisting him also groaned upon getting up.

"Don't worry, Lydia. Just need to learn how to warm up your body or stretch some more!"

"You make it sound so easy."

"Training makes it easier." Erik left the room and went out into the new residence he lived in, a large manor with all the necessary facilities.

Lydia and Rimy followed him.

"Mission Hall?" Rimy asked.

"Yeah, need to turn in the pill."

The servant manning the teleportation formation sent them to the Mission Hall.

Erik walked up to the counter, pulling out a pill bottle and a slip of carved wood, putting it on the desk.

The woman looked him up and down through the side of her eye, keeping the sneer from her features. Erik's smile only widened.

She clicked her tongue and took the piece of wood and pill.

"High Expert grade pill received. Mission is completed. Medallion?"

Erik put the medallion on the table. She grabbed it without looking and frowned. She opened her hand around the medallion. The picture of shock and confusion on her face made Erik's smile even brighter. He could see the internal war in her features, not sure how she should treat him.

He waited for a few moments before he pulled out several boxes.

"I also have these to turn in. If you could keep the stars quiet?" Erik smiled.

"Uhh, yes, sir."

"Thank you, and I do not want contribution points, but I would like these materials instead, the ones underlined. Please give me amounts of each in quantities equal to the contribution points."

He put a piece of paper on the desk as she searched through the boxes filled with pills and powders, as well as associated slips.

"Could you have those delivered to my accommodations? I'm not in a hurry and there are a number to complete."

"Uhh, certainly, sir." She gave a meek smile of relief.

Erik held out his hand, and she put the medallion back in his palm.

"Don't judge a book by its cover." He held her eyes, smiled, and left.

"You having fun torturing the staff?" Rimy asked.

"Ah, have to have some fun in life."

"More pills next or patients?" Lydia asked.

"Patients I think. Getting stuck in that small room all day can make someone feel a little cramped."

Erik moved to the wall and formation that listed out all the different kinds of ailments and issues that people were suffering from. Some even included seer formations that stored a scan of the patient.

He went through the boards, selecting different patients.

"All right, let's go."

A few hours later, Erik stepped out of a carriage outside of a grand estate. A large wooden gate stood in their way.

Rimy activated a formation next to it.

Several minutes later, part of the door opened to reveal two blue eyes.

"Hello, might I ask you what business you have here?" a servant asked.

Erik held up the slip and put it through the opening. She took the slip, closing the eye slot and opening the gate seconds later.

"Please, come in." She smiled.

She locked the gate behind them and escorted them into the estate. It was a simple building of angles, but it looked like it would weather the next century without any sign of wear and tear.

They entered through a foyer, passing through different rooms before arriving in a warm sunroom where a man sat in a wheelchair, looking out at the world.

A guard stepped out next to the door, stopping them.

Another servant hurriedly cleaned up the man, hiding the bowl of food she had been feeding him from. She cleared her throat and stood beside the man.

"These two stay outside," the guard said to Rimy and Lydia.

"I'll be fine. If they raise an issue, they'll be dealing with the might of the Mission Hall and Alva," Erik said.

The servant that had greeted Erik led him over to the man. "This is your patient."

The man's eyes were crystal clear as he looked at Erik.

"I need to confirm some things. He tempered his body with the fire element, but not Earth or Metal, correct?"

"That is correct."

"He has lasting damage from trying to open an acupoint and it's reflecting back on him?"

The maid nodded. "Correct."

"He can control Fire to a great degree and can still write concise messages, but his control over his body, and his mana, has decreased."

The woman looked at the man. His eyes flicked over to her, to Erik, and then to the garden, disregarding them as if he had been through this a dozen times.

"Correct."

"Sir, please look up and down if it is okay for me to touch you." Erik said to the man.

He did so.

Erik grabbed his wrist and ran a scan through his body. He reached around and touched the back of the man's neck. "You might feel an odd sensation. Don't worry."

He sent a spark of lightning into the man's spinal column that should have moved his fingers. Erik traced the lightning as it faded out, never making it through. The connections were broken.

Erik sent a few more flashes of lightning through the man's body. "I think I know what this is. We need to lie him down somewhere before I can get to work."

The man looked at the attendant that had been feeding him. She pulled out a piece of wood and put it near his hand. In flowing script, words burned into the wood. "What are you going to do?" the man asked.

"First, I want to clear the blockage to your acupoints. Acupoints are very similar to mana gates, and I've been known to open a few of those in my time. I will heal your acupoints first, then you will temper your body with the Earth element and then the Metal element." Erik looked at the attendant. "I will check the method to make sure that it won't create issues."

His eyes returned to his patient. "With that, you should be able to recover quickly from what ails you. It will take me a few days, so I will come here every morning to check on you. Should be completed in two weeks. Shall we proceed?"

Do it."

"Very well."

The attendant and guard moved the man to a bedroom. Erik waited downstairs with Lydia and Rimy, giving the man some privacy and respecting his dignity.

"How long will you be?" Lydia asked.

"The acupoints aren't too badly injured. It should only take a few minutes. Should be seeing our next patient in an hour. We'll go to the ones in the worst condition first."

"Make sure you don't pick up another batch of patients when we return, or you won't be done in a month," Lydia said.

Erik smiled as the servant appeared. "He's ready for you."

"Thank you." He tilted his head toward Rimy. "Do you have the concoctions and materials needed for his Earth and Metal tempering?"

"I have sent the servant out to gather them. She should return shortly. Are you sure tempering his body won't harm him?"

"I was asleep for a lot of my elemental tempering. What matters is to make sure that you're helping more than you're harming." The servant appeared with an ornate box.

Erik went through the servant's potions and concoctions, laid out in a box. "Okay, this should be enough. With the Metal elements, you will want to go further. This will allow him to temper his body with the Metal element but won't allow him to assimilate it. You'll need to get three times the dosage of this Metal tempering kit and have him in a Metal element gathering formation to make sure that he progresses, and the Metal element builds instead of reversing."

The servant backed away with the box.

"I'll be right back." Erik went upstairs. He pulled out the prepared needles and took out a needle, injecting a potion through an open acupoint into the mana channels. "That should make it a bit easier."

He dipped a needle into a mana cultivation potion. Checking his scans, he studied the network of fine hair-like acupoints across the man's body. He took the needle, lining it up, and tapped it into the small acupoint. Feeling the hardened blockage of his acupoint, he twisted it to drive in deep.

"One done." Erik worked, hitting the other four in the area that had been badly affected.

He checked his work. Already, the needles were starting to work, releasing the blockages. He left the room, finding Rimy and Lydia waiting with the guard and servant.

"Here is my sound transmission mark. Take out the acupuncture needles in four hours. Call me once he has completed his Metal element tempering."

They exchanged information and left.

"So, what's wrong with him?" Lydia asked once they were away from the manor.

"He has a neural issue. Parts of his nervous system have shut down. When he had the backblast of the mana gathering cultivation, his body was dealing with the damage and his nerves started to retrograde. Even with the healing concoctions, it wasn't as strong as his own healing abilities. Once they started going, the body thought that they shouldn't exist, and healing didn't help. He needs to go through Metal tempering because it will temper and renew his nervous system, rebuilding it. Fixing his acupoints means that his body will be under less stress, so it should be easier for him to go through his temperings."

Lydia pursed her lips and nodded.

Erik hid his grin. "There are few things that are better in the world and more rewarding than healing someone." He pulled out notes on his next patients. "And there are plenty of others that need our help!"

The next three days were spent going from patient to patient before Erik returned to his accommodations.

The compound had been taken over by the Special Teams. In its depths, Erik found several cultivation pods and a familiar face.

"I hear you've been off healing everyone," Jen rose from her desk.

"Shouldn't the head of Alva's medical studies be off in Alva?"

"Some in-field training never hurt, and my staff have things well in hand. Up here, I get to be on the bleeding edge of cultivation and there are plenty of bookstores, healers, and alchemists that are willing to exchange information." She grinned.

Erik snorted, hugging her. "It is good to see you."

"And you. So, tell me about your patients."

They discussed his patients' ailments and the different ways he was trying to heal them, losing track of time.

"The man with the nervous system. How did you know what he had?"

"We have issues like it, or the same back on Earth. People who are completely cognitive, but their bodies betray them. It's nasty to see. Sharp as a whip, but their body turns into their own prison."

Julie shook her head. "That's horrible."

"Yes, it is. Glad that I'm able to help him here, at least. Anyway, I was told that you're the lady to talk to about supercharging my mana gathering cultivation?"

"Get in the pod and roll up your sleeves." She smiled.

He obeyed as she attached IV bags to the pod and moved a table over with the catheters, needles, and tubing she required.

With quick deft movements, she set up IVs in both arms.

"Okay, got the drip going. Just get comfortable and circulate your mana, condensing as you do so." Julie checked the last of the IV lines and pressed the command, tilting Erik backward as the glass closed over him.

"Have a good sleep. Shouldn't be long now till you get your Five Aperture heart. I've added in Fire, Earth, Metal, and Water elements as well to increase your bloodline and your Water tempering slowly." Her voice was muffled by the glass covering.

"Thanks," Erik said, giving her a thumbs up as mana rushed into his pod and he closed his eyes.

# 11
# Rising Tensions

"We can't let them continue to stroll through our corridors as if they're above the Imperium!" Gars slammed his hand on the desk.

He sat at the head of the table. The other department heads sat in the seats around the table, broken into sectors based on what they taught and by generation and ranking.

Teachers worded their agreement. Mueller held back from responding, looking at Academy Head Serkin. He sat back in his chair, holding his elbow as his finger traced down the blue and green scar running down his cheek into his salt and pepper beard.

"We cannot go too far. This is the academy of Avegaaren," Wahida said in a stern tone. "While many of us are from the Associations, the school exists to prepare people to fight in the Tenth Realm to defend the Realms. It does not matter where someone comes from."

"Training? What training have they had? They go to the lectures and the library to suck away our knowledge!" Meng, a fighting trainer, said. "This is a play by the alliance to make us look bad and establish their strength. We are dealing with a big problem, indeed."

"So, they're strong and talking to their people in the lower realms. So what? Do you not send information to your family?" Wahida asked.

"Of course I do, but they're stealing our information!"

"What makes it ours? Are we not the caretakers of the Academy?"

Meng grasped for words as Gar came to his rescue.

"We are all training people to fight in the Tenth Realm. There have been problems with the lower realms in the past, and we must make sure that we are not being pulled into a fight that could affect our mission to defend the Realms."

Wahida looked like she'd sucked a lemon while Meng tilted his head in thanks to Gars.

"Alva has their own academies. They don't teach the same principles we do. This could be a play for them to try to bring more students to their ranks, away from Avegaaren. Those that do not make it into the academy now have an option," Gars said.

"People who have not gained their will, that do not know why they do what they do. If you do not know who you are, how do you know what you will become?" Meng shook his head.

"And what about their four-star ranking, or are we turning a blind eye to that as well?" Wahida growled.

Some of the teachers shifted uncomfortably, looking at one another with unspoken questions.

"They reside in one of the Gnome dungeons. They're lucky the Gnomes didn't take it back from them for stealing it," Gars huffed.

"What the Gnomes do is of little consequence to you," Kronin, an elderly Gnome, spoke lightly, his smile soft, taking all the wind from Gars' sails.

"Sorry, Master Gnome. I was too hasty, angered that others might steal your lands."

Kronin gave out a breezy laugh and shook his head.

Gars cleared his throat. "They activated the dungeon created by the Gnomes, a master work creation. All they did was power a drill, and it opened up the ley lines. It affects the whole of the First Realm. I won't disagree, but if we were to just supply mana stones to machines, then couldn't we all be four-star heroes?"

The teachers muttered to one another. Wahida grimaced as they fell on Gars' side.

Serkin rapped his knuckles on the table, all eyes moving to him.

"A time of change is upon us. To excel or fall behind, it falls on our shoulders to usher our students into this new future. I will remind you that Avegaaren's purpose is to teach anyone that makes it into our academy, to rise up the Realms, and make sure that we can defend against the Shattered Realms."

He sat back in his chair. "For the next three months, all challenges will be stopped. A tournament will be held with all current students. It should shake up the rankings and we can see exactly where students stand."

A ripple of mutterings ran through the room. His raised hand stalled them.

"The lower realms are uniting in a way that we have not seen in the past, ushering in peace. Whether it will last remains to be seen. We have had more incursions and tears in the Ninth and Tenth Realm than in any previous year, and the number of people that come to the academy has continued to decrease." He glanced around the table at each of the teachers. "Even among the Associations, many do not want to reach the Ninth Realm, knowing that they will have to join the academy. They feel that they will be forced to serve in the Tenth Realm away from their families. Our students are mostly people trying to escape from the lower realms, rather than the Associations. Make sure to keep that in mind. the way it was in our generation is not how it is in the current time."

Rugrat sat in Weebla's forge, tucked into a side room off the training room, the door looking like a section of the wall.

"Now, you've been forming blades of mana and elements. Don't forget that you have other elements at your disposal, and you can use them to make enchantments. You don't need to make blades of just mana."

Weebla held out her hand and the flame from the forge twisted and turned into a swirling blade as water daggers condensed from the air. A stone spear flowed from one hand as lightning traced the outline of an arrow. "Every element, while they are different, is stronger or weaker in different situations. While you are disrupting people's mana and the elements around you, someone can easily do the same to you. You need to know how to adapt and use what is around you."

"Still a lot to learn." Rugrat laughed.

Weebla smiled and dismissed the weapons. "There is always more to learn. It is one of the greatest things about living. Now, you create some elemental weapons."

Rugrat raised an arrow of fire, a spear of earth, and a round of mana.

Weebla studied their fuzzy features. "As you grow, you will start to incorporate more of your smithing into your skills. They will be sharper, their form stronger, the enchantments using greater power. You've learned how to forge mana into different shapes. Now you need to do that with the elements. Use what is around you. Forge the Ten Realms into what you need it to be."

Weebla got up from her chair and patted Rugrat on the shoulder. "It's been a quick two months, Master Smith Rugrat." They shared a smile. "But I think your combat teacher wants to have a few words by the way he's hopping around out there."

Rugrat followed her out of the forge, nearly hitting Xun Liang with the door as they exited.

Erik stood in the training room behind him.

"All right, well, that was a productive two months!" Xun Liang clapped his hands together. "Now you two need to get ready for the coming tournament."

"Tournament?" Erik asked.

"You hear that? I think there's an echo in here. Yes, the tournament! It's the talk of the Academy!" Xun Liang beamed.

"Been busy with other things," Rugrat said.

"Polite way of saying there's no one but you and Weebla that would tell us anything that's going on in the Academy," Erik said.

The mood stagnated quickly.

"Well, you're hearing it from me. This is your chance to show just what you can do."

"One big middle finger," Erik laughed dryly.

"They aren't going to look too kindly on you for helping us and if we didn't have a target on our backs before, we sure do now." Rugrat shook his head.

"Are you just going to bow out because some people don't like you? This is a challenge, a way to show them that they're wrong. To shove it in their faces. You just going to roll over?"

Erik's and Rugrat's glares made Xun Liang's smile widen. "That's what I thought. Win or lose, forget them. Fight for yourselves and dig deep." Rugrat and Erik's faces reflected Xun Liang's smile.

"All right then, so Telarri?" Erik asked.

"Naturally. Need to make sure you two haven't gone soft." Xun Liang led them toward the teleportation formations. "You're only allowed to use attacks that meld with your crafting techniques. Each time you come out, you will switch roles: one long range then short range."

"Got it," Erik said.

"Copy," Rugrat said.

"What have you been working on?" Erik asked Rugrat before they stepped onto the formations.

"Shaping elements and forging mana into weapons and spells. You?"

"Creating elemental and mana beasts to perform alchemy. Flames are still my strongest. Do you want to just work on fire element, then compare notes? Then mana, then Earth element. that should allow us to go through them all in greater depth."

"Yeah, I've been thinking that our knowledge of our elements and mana isn't as deep as I want it to be."

"Same here. How did your tempering go?"

Rugrat smiled and held out his hand. Metal spread from his shoulder and down his arm. "Workable."

Erik laughed. "All right, here are a few tips and tricks I found with the Metal element."

Xun Liang and Weebla added in what they had learned about the elements. That took the rest of the afternoon.

Erik tested out what he'd learned in the forests, coming out to discuss it with Rugrat. Weebla and Xun Liang adding in their knowledge. Then they went back in again to continue fighting and testing out what they had learned.

"Do you think this tournament has been created because of Erik and Rugrat?" Delilah asked Roska as she finished giving her briefing.

"I think that it might."

"How safe are they?"

"We have plans for immediate extraction and if they try to stop us, we have the first trans-realm communication devices that will allow us to report the situation to the Seventh Realm and Celestial-level bombs. If they try to take the teams, or Erik and Rugrat, then we can threaten them right back."

"How bad could this get?"

"Depends how far they go with it," Glosil said.

"With the materials sent down by Erik and Rugrat, how is the development of the fleet going?" She looked at Edmond sitting behind Glosil.

"We completed about fifty percent. We started with the smallest ships and worked up from there. We'll use what we learned to build the later generations and larger craft."

"And our personnel?" Delilah looked at Glosil.

"The military has over three hundred thousand full-time military members, another four hundred thousand in active reserve. Five hundred thousand to a million that are ready to serve across the guild and empire." He looked at Blaze and Aditya.

The empire had swelled to six million Alva citizen applicants. Another three million were confirmed Alvan citizens.

"For once, our people are trained ahead of their equipment. We have crews switching out on the different warships to train around the clock inthe Crow assaulters, the air force wings, and the Air force fleet."

The fleet had fallen under Kanoa's umbrella. He and the other Earthers that had served or knew about fleet tactics and aerial tactics had put their heads together with the ex-Sha officers.

There had been some tension with the Sha when they'd given up their warships and joined Alva. Some had joined as citizens, while others had spread across the lower realms. The tension had subsided after they understood what their warships would be turned into.

"What about our allies? I heard there were a few that have been using the threat of the alliance to get away with criminal acts." Delilah looked at Alva's police chief.

"Yes, unfortunately. Some have been dealt with by external sources, like the Mission Hall. Others we've dealt with internally. I have some letters for your signature to be passed out to our mainstay allies about adding new people to the alliance and new rules that groups going against the morals of the alliance will be excommunicated."

"Good. Elise, how are we looking financially?"

"Our infusions of capital into the smaller businesses starting out have paid off, and many of them are showing profits. Factories are moving out into the empire with the increased cost of real-estate. There have been some issues in the other realms with people holding up Alvans, and there was the hostage situation a month ago. Thank you for your assistance there, commander." She smiled at Glosil.

"It is our job to secure the safety of Alvans. Fortune favors the strong, so we cannot be weak toward others. Still, I only sent the Close Protection detail out. I will pass on your thanks to the team lead."

"Thank you." Elise looked back at Delilah.

"Egbert, Miss Jia Feng, how are the academies doing and what is the impact of the information we're getting from Avegaaren?"

"We had to expand the academies. Old Quan has broken ground on a new academy in the empire. It should be completed in another month. The city is devoted to the academy within. There is only so much that we could increase Kanesh and the old Consortium in King's Hill," Jia Feng said.

"It will also have its own dungeons and areas underground, and there are plans to build upward, allowing the academy to expand rapidly," Egbert said. "With the information we are getting from Avegaaren, it really depends on which area people are in. We have furthered our information on smithing, healing, alchemy and fighting in a big way because that is what Erik and Rugrat are focused on. They have gathered information from other areas, but they are not experts in these areas, so the information, while good, sometimes misses the point. The Special Teams have been purchasing books, working in the Ninth Realm Mission Hall to gain more supplies and items that our teachers and department heads can study and learn from. I am pleased to announce that Julilah is our first Star-level crafter, and Qin and Taran should not be far behind her." There was a smattering of applause as Egbert smiled like a proud parent. "Don't tell her I told you. She's rather embarrassed about it and just wants to be left alone to do her crafting."

"Sounds very Alvan to me," Delilah said dryly.

"We should make sure to celebrate it, even if in private," Momma Rodriguez said.

"Couldn't agree more." Jia Feng smiled. The two were close friends and had a motherly disposition toward all Alvans.

"Also, I wanted to bring up the mana well. With the elemental mana coming from the well created by the mana drill, we have been able togrow our dungeon cores rapidly and increase the density of Alva. We cannot hold all the mana, even with the mana gathering formations across the empire. Several locations across the realm are releasing higher elemental mana. Should we send people to these locations?"

"We cannot take everything for ourselves. We will not lay claim to those areas and will allow mana to leak from the empire. We don't need it all, and it increases our ties to those around our borders."

"Shall we continue with the ten percent Sky Realm grade mana stones for the fleet?" Egbert asked.

"Is that enough?" Delilah asked.

"Yes ma'am," Glosil said.

"Understood, that's all I had to say."

"Then unless there is anything else, we are all done."

No one had more to add, bringing the meeting to a close. Momma Rodriguez gathered Delilah, Egbert, Jia Feng, and others with her eyes. Planning out something for Julilah, undoubtedly.

Delilah's thoughts turned toward Rugrat. *Stay safe, you big lunk.* She pictured him training and shook her head. A small smile appeared on her face. It quickly dimmed, her stomach turning as she remembered her last thoughts as he had left.

*I hope he doesn't think I hate him.*

The Avegaaren library was a grand building of polished wood floors and shelves filled with books. Teleportation formations, stairs, and elevators weaved through the building from one section to another.

Erik continued reading, his domain capturing the four librarians that had been putting books away in his vicinity and clearing shelves, watching him the entire time. He used it as extra training as he made notes from the Water element book he was reading.

He sat back, tapping the back of his pen against his chin. "So, the Water element, water cycle, heating and cooling changes form. Water will wear down the strongest material in the world given time, and it is constant. Water is in the body, blood, muscle, movement of nutrition through the body. Water and heat create air type reactions. Ice, vapor, water. Pressurized water can create a cutting force." Erik had been studying Water tempering for weeks. A Water tempering needle was stuck in his right thigh. With the new formations, he only needed one needle to maintain his tempering.

He stopped tempering with the element, wanting to learn more about it. The Water element filled all his cells. He felt like he was fit to bursting. He was on the cusp.

Erik drew on his elements and mana as a male librarian charged in like a bull. "All right, that is *it*! You are *banned* from the library for your infractions!" he yelled.

"What for?" Erik said as the librarian grabbed him and pulled him out of his chair.

"You have come in several times, creating a disturbance with your noise with that other lower realmer!"

"Hey, let me get my notes."

"Just want to steal our books," another said.

Erik reached out with his mana, grabbing the papers and storing them away.

"Fuck you." Erik gave him the middle finger and a smile.

The bullheaded librarian pushed Erik. Erik floated through the air, turning, and leaving the three librarians dogging behind him.

They moved to corner him between the three of them.

A group of students laughed at something one of them had found. Erik paused, looking at the librarians and the group, then back at them again.

"Please don't make a scene. We don't need you lower realmers messing up everyone else's studying." The one who had muttered about him stealing books sneered and the bull-headed one crossed his arms.

A smile pressed over Erik's face as he pulled out a blue and purple needle from his storage ring.

They looked at him, unsure what to do.

"You know, it is school rules like that one that can interfere with a student that is cultivating. And I do so love to make a scene."

Erik smacked the needle into his shoulder mana gate. He breathed in, embracing the thrill of mana.

The potion ran through his mana channels, twisting with his burning rage.

Power tore through his body. He reveled in the pain, accepted it, the forces of mana breaking through his body, tearing him apart as black blood pushed out of his pores; he looked like the devil. The librarians tried to pull out formations.

Erik drew in more mana, expanding his domain to the limit. Mana and elements rushed in. Books tore from the shelves and people yelled as the room danced around Erik, a bloody demon in the midst of it all.

Someone ran at him; Erik reacted. He shifted across the room, turning their fist, breaking their arm, hitting their knee backward, and hurling them away with their own motion. Lightning strikes made them convulse as they lost control over their muscles.

Erik felt a barrier crack, and the realm came into focus. His mana channels and core altered, connecting directly to his elemental core, to his body, changing from a Mana Heart to a Five Aperture Mana Heart. His mana heart connected to his body, the library caught in a tempest around him. His domain expanded outward as he felt a sense of peace, becoming connected with the Ninth Realm in a deeper sense.

Pages torn from books settled down in the middle of the library.

"Seems this is only a library for the slaves of the Association. All others beware the un-benevolent Associations." Erik laughed. "Hasn't it always been the way, looking out for yourselves?" Erik shook his head.

"Ah, I think it is time we stopped our dance. My teacher will be displeased." Erik stepped upon the wind and shot out of the library. Papers created white flurries in his path.

Students and librarians ran after him, but he left them trailing behind.

Eli'keen read the report from Avegaaren. "So, Lord West is showing his colors."

Beatrice pushed a piece of paper across the table. "A tournament has been called, undoubtedly targeting him and Rugrat. People are purposely using a moniker that Rugrat does not like. The infractions against Erik and Rugrat are greatly inflated, and they have been harassed constantly."

The windows rippled around Eli'keen with his anger. He took a deep breath.

"Sorry about that, Beatrice."

"No sir, I know that you like fairness above all else."

"Serkin?"

"He is monitoring the situation. He has not taken an active role. He could be using this."

"It might be the case. He has been fair in his assessments so far." Eli'keen picked up the piece of paper she'd put on his desk and read it.

"The empire banned all Associations from the First Realm?" Eli'Keen shook his head. "I guess there is little we do in the First Realm. Hiring is rare, and we are mostly just looking for rarities to sell in the higher realms and offload junk."

"It's signed by every nation leader in the First Realm," Beatrice interjected.

"*Every* nation? That would mean that they control the first realm. What are the implications?"

"They control the Mortal, Earth, and Sky realms. All of them listen to Alva. They are allied with so many and offer teaching to all. No one wants to bite the hand that feeds them. Military somewhere around a million, at least. Strength, unknown."

It was more control than the Imperium had ever been able to spread over the realms.

"How can we not know?"

"Alva citizenship is hard to gain. Their people are incredibly free, and they provide basic securities and necessities. Their military is a core part of their identity. Half of their nation has been in the military or has someone in the military. Their intelligence department reaches across the Ten Realms. When they appeared two years ago, they fought the strongest alliance of Sky realm and lower sects that the Ten Realms have seen in generations—by themselves. They have an unknown number of Experts, and they sell Journeyman equipment as if it's going out of style." Beatrice put another piece of paper on the table. "This is a report on Emperor West and Rodriguez's security detail."

Eli'keen rubbed his temples. "There are forty people here. They're all working for Erik and Rugrat?"

"They should be the strongest of Alvans."

Eli'keen snorted. "At least there's that. I would expect to see these cultivations in the highest rankers of Avegaaren. We also know that their warships and technology are much more advanced. Even someone without a cultivation with the Alvan gear could take on people realms stronger than them."

Beatrice nodded.

"I don't know what is more worrying: that they have so many power houses, or the fact these people could have joined Avegaaren but didn't."

"This is not the first or even second time that the Association has been seen in a bad light by them." Beatrice pulled out more reports.

"An Association member tried to take control over their second city. Associations tried to pressure them into giving them greater concessions to end the fight at Vuzgal." Beatrice took a breath.

"Vuzgal was a place where people from all the Associations went to craft and to train. We have seen many of the Association members in the lower realms leaving after their contract finishes, joining the Alvan equivalent, over the treatment of Alva. People that have interacted with Alva and Vuzgal—realm heads, managers and association heads—have all expressed their frustration. Hiao Xen, an up-and-coming leader in the Blue Lotus, and previous acting head of Vuzgal, has declined several promotions, and is withdrawing to join the Alvan mercantile. His son, who was healed by Erik, is also ending his term and planning to join Alva's adventurers and military if they let him."

"So, everyone that's come into contact with them is leaving the

Associations to join them. Others are allying with them as fast as they can and they're educating the next generation." Eli'keen sucked in a breath. "I would applaud them. I want to, but this puts the Associations and the Imperium at great risk. I was hoping I could just deal with this as students of Avegaaren, but this is a political nightmare. I pride myself on the fact that we treat everyone equally in the Associations. This flies in the face of that."

"Is it worth doing something? It will weaken your position."

"We are supposed to be above the squabbling that the sects go through."

"If I show my support for Erik and Rugrat to punish those that haven't been doing their jobs as teachers and administrators, the traditionalists would say that I'm being unfair. They want them to fail and to disappear." He shook his head. "Though if I let this continue, and Erik and Rugrat have every reason to distrust us. It will only lead to a great schism between them, the Imperium and the Association.

"Maybe in a year, five years, or ten years, we will have the Alvans stepping up into the Eighth and into the Ninth Realm in numbers never seen before. We can't stop them. Then what? Each time we have someone who's not from the Association, we bend the rules to kick them out? What happens when there are more applicants not from the Associations?"

Beatrice gave him an apologetic smile.

"I hope that some answer comes about."

"Do you think that the Imperium Head will show up for the tournament?" Beatrice asked.

Eli'keen snorted. "Rekha is his student. When has he failed to show up to cheer her on?" *I'm sure he'll show up for that, at least.*

"He might not be the most delicate about these things, but he has the strength to pull Avegaaren together."

"Or, as he would say, give them a smack and pull their collective heads out of their asses. He's always been critical of how they treat people not from the Associations."

# 12

## Tear Clearing

Rugrat checked his map, leading Special Team Two, Five, and Erik.

"So, these tears are openings into what, another world?" Erik asked.

"Yeah, so the Shattered, a group that lives beyond the Ten Realms, use them to get into the Tenth Realm. Then they can use them to descend the realms."

"Great, fighting alien invaders on an alien world."

"They look like mutated or screwed-up monsters, for the most part."

"That helps." Erik shook his head.

Rugrat led them to a courtyard near a teleportation hub. Three groups waited there already. Two groups wore student emblems on their chests.

Two more groups entered behind them, led by an Elven warrior with striking lilac eyes that seemed to glow and with matching rich purple hair that she had braided tight to her skull, leaving her Elven ears bare.

Her team was mixed across races, each of them holding themselves with ease.

Rugrat couldn't pull his eyes from her. The hairs on the back of his head stood on end.

She looked at him, frowning, shook her head, and surveyed the rest of the courtyard. "All right, looks like I'm in charge of this mission."

"Wait, why are you? There are ten teams here," a girl from the student groups said.

Rugrat saw all the guys in her group staring at the Elven leader with lust. A flare of anger made the mana around him shift like angry clouds before a thunderstorm.

Erik cleared his throat and looked at him with a raised eyebrow.

*What the hell is wrong with me?* Rugrat calmed his mana as others looked at him. His domain had reached over the entire courtyard and evaporated the very next second.

"That's the way of it. Go join another team if you won't listen to my orders. I don't need hangers on. Come on." The Elf turned and walked away as if nothing had happened. "The longer we leave the tear open, the more Ravagers can get through, or even a Devourer."

"What's your name?" Rugrat asked.

"Kay'Renna." She glanced backward, and kept walking.

She led them to the teleport pad. Despite the other girl's words, her party joined the others and traveled through the teleportation formation.

They arrived between pillars of white bleached stone.

Ray'Kenna talked to people in her group as they led the way through a small archway and into the sun.

Rugrat pulled out his helmet and put it on. It adjusted to the light as others wrapped scarves or used formation-engraved hats.

Plants of vibrant blues, reds, and purples stood in shock contrast with the white world around them.

"Mount up!" She called out a beast that looked like a cross between a bear and a gecko. She tossed the mean beast a slab of bloody meat, patting its scales as it snapped and tore the meat to shreds. She swung up onto his saddle, the rest of her group following suit.

The Alvans mounted their panthers and various beasts. Few Alvans changed their mount unless their previous one had died. The Special Team did their best to not get close to their companions, but it was hard.

Kay'Renna sent out four scouts ahead and turned to the others.

"Party leaders on me. We're moving out."

She clicked her tongue, rolling with her mount's motion as the group set off along a path of compressed stone that cut through the outcroppings of stone and plants. They quickly picked up speed, their mounts moving as fast as a sportscar on Earth, raising a plume of stone dust.

"I'll hang back," Erik said, smiling at Rugrat as dust started to pick up from the lead mounts.

Rugrat grunted and tapped the top of his head. Gong Jin and Yawen rode up beside him, discussing before they rode to the front of the group together.

The other group leaders had arrived before them, among them the girl that had spoken out, and two guys from the non-student party and student party.

The Alvans rode up, settling alongside Kay'Renna.

"Tear was detected this morning. I expect it's been open for two days. No Devourer spotted yet, so probably just Ravagers, but that could change at anytime. It's four hours' ride from here. Who are you and what are your teams like? So I know how to use you."

She looked at the girl first, being the furthest away.

"Buffing mage, three tankers, two ranged, one bow, and one spear."

"Star level?"

"One."

Kay'Renna gave a brisk nod and looked to the non-student party leader. He drew himself up in his chair, while Rugrat slumped.

With her presence and looks, Rugrat was sure that she had been hit on so many times that she'd lost count.

"Three sword and shield users, elementally enhanced attacks, two spear users. Two-Star."

She looked at the other man leading the remaining student group.

"Mages, all with Fire tempering." The others looked at him in surprise as Rugrat checked his cultivation.

*Five aperture heart, eight mana gates open, has low fire body tempering.*

The boy grimaced at his next words. "We have two one-stars, and the rest are looking to get their qualifications for the hero hall. They have all seen combat before."

Kay'Renna raised an eyebrow, seeming to consider something, and nodded, looking at Rugrat and his people. "And you, our mysterious masked leader?"

Rugrat couldn't read anything into her tone.

"Trained in close range, long range and mid, combat mages and melee fighters, healing training, two-stars."

"How many?"

"All of us," Rugrat said. That caused a stir as the other's eyes narrowed.

"You'd best get that probing mana away from me." Gong Jin turned his head to the other hero party.

The man coughed and bowed his head in apology.

"Combat?" the student boy asked.

Rugrat looked at his armor. It had been repaired, but the stitching and scratching told its own story.

"Alvans." The girl said the word as if it fouled her mouth.

The boy snapped to her, frowning.

She nodded, his anger growing.

"Fucking gatekeepers. Come out here to hide from the school? Don't worry. We'll keep a *close* eye on you. You should watch out for them, Lady Kay'Renna. They'll stab us in the back when we're not looking."

"Alvans." Kay'Renna rolled the word through her mouth. She cocked her head to the side, looking at the three of them. "I heard that your lords took out a corvette with a bathtub."

Gong Jin snorted and looked away while Yawen shook his head.

"It was *not* a bathtub. Just a..." Rugrat moved his hands, trying to describe the shape without calling it a bathtub.

Kay'Renna laughed against her hardened demeanor.

"It was a glider with cramped seating. We rammed one corvette into another and crashed them. Then Ubren, this general in the other corvette, tried to kill us with a spell scroll. Chaotic something. Something nasty."

"Chaotic rending pillar. Expert level spell. Peak Sky Grade," Yawen said.

"Shit." Kay'Renna grimaced.

"Thus the bathtub with wings," Rugrat said.

"So it *was* a bathtub?"

Rugrat could see the joy dancing in those eyes as he worked his jaw. "It might have been a bathtub to get away from the chaotic bomb thing! But we didn't take out a corvette with a bathtub."

Gong Jin let out something that was very close to a snort of laughter. "And who was it that used a damn shield as a punching glove in the defense of Alva because they lost their arm and sword?"

"Improvising!" Rugrat threw his hands up.

"That's what I'm saying!"

"Fist of fury." Yawen snorted.

"Shut up," Gong Jin growled, apparently displeased with his nickname.

"We don't pick our nicknames. They're given," Rugrat explained.

"Like the bathtub knights?"

"Hey!" Rugrat turned back to Kay'Renna, fumbling with his words. "You had to be there."

Kay'Renna smiled and looked ahead. "They're fine with me. Alvans, you take up the rear. My guys will take the front. You second, your mages third, and you fourth." She pointed to the hero leader, student boy and student girl.

Rugrat turned off to the side, letting others pass.

"We're in the rear with the gear," Rugrat said to the team's second-in-command and Erik.

"Security, three fire teams, flanks, and rear security," Erik said.

The Alvans fell to the rear, trailing behind the white dust kicked up by those ahead. They staggered back further to keep their mounts out of it as they scanned the horizon.

Rugrat came back to ride next to Erik.

"It's places like this that remind me that we're on another planet," Erik said.

"Like a desert of stone, and the plants are weird."

"I think they're cool."

"Says the guy who spends his time messing around with plants and comes out like burnt rubber."

"You know that rubber comes from a tree."

"It does?" Rugrat looked at Erik.

"Yeah, some tree, I think."

"Huh." Rugrat turned it over for a few seconds and shrugged.

"So, you got the hots for our leader?"

"What, do you?"

"Dude." Erik turned his helmet on Rugrat.

"All right, I might be interested, but we've got a mission to do first."

"And afterwards?"

"I dunno." His luck hadn't been the best with women in the Ten Realms. It hadn't been the best on Earth either.

"Worth a shot."

"Says the perpetual divorcee," Rugrat muttered.

"I think that once you get divorced the first time, you get the title for life."

"Sorry, that was a low blow man."

"Dude, it's true, and I'm not telling you to marry her. Just saying that if you like someone, you should talk to them a bit more and see if they'd like to go on a date. Easier than trying to figure out what they're thinking."

"I was hoping with all this magic crap, I'd at least get some telepathy. Can you teach me that heartbeat lie detector trick?"

Erik stared at Rugrat.

"What?"

"For both of our sanities, let's agree not to have us stuck in a room with me trying to teach you the medical minutiae of someone lying."

"Urgh." Rugrat pulled his neck back.

"Nice chins."

"I'm wearing a helmet!" Rugrat reached for his neck and felt the covering. "Dick"

Erik snorted and rode with the movements of his mount.

"Well, might as well give it a shot later if you're really interested." Erik's voice became heavy.

"What do you mean?"

"I mean that we're not young guys just out of basic anymore. We're emperors of a nation that has pull on several planets. Millions of people under our protection. You date someone, you think about marrying them, you have to make sure they would be okay with that kind of life."

"Well, you're quite the buzzkill. Who would have thought getting power might be a cock block?"

Erik shrugged. "Better to go out with someone that likes you for you than your power."

"I don't want to just look for someone for a little while anymore," Rugrat said a few minutes later in a small voice.

Erik was quiet for so long Rugrat thought about repeating himself.

"That's a big step," he said and patted Rugrat on the shoulder. "Looking for someone to live your life with, not just a few moments and your bed."

Rugrat shrugged, and they rode along together.

"That mean you can stop stealing my damn cot to sleep in when I'm out?" Erik asked.

"Pfft, no. Why would I do that?"

"Take your damn boots off when you use it at least! Or use a spell, *one* spell, and it wouldn't have dust all over the end of it."

The four hours went by quickly, with the scouts returning and changing over every hour to keep them fresh. Erik had offered to go out and scout but been turned down by the Special teams.

*Being an officer comes with benefits, some say.*

After three hours, Kay'Renna led them off the road they'd been travelling down. They slowed their pace, moving between rock outcroppings and plants.

"Halt up here and dismount. We'll go the rest of the way on foot. Five minutes to get ready. Team leaders on me."

"Get up there," Erik said to Rugrat, sliding from his mount and grabbing Rugrat's reins.

"All right."

Erik guided the mounts over to where the rest of the mounts were being rested. A clean spell took the stone dust from their bodies. He tied them up to a stone post that was formed from the ground.

Erik put down his water and moved to Gong Jin. A beast handler among the team tossed out meat. The beasts tore into it as Erik crouched next to the kneeling man.

The tree cover here was thicker and there were larger rock outcroppings, creating shade in the afternoon sun.

"Bright as hell and as cold as the backside of the moon," Erik muttered. He pulled off his helmet and tousled his hair.

"How the fuck did dust get in my helmet?"

Gong Jin shrugged, clearing out his helmet too.

They pulled them back on and Erik sucked on his water tube as Rugrat jogged back over. Yawen moved to join them as well.

Rugrat put down the map. "We're along this line of trees here. The tear is about here. Area has been cleared by Ravagers. They've been fighting one another, leaving trees and shit down all over the place. They're blood thirsty rams the size of a deer. About fifty of them. Probably more. No Devourer seen. Plan is to cut off the tear so no more can make it down here and clean up the rams."

"So, keep the rams back, break the tear, and go home. I like simple," Gong Jin said.

"Why so many people then?" Erik asked.

"In case there was a Devourer," Rugrat said.

Erik grimaced, thinking of Aziri. He checked the rough lines drawn on the map.

"Yawen and half of Gong Jin's team on this line will be our firebase. Right side, Gong Jin, make sure we don't get flanked. The girl and the guy not with Kay'Renna on our left flank?" Erik looked up.

"Yeah, they're going to have the combat mages shoot at the tear, close it. Kay'Renna is holding her people in reserve," Rugrat said.

Erik nodded; the plan was simple but effective. "Move up in an extended line, nice and quiet. Tet into position and greet the Shattered Alvan style."

Several stealth spells later and they headed through the sparse forest with twisted branches ending in brightly colored fern-looking leaves.

Erik heard stones crashing into one another, lowering himself to his crouch to his knees, his rifle ready.

The crashing continued.

Erik signaled to keep moving.

The line pushed forward, and Erik saw where the noise was coming from. Two rams were smashing into one another, locking their horns. There were several of the oversized rams on the broken ground. Several ate the colored ferns. Others were laying down, mana currents swirling around them like water down a sinkhole.

The rams had blackened coats with predominantly red colorations.

*Demon rams.*

In the middle of the area they'd claimed was a tear. It looked as described: a tear in the air that touched the ground, thin at one end, widening to reach the ground, and then presumably thinning below.

On the other side, it was nighttime, but with signs of morning approaching, distorted by massive elemental storms eating their way through a forest and the mountain underneath.

Erik felt a chill at the almost calm destruction, unable to hear anything through the tear. *I guess that's the Tenth Realm.*

A ram appeared on the other side of the tear and pushed through, appearing in the Ninth Realm.

The tear, while large, was as thin as a dinner plate on one side. Another ram bleated at the new arrival. The new arrival bleated back and tossed its horns. It seemed the other didn't like the noise and charged. They crashed into one another, making two fights in the opening.

The groups stopped, placing down trap formations, preparing positions quickly and silently. Erik placed several of the new claymores and checked his rifle, scanning the other Alvans.

"We're in position," Erik reported to Kay'Renna.

Erik checked their left flank as the parties moved into position.

"We're here," the girl said.

"In position," the other Mission Hall leader said.

Rams started appearing on the other side of the tear and coming through in a herd, like water out the side of a cut kid's pool.

Erik raised his machine gun.

"Hit the tear now! Attack!" Kay'Renna yelled.

The Alvan line fired, their silenced guns spitting rounds through the undergrowth. Rams fell without knowing they were under attack. Something exploded.

"The fuck was that?" Erik hissed.

"A ram. One cultivating, just popped!" Rugrat yelled.

Another exploded as spells struck the tear. The tear shook and wavered

A demi-human ram, horns curled around his head, crashed through several rams as it charged through the tear. Its body was ash and magma turned flesh, wearing red armor veined in black.

"Fire on the tear! Devourer!"

Erik fired into the tear; it flexed and bent but didn't break. The Devourer tore free as it snapped closed. The beast roared as it lost a leg.

"Cover us!" Kay'Renna barked.

"Shift fire! Watch for friendlies. Focus on the rams!" Erik yelled.

Rams rushed the attackers as the area seemed to gain an arctic chill. The Devourer gathered it across his body, unleashing it from his horns. A block of the forest was incinerated in seconds as he threw his horns to the side.

Several spells hit him, and arrows burned up in the air around him.

The rams found the trap spell formations ahead of the Alvans. Magical claymores. They tore through the ram's lines.

Clouds gathered as rain began to fall.

Alvans fired into the teeth of the fams, cutting them down, but there were more coming.

"Right flank!" Gong Jin roared.

Spell scrolls tore through forest and stone, burning through ram lines.

Machine guns worked with lethal efficiency, their silence spells falling away. Tracers cut through the underbrush.

Erik reached out with his domain, cutting down rams. He drew up spikes across the lines and tore the bullets from the downed rams, throwing them upward and into the rams jumping over their bodies.

Kay'Renna and her two teams hacked and slashed at the Devourer. They'd taken its new leg and an arm, chipping a horn.

A combined spell hit the Devourer, spinning it away.

It landed on all fours and expanded into its true form. The clouds boiled and steamed. Flames danced in his eyes as his blood hissed, magma hot against the stone underneath. Its attack made its incineration beam look like a party favor.

Fighters dove for cover, using movement techniques as Kay'Renna *charged*. She slid under the beam, throwing a spear and hitting the Devourer in the leg. It roared as elements were torn out through the spear, dropping to one side. Kay'Renna was up already, a sword in her hand as she jumped up, aiming to cut off the beast's head.

It lowered its head and her blade hit horn. She released her sword, a spear appearing in the opposite hand as she grabbed the horn, swinging around. Mana drove through her body as she stabbed the spear into the back of the beast's neck. She planted her foot on its shoulder and jumped free.

She turned and rolled, drawing a shield as she called on her metal elements. The beast turned its horns on her, breathing out his flames as the weapons she'd dropped, rose and stabbed into its unprotected sides.

It howled, revealing her polished shield, now blackened with ash.

Erik finished the last target in his area with a burst of his machine gun.

He turned as Kay'Renna's party unleashed their attacks.

The Devourer tried to heal under the attacks, but it was *dismantled* under such an onslaught and crumpled to its side.

Kay'Renna stood, a sword in her hand and a wide grin that was at odds with her Elven grace but seemed to fit her perfectly.

"Check your area. Make sure none are left alive," Erik ordered.

Rugrat wandered over to him.

"Little more than we thought," Rugrat muttered.

"Well, at least we had good parties with us." Erik checked the area as people moved through the Ravagers, using spears to make sure they were dead.

Rugrat waited as Kay'Renna finished talking to her party and they broke apart.

"Well, no bathtub this time," she said as she walked over to him.

"No," Rugrat said, taking off his helmet.

"I was wondering what was under there." She smiled and turned to stand next to him, looking at the Devourer.

"They always like this?"

"Devourers? Nah, they come in all shapes and sizes of ugly. Look like beasts we might see here sometimes. Most, they just look *wrong*. Elements went and twisted their bodies."

"I meant the tear clearing missions."

She shrugged. "Some better, some worse."

"First Elf I've seen out here fighting."

"There are plenty. Just so many of you humans out there. Some Elves hide their identity too."

"Not you?" Rugrat grinned. "No one's been stupid enough?"

"Oh, there are plenty of idiots in the realms." She rolled her eyes. "But being a three-star hero gives you certain protections by law from idiots." She patted the daggers on her hip.

Rugrat laughed and looked at the battlefield. "But the tears, they're usually the same? Take out the tear, then the Ravagers? Devourers if they show up?"

"If you don't close the tear, more can flood in. Once a Devourer makes a tear, they can last days, weeks, or months. Place like this, not much ambient mana. Could have been weeks before it closed on its own. Tears in the Shattered Realms can last for years."

"So. you just hunt down tears? Or any missions you can get?"

"Tears pay the best and plenty of people will pay good coin to have some backup." She tilted her chin toward her group.

"They your party?"

"We've known one another for a while now, but I don't have a group."

"Just a solo hero."

"Makes it easier, not getting tied down." She looped her thumbs into her belt and sighed.

"Yeah, I can understand that."

She studied him closer. "A big emperor, out here?"

"What you think I was doing out here?"

"Maybe a hunting trip. Boredom?" She shrugged.

"Maybe the second. Nah, wanted to learn more about these tears and everything that happens in the higher realms. Used to be just a grunt. Now they say people look up to me." Rugrat leaned back, a cocky smile on his face. "But I guess it does come with the height advantage."

Kay'Renna glared at him with one eye, shaking her head in a failed attempt to hide her grin. "You're different from most. Haven't seen someone like you in all my years."

"See, my momma always said I was unique."

"A unique pain in my ass," Erik's muttering carried over.

Rugrat flashed him the bird and returned to how he was, as if it had never happened.

Kay'Renna laughed. "Seen some emperors in my time. None quite like you two."

"Thank you? I think?"

She smiled without clarifying.

"Well, I'd say we stay the night and head back tomorrow, get out of this stink. The white forests have their own dangers to worry about."

"Sounds good. I'll let my guys know."

They camped out for the night, having fire watches, but few of them needed to sleep for more than a few hours and spent the night playing games or talking.

Rugrat found himself with Kay'Renna, talking about the Devourers, tears, the Mission Hall and beyond. Even sparring several times. Erik joined in, his speed surprising Kay'Renna.

They packed up at first light and headed back to the teleportation hub, reaching the same courtyard they'd met at the day before.

Rugrat and Kay'Renna caught up to one another before they disappeared.

"Would you be interested in going on a date with me?" Rugrat asked.

"A date?" She crossed her arms and leaned to one side. She looked up, debating it. "Sure, why not? Not gone on a date with an emperor before."

"Uhh, that's kind of the thing, say in two-ish months?" She raised an eyebrow. "There's this tournament... We've got some free time to do missions, but for the next two months, the sadistic bastard training us will probably only let us rest when we pass out from blood loss."

Kay'Renna laughed and shook her head. "And you're not even joking. Sounds like a good trainer."

"What about blood loss and passing out sounds good?"

"Well, you woke up?" She grinned and passed him a note in her hand. "When your tournament is over, send me a message. My sound transmission device number is on there. Much better you asked me." She winked and left.

Rugrat held the paper, mental gears moving. "Wait, were you going to give this to me anyway?"

She raised her hand without looking back and kept walking.

Rugrat turned to face Erik with the paper still in his hand.

"You wanna pick your jaw off the floor and save that in your sound transmission device before you lose it?" Erik said.

"Ah!" Rugrat pulled out his sound transmission device, plugging in the information.

# 13
# Training Demons

"Take a break," the training teacher said. Cayleigh groaned and dropped to the ground in a pile of armor. Rekha wiped the sweat from her face, taking an offered canteen from a waiting servant, having to pause between gulps to breathe.

Sam moved to the waiting chairs, grabbing Cayleigh and dragging her over.

Rekha panted, passing the canteen back, and slumped into another chair.

Sam sat in his chair, pulling Cayleigh to sitting with her back against his legs. He took out a leg of chicken and gave it to her.

Cayleigh sat up taller, eating with pleased noises.

"Two months to go untill the tournament now," Sam said.

"Third tournament while we've been at school. We reached the top of the school with the last one. There's bound to be others who'll try to take our spot," Rekha said.

"They think they can defeat us with five people or ten, they're welcome to give it a shot!" Cayleigh waved her chicken leg.

"Do you really think the Alvans will challenge us? They're six thousand spots away," Sam said.

"You heard about the library incident. Five Aperture Heart left everyone in the dust," Rekha said. "You and I have started to open our acupoints and tempered in the Metal element, Cayleigh is at Mana Heart but tempered in all the elements. We have the highest cultivation in Avegaaren and in the Associations, other than my master."

"Still, there are others on the same level as them in cultivation and should be more skilled."

"Yes, but I have a feeling," Rekha said.

"You want to beat them and make your master proud?" Cayleigh said.

"Well, that could be a part of it," Rekha admitted.

"Don't worry. No matter what other crap is going on, we're up to fight whoever challenges us!" Cayleigh grunted and got to her feet. "I need a shower and a slab of cooked meat." She kissed Sam and grabbed her axes, putting them on her shoulder.

"A shower sounds good."

Rekha groaned. "Can you two be a little less PDA?"

"Could you please get laid or find a boyfriend? You've got the pick of the school."

"Of the Realms." Sam stood, and the two walked off.

Rekha shook her head, pulling her helmet off.

"How long have they been in there?" Weebla asked.

"It's been three weeks now since Erik broke through to Five Aperture Heart, and Rugrat broke through and tempered his body with the Metal element last week." Xun Liang's smile was missing as he watched the duo training. They were as savage to the Telarri as they were to themselves.

"The Special Teams have turned Erik's accommodation into a fortress, and they've evicted the servants. They've continued to take on missions from the Mission Hall, but only for materials. They keep none of the contribution points."

"Just two months until the tournament comes. All because of the short-sightedness of people. They come from the lower realms, so they just have to be another sect creating problems and trying to overthrow them." Xun Liang scowled. "They're threatened because of their own prejudice. They'll make it come true if they keep this up. Honestly, if I was Erik and Rugrat, I'd be out there kicking their asses in more than just the arena."

"Those two aren't saints."

"No, but they're good people that are just trying to learn."

Weebla let out a tired sigh filled with regrets. "The sand falls through the hourglass, and new things become old."

"Some more ancient than others." Xun Liang yawned and rested his head on his hand. "Ow!" He rubbed his head, glaring at Weebla.

"I am not ancient! I will get some manners into that thick skull of yours one of these days. Never joke about a lady's age!"

"You're hardly a la--!" Xun Liang jumped out the way of a clip and his seat. "Hey!"

"Stay still so I can give you a proper education!" She imbued the air elements as Xun Linag hopped away.

"Weebla! Weebla!" He dodged and ran as she scurried after him around the training hall as fast as her short legs could take her.

Erik and Rugrat appeared on the teleportation formations, bruised and bloodied. They gathered themselves, taking stamina potions and drawing in the mana and elements around them, accelerating the healing process.

Erik held out his hand. Miniature beasts of fire, mana, earth, and metal condensed in his hand and walked up his arm. He concentrated, creating a weak beast of water. It turned and folded in on itself, but it was stable. Without tempering fully with Water, it was hard, like he was working with mittens on his hands.

The others were all lifelike, gaining an intelligence to their eyes that hadn't been there before. He released them, and their elements sunk back into his body as he studied his elemental core. He had actually reached the Divine level with Earth while his Fire element was at the Celestial level and Metal, the latecomer, had reached the high Sky level. As they increased, his control and resistances toward the elements became higher.

"Nice," Erik muttered. "Leveling up isn't as big as it was in the lower realms."

He checked his mana cultivation changes and his stat sheet.

| Quest Completed: Mana Cultivation 5 |
|---|
| The path to cultivating one's mana is not easy. To stand at the top, one must forge their own path forward. |
| **Requirements:** |

Reach 5 Aperture Mana Heart

**Rewards:**

+320 to Mana

+320 to Mana Regeneration

+500,000,000,000 EXP

---

**589,285,913,157,831/1,168,160,000,000,000,000,000 EXP till you reach Level 105**

---

**Title: Mana Reborn V**

Your body has undergone a deep transformation, bringing you closer to Mana, reborn with greater power and control over its forces.

Mana channels are transformed into mana veins. Your mana sense and control increases greatly.

You can now convert stamina into mana and vice versa.

---

**Quest: Mana Cultivation 6**

The path to cultivating one's mana is not easy. To stand at the top, one must forge their own path forward.

**Requirements:**

Open your 72 acupoints

**Rewards: ?**

---

**Name: Erik West**

*Level: 104*

*Race: Human-?*

Titles:

*From the Grave III*

*Blessed By Mana*

*Dungeon Master V*

*Reverse Alchemist*

*Poison Body*

*Fire Body*

*Earth Soul*

*Mana Reborn V*

*Wandering Hero*

*Metal Mind, Metal Body*

| *Sky Grade Bloodline* | |
|---|---|
| Strength: (Base 90) +88 | 1958 |
| Agility: (Base 83) +120 | 1218 |
| Stamina: (Base 93) +105 | 3267 |
| Mana: (Base 637) +134 | 8028 |
| Mana Regeneration (Base 660) +71 | 468.84/s |
| Stamina Regeneration: (Base 162) +99 | 59.52/s |

"It might give you fewer attribute points, but it is no less useful. Leveling up and going through the totems is literally what's keeping you together," Weebla said.

"What do you mean?"

"I guess that you haven't been learning much from the academy." She sighed. "When you level up, that is the accumulation of experience in your body. It would be easier to say that experience is actually the energy from the Ten Realms changing you."

"That explains why we didn't get any experience when we were in the Undercity and when we came back, we were filled with it," Erik said.

"I wondered when we were on Earth, the way we changed, it felt like experience," Rugrat said.

"But why is it changing us?" Erik asked.

"So that your bodies can cultivate and temper with the elements and mana without becoming a Ravager," Xun Liang said.

"I think you're going to need to go back to the beginning," Erik said. "So, we gain experience and that's the Ten Realms changing us?"

"Think of it like mana fueling a spell. You gain experience, and that fills you up, and then every ten levels you go through a totem. When transiting to a higher realm, a formation within the totem is imprinted upon you. Every time you go up a realm, that formation becomes more complicated as it develops your body more, increasing your ability to hold elements and mana and the stability of your body."

Erik snapped his fingers. "That's why people who went to the higher realms weren't having a problem with increasing their cultivation, but people who didn't were having all kinds of problems in Alva. Sent them to the higher realms, and they came back down. We thought it might have something to do with the increased density of mana. We were still trying to figure it out when I left," Erik said. "So, each realm we go to, a new formation is imprinted upon us with our experience as fuel. Why would we be Ravagers without it?" Rugrat asked.

"Well, instead of your body guiding you, you would have to come up with mana channels, elemental cores, and mana cores, or whatever system you can think of to control that power. Now that you've gained your will, you can control some of the changes in your body. Going to the Tenth Realm, there will be no more formations. Instead, you need the ascendant platform," Xun Liang said.

"And that is?"

"It's an inverted tower. You must have tempered your body with all the elements, reached level one hundred and cultivated your seventy-two acupoints. Then, as you progress through the tower, you will be tested and you will be refined. You must descend all the way to the bottom of the tower where the last formation will be pressed upon you. Then you will become as powerful as the Thirteen."

Weebla saw the duo's blank looks. "The Thirteen cut off the Ten Realms from the Shattered Realms. They connected to Earth and created the Ten Realms system that works to stabilize the Realm and incite growth in the people of the Ten Realms."

"So, are there any ascendants walking around?"

"No, they died creating the Ten Realms, and since them, there haven't been any others."

"Must have been a few that tried?" Erik asked.

"Yes, but the trial is not an easy one, and it tests the mind as much as the body. While the Eighth Realm wants to know why you fight, the Tenth wants to know who you wish to become and if that is who you want to be," Xun Liang said.

"Got to love me some riddles." Erik sighed and stood. "Again? I'm just getting into the groove of my new movements, and I'm up front this time."

"Nice to not get a lightning bolt to the ass!" Rugrat grumbled.

"That was three days ago, and you turned out fine."

They appeared in the forest, circulating their mana as Erik floated up into the air. Manipulating mana to fly had become second nature now. They scanned with all their senses, including their domains, and circled one another, watching outward.

The first yells rang through the forest. Heat spread through Erik's limbs as the Telarri moved into his range.

"Going for it."

Mana and lightning raced through his body, crossing a dozen meters in a blink of an eye, using the attributes of the Water element to transfer his force through his body to his hand as it smashed into a tree.

Shards of tree as strong as Sky grade iron tore through several Telarri as he blurred away from their tombstones. A line appeared in the ground as he launched a spear of earth, cutting through several Telarri. Erik ducked as Elemental blades crossed where he had been, causing rolling destruction through the fog covered underbrush.

Erik glided into the air and turned. A flaming whip with the face of a serpent unraveled from his hand, cutting through Telarri rushing out from below.

Telarri touched one another. Like shadows reclaimed by the night, they combined together.

"Looks like things are going to get spicy," Erik said.

"*Muy caliente!*"

Erik rushed forward, appearing across the battlefield, clipped words or phrases enough for him and Rugrat to coordinate.

The Telarri combined again, blurring in their movements and using different elements.

"Starting to get interesting!" Rugrat said, sending a bolt of formed lightning past Erik. The ground exploded, killing the Telarri moving through it.

"You did that on purpose."

"Nah, why would I do that?"

Erik called upon the earth. Beasts of dirt, stone, and grass roared out of the ground, biting the Telarri and dragging him back under.

The Telarri slashed and hacked the Earth formed beasts, tearing apart their limbs and faces, the dirt congealing back together seconds later. Erik formed a blade of mana on his fist, hitting the Telarri in the head and jumped away.

It slumped. The beasts stilled and collapsed as Erik dodged an elemental attack. Flames raced down his arm like sparks from a fire log. Dragons, phoenixes, beasts of the flame eaves formed into a spiral, burning a hole through the attacker.

Fights were short and vicious. Erik's and Rugrat's moves had acquired a brutal elegance, using the minimal amount of mana, elements, and work to wreak the most damage.

The Telarri continued to combine, becoming smarter and gaining control over more mana and elements.

"Need to get their blueprint in Alva," Rugrat grunted, weaving through a Telarri's attacks.

"No fair!" Erik used lighting in his attacks, numbing the creatures' nerve clusters. He drew his poisoned blade across the creature's stomach and stepped away.

The Telarri shuddered and took two halting steps forward before collapsing.

Rugrat had learned to fight with small daggers and chains, while Erik had practiced to fight with his fists under long brutal hours with Xun Liang.

Erik reckoned the man knew how to use every weapon to an expert level.

A half day later, Erik and Rugrat were laying bruised and exhausted on the teleportation pad.

"What is my number one rule?"

"You stole it from us," Rugrat said.

"Keep it simple, stupid." Erik groaned, pained, as he sat up.

"Rugrat, blades and guns. Erik, fists and guns. Rugrat, mana and elements combined into weapons and spells. Erik, elements and mana into beasts. Erik, speed. Rugrat, power. Focus on the basics. You start doing all this complicated shit and you'll get confused in a fight. Act and react!" Xun Liang growled. "Come on." He headed into the training area.

Erik and Rugrat dragged themselves off the ground and into the sparring area, both taking stamina potions and cleaning the blood from their clothes.

Xun Liang stood facing them and waved them forward. "Come at me."

Rugrat looked at Erik, who groaned and shot forward. He drove his body as fast as he could, transferring instead of pushing the force through his body, using the explosive speed of detonating close-range fireballs.

Xun Liang was a slippery eel. Erik couldn't even catch the shadow of his robe.

"Over extended. with you flowing the force, your body is going to push forward more than before. Control it, use it, add the reach instead of being led by it." Xun Liang threw Erik and moved to attack Rugrat, who used his blades of elements and rushed forward.

Erik got up and jumped into the air.

Xun Liang fought them both breathless, giving them pointers along the way. They'd lasted three days in the training dungeon. Here, they lost thirty times in ten minutes.

He countered their attacks without turning or looking, using his arms and legs to counter.

Xun Liang had a smile plastered to his face as he gave them pointers, diverting attacks.

"Make sure you're done in time for dinner. We're out of leftovers!" Weebla said from her rocking chair as she studied the armored pants she'd knitted together. They were utterly seamless; one couldn't tell that they had been weaved together, or that they were metal from the way they moved.

"All right, we should speed things up then!" Xun Liang, who had been enhancing himself with elements, now used them externally.

Erik felt like a punching bag as he rushed to defend and tried to get in a blow in.

A handful of minutes later and he and Rugrat were embedded into the ground with the fight out of them.

"At least you only hit the floor this time. You're going to leave dents in the ceiling otherwise," Weebla said as she put the pants away and started to work on another creation.

"I think that's enough for now. I'll get dinner going." Xun Liang dusted off his hands.

Erik moaned as he put his left leg bone into place. He opened his eyes to not find Xun Liang.

Moaning and grunting, Erik and Rugrat put themselves back together. A quick earth and metal spell and the floor looked no different from it had when they'd started.

Erik grunted as he stood fully upright, feeling his years as his body continued to pull him back together. "I think we're better at dealing with pain now."

"You say that like it's normal or a good thing."

Erik shrugged, and they headed toward where Xun Liang was cooking. He'd already set out a table and chairs for them.

Erik held up his glass over the food. The mixing aromas reminded him how long it had been since he'd had actual food instead of stamina concoctions.

"Congratulations for making it through fifteen months!" Xun Liang clinked his glass with theirs.

"He forgot to congratulate you on being here for a year," Weebla said.

Xun Liang held his chest as if he was mortally wounded.

Erik and Rugrat laughed, tapping their cups to the table and drinking.

"Fifteen months. It's gone by quickly," Erik said as he started pulling some fish onto his plate.

"Well, we had to get rid of that crap you call fighting and teach you how to use your elements. You've still got more to go, but your foundations are solid now," Xun Liang said, picking up some thinly sliced vegetables and snacking on them as he picked out more food.

"Are you going to talk about training all dinner, or you going to eat? Enough time tomorrow to deal with that." Weebla smiled as she dove into her food.

# 14

## Placing Round

Erik, Weebla, Xun Liang, Rugrat, and their protection detail arrived outside Avegaaren's main arena, built to hold hundreds of thousands at the same time. It was bigger than some of the mega stadiums Erik had seen in the States.

Contestants and spectators from the cities created a shifting hum of noise, spectators streaming in through hundreds of entrances.

"There's the contestant entrance." Weebla pointed to an entrance leading down with guards checking medallions. "I'm going to find a seat. I'll be watching." She looked at Xun Liang. He looked like a silk merchant that believed in wearing his wares instead of storing them away. He had even done his hair into a turban that was several times larger than his head. "I'll catch up with you. Come on."

He led them through the entrance, gathering stares as they did so. How Xun Liang didn't trip, Erik didn't know.

They presented their medallions to the guards.

"Your fight is in an hour."

"Nice, means we can watch some of the other fights. Come on!" Xun Liang led them inside, through corridors and stairs to a room covered in views of different fights.

"There, look! That's the Wrekha team. The W is silent." He pointed at one of the larger displays.

"Isn't their leader Rekha Bhattan, the number one student in the academy and the apprentice of the Imperium Head?" Erik asked. He looked over the seating.

A woman at the rear used a blast of wind, throwing an opponent to the side as a smaller woman with axes finished off another. A male mage took out the flying opponent, sending them up and away.

"Shorter one is Gnome Cayleigh. He must be Sam, and Rekha's in the rear," Rugrat said.

Cayleigh raised her axe. Sam hit it with a spell. She swung it to meet her enemy's sword. The explosive spell went off, throwing the man wide. Her other axe killed him as his barrier went up and he crumpled to the ground.

Twin stone vipers crushed the remaining opponent as Rekha lowered her glowing staff.

"Good teamwork and control," Erik muttered.

"Come on, let's get moving before she spots us. She's a monster." Xun Liang shook his head and moved away.

Some of the metal in his egg-shaped covering must have drawn her eyes as she glanced up at Erik. Erik caught her eye, their faces impassive as they revealed nothing.

Finally, Erik's expression widened into a grin. He carved a flamboyant bow. She snorted as he turned and waved.

His heart beat faster. *Maybe I am a battle maniac.* Erik couldn't help but be excited about fighting a group like them.

Erik secured his helmet as Rugrat went through his gear, checking his upper armored pants.

"You going to be okay with that in there?" Rugrat tapped Erik's left armor plate over his Water tempering needle.

"At least this time I only have one in my leg and I'm not bleeding mercury all over the place."

"Why aren't you?"

"I tempered slower, and I can use my will on it. I'm guiding it through my body instead of just washing my body in the element. I'm injecting it slowly and spreading it."

"All right, but if there are any issues, then you pull it out, got it?" Rugrat raised his arms.

"Yeah, yeah." He finished checking his rig and gear, hitting him on the shoulder.

They looked at Xun Liang as the red light turned green and the door opened.

"Well, don't lose now."

Erik and Rugrat bowed to him. They walked up the short ramp to the arena.

"You think they banned guns because of us?" Rugrat asked.

"It's the gesture that counts."

"Aw, they shouldn't have. Really, they shouldn't. I miss the Beast."

"If I was a betting man, I'd say you sleep with a gun in your bed more than you do with the ladies inhabiting it," Erik said.

"Why, thank you." Rugrat raised his arms and made kissing noises on his biceps.

"Fuck sakes." Erik laughed as Rugrat flexed and struck his best pharaoh. The boos of the crowd took on a note of confusion, leaving Erik snorting in his helmet.

"Redneck beauty contest. Welcome—" He changed position. "—to the—" Another change. "gun show." He took a knee, turning and flexing his biceps.

The boos had almost died down. People looked at one another with concern.

Rugrat stood and air-wiped his helmet. "Wooh, I am a beauty, if I do say so myself."

Erik couldn't see Rugrat's eyebrows, but he could *feel* them moving behind his helmet.

"Oh, God." Erik shook his head, a smile plastered inside his helmet as their five opponents walked out to cheers and celebrations.

"You think they're compensating?" Erik asked.

"What do you bet they are? I think two casters and three melee." Rugrat crossed his arms.

"I'd say." The largest muscled man wearing a blue set of armor pulled out a green and blue mage's staff with silver runes that weaved into an oblong crystal at one end.

Erik leaned his fist on his hip. "Now that is overcompensation."

"You think *his* head or Xun Liang's is bigger?"

"I'm surprised he could get through the damn door with all that. Oh, look, there he is, nondescript," Erik pointed him out as Weebla tried to shuffle away from him. The stands were rather empty as they shuffled down the stadium bench that ran around.

"Get this over with before they do a lap?" Erik asked.

"Guess so. What do you think, mages and melee?"

"Three and two the other way."

"Alright. You do defensive, I'll go offense."

"Just make sure those mages don't blindside me."

"Yeah, yeah." Rugrat waved off his worries.

"Begin!" the proctor yelled.

Erik surged forward. Rugrat stayed with him, back and to his right.

Spells crossed the space to Erik as Rugrat covered him with his own.

"Distance," Rugrat said as two charged Erik.

"Looks like I was right," Erik said.

"Just kick their asses already, will you?"

Erik and one brawler crossed attacks, his sword cleaving through the air as his shield slammed out to catch his side. Erik moved through the attacks, hitting back.

Rugrat was in his own fight. The mages in the rear avoided the melee attacks and tried to move to get a clear shot, spreading out.

"Rugrat!"

"Take 'em!"

Erik released lightning beasts, attacking Rugrat's opponent and darkening their barrier as Rugrat threw out stone needles that tore through a mage's defenses, killing them and dropping them to the ground.

Erik's fighter seemed to not like it, attacking rapidly and then dropping out of view.

Erik shot to the side. A blast passed the man before Erik blurred back as the man was getting up. He drove his knee into his face, knocking him out and taking him out of the battle.

Erik punched the ground. Stone cracked up to another mage, but he'd transferred heat, not Earth element, through the ground as the fire shot up. Rugrat turned it into blades that killed the last two mages.

The lighting beasts moved around the man who'd been their opponent. His eyes were moving, but his body didn't.

"You taught them to target someone's nerves." Rugrat floated to the ground and poked the man's head. He fell over like a domino.

"Well, I thought that it might be helpful."

"The Door Kickers win." The proctor sounded like he wished he could rinse the words out of his mouth.

Erik and Rugrat returned to the waiting room and met up with Weebla and Xun Liang.

"Nicely done. A little wasteful, but it worked," Weebla said.

"What does K.K.M.F. mean?" Xun Liang asked, looking at the new patch on their carriers.

"Pretty nice, isn't it? Erik came up with it."

"Knock knock, mother fuckers," Erik said. "But say it in a whisper, scares people more."

"Cause the next thing they hear is a breaching charge through their wall."

"Oorah!"

"Oorah." They tapped fists and kept walking. Weebla and Xun Liang staring at one another before following.

"Knock knock, mother fuckers. Has a ring to it."

# 15

# Training...Training Never Ends

Rugrat quenched what he was working on, the steam rising in the forge as he wiped his brow.

"And another master smith was created," Weebla said.

"I haven't charged it yet, and it still needs some formation work," Rugrat said.

"I don't have a doubt when you finish it." She smiled.

Rugrat looked at the gauntlet parts in the bucket. Each had been crafted to fit his left hand.

"Why are there no crafters in the Ninth Realm?"

"There are plenty of crafters here," Weebla said.

"No, like how come there is no one who does crafting as their primary pursuit?"

"Oh." Weebla put down her knitting. Her type of smithing combined knitting and metal with smithing and tailoring.

"Well, the Thirteen needed people to fight for the Ten Realms. Having two realms filled with people that were able to fight should protect the crafters in the lower realms."

Rugrat sat down on a rolling chair. "But they don't gain access to their will."

"Back then, everything was about survival. You can overlook a few things and it might entice people to learn how to fight."

"Can you change that?"

"Maybe, if I were a god." Weebla laughed. "You can only change the Ten Realms and the rules of the Ten Realms if you ascend."

"And no one has ascended since the Ten Realms were created."

"And don't think that you could change it with your request to the gods. People have tried," Weebla said.

"Request to the gods?" Rugrat thought to one of the first notifications he had ever seen.

"You reach the gods of the Tenth Realm, and you can give them a request. Return to Earth, to heal someone. Like the Eighth Realm Trial, even if you leave the realm, you can make the request. But there's a price to pay." Xun Liang's voice was grave.

"What's the price?" Erik asked.

"Equivalent exchange. You want to bring back someone that is badly wounded, then the Ten Realms will consume your power to heal them. You want to return to Earth, it'll cost you nearly all of your cultivation." "Any more questions or can we get to assembling your gauntlet? I'm rather interested in what it will do," Weebla muttered.

"What about the Elves, the Gnomes, and Humans? How did everything turn out this way?"

Weebla sighed. "They really didn't teach you shit." She cleared her throat and organized her thoughts. "The Shattered Realms connected to the Gnomes' and Elves' home planets around the same time, the current Ninth and Tenth Realm. The Gnomes were good manipulators of elements and the Elves had magic.

"They created an alliance to fight against the Shattered Realms. It was a losing battle at the start. Most of the planets were destroyed, and they had to retreat through several planets, but they got stronger and figured out the secrets of mana and elements. They created the formations and altered their people. They rapidly became stronger and reclaimed many of the lost realms. The fighting had been going on for decades and the populations had been whittled down."

"Why do the Shattered, Devourers, and Ravagers want to kill the Gnomes and Elves?"

"They live to get stronger. Eating a gnome gives more elements. Eat an elf, you get mana. Mana is one of the rarest substances to find in its pure form unless you have a way to refine it."

"Dungeon cores."

"You want to tell the story, or me?"

Rugrat made a zipping motion over his lips.

"Right, so the Elves and Gnomes, they fought a terrible series of battles, but they were nearly spent. While they were securing the Ten Realms, a group of Devourers escaped through a tear into a different kind of realm. A realm without the elements and mana. It was called Earth by its inhabitants. They called themselves humans. The Gnomes and Elves helped them to fight the Devourers. Then the humans made a deal with the Gnomes and Elves, a three-way alliance. They would need time to become stronger, but they had numbers and you humans are great at creating descendants." Weebla took out some tea and sipped it.

"They agreed that every few hundred years the top fighters and smartest of the humans would join the Ten Realms to add new blood."

"The Two-Week Curse," Rugrat muttered.

"Anyway, that's how the realms came to be."

"What about the Elves and the Gnomes?"

"Elves and Gnomes worked in the higher realms to make sure we could hold the realms. Left the humans alone for a few hundred years. We didn't take into account the short human lifetime. They figured out how to cultivate and temper their bodies on their own, fought wars across the realms, and advanced. When they met the Gnomes and Elves, a war broke out called the Rising War. It hurt the Gnomes and Elves badly. The Associations were created, and we still needed people to defend the Ten Realms, so Avegaaren was opened to humans. It stabilized the Realms."

"So, what about the Gnomes and Elves?"

"There are still Gnomes and Elves in the realms. Gnomes, we like our warm homes in the ground, like your Alva, and Elves are powerful mages. 157hey control nations in the Seventh Realm and there are many of them in the Ninth. Anything that is different is bound to create friction, even among races that have coexisted for hundreds of years."

Rugrat took it all in.

"Now, will you finish your gauntlet? You have a week before your next battle and Xun Liang is eager to give you more training."

"All right." Rugrat fished out the different pieces in the bucket and put them on the workbench.

He took out a fingerless left glove that Weebla had knitted for him. He put it on his hand and attached the different pieces of metal. He'd enhanced them differently and formed them so they allowed him flexibility. Piece by piece, he fused them to the glove.

| Mana-pulator |
|---|
| Weight: 0.4 kg |
| Health: 1000/1000 |
| Charge: 1000/1000 |
| Innate Effect: |
| Increased control over Fire element by 5% |
| Increased control over Earth element by 5% |
| Increased control over Metal element by 5% |
| Increased control over Water element by 5% |
| Increased control over Wood element by 5% |
| Enchantment: |
| Mana manipulation — Increased control over mana by 20% |
| Requirements: |
| Mana 100 |
| Mana Regeneration 100 |
| Stamina 75 |

Rugrat tightened his grip, compressing the elements and mana within his hand together, creating a tiny pebble swirling with colors emitting light.

| Skill: Smith |
|---|
| *Level: 100 (Master)* |
| You are a Master within the forge. Stamina increases by 30% when forging. Product will be 20% stronger. Innate abilities are 10% stronger. |
| Upon advancing into the Master level of Smith, you have been rewarded with one randomly selected item related to this skill. |

| |
|---|
| You have received the book: Multi-part systems. |
| +1,000,000,000 EXP |

A light flashed, and Rugrat caught a hefty tome with a mana spark and gear wheel intersecting one another on the cover.

"Nice!"

"What is your little glove thing supposed to do?" Weebla asked.

"Manipulate elements and mana easier. I can actually grip the elements and mana in my hands. Should allow me to understand them more so I can improve faster."

"You know most people would say you're crazy trying to hold elements and mana in your hand, probably because you're liable to blow your fool hand off!" Weebla shook her hand at his smile, unable to keep the corners of her mouth down entirely. "Pass it over here so I can test it out!" She scowled.

Rugrat laughed and threw it over. He opened the book and started reading. "Hmm, mana and different systems working in concert, mechanical systems... Oh, pneumatic systems, too. Making trains here," Rugrat mused through the book and the ideas contained within. At times, he pulled out other information books, consuming them, and went back to reading, the knowledge clicking together.

It was several hours later when he put a bookmark in and closed the tome.

Weebla looked up from her knitting. Rugrat was looking at what she had made. The metal yarn was woven so tightly that air couldn't get through. It moved like scaled skin. His improved senses showed it practically vibrated with elements, fused into the very fabric of her work.

He gave her a tired smile.

"Something on your mind?" she asked.

Rugrat took in a breath.

"Just remembering the first time I was introduced to smithing. It was in Alva. Egbert had these imprinted personalities, Gnome teachers that had helped to build Alva." Rugrat frowned and looked at Weebla.

"Do you know why Alva was created?"

Rugrat's brain caught up to his mouth as he grimaced and rubbed his head. "Sorr—"

"Alva was created as a two-fold experiment. One, to open the blocked ley lines across the planet and two, to connect with the people in the Second Realm, teach them, and raise them up. They were a group of crafters, not able to enter the Eighth Realm. They created the facility and begun experimenting, working on their cultivations, making a better and stronger drill to tap the ley lines. They theorized that if they were to create a mana well, the change in pressure would force open the mana blocks across the First Realm or create new ley lines." Weebla set down her needles. "Things did not go as planned."

Rugrat had the distinct feeling this wasn't from some book. Weebla had *lived* this.

"The blockages occurred across the realms; without an ascendant we couldn't easily clear them. There were many theories. None worked out, at least until you powered up the mana drill again."

"What are blockages?"

"Think of a planet as a much larger version of your own mana system. The mana channels are ley lines. Elements and mana move through them, cycle through the planet again and again. A build-up can occur with elementally heavy mana. Takes millennia, but just like someone who doesn't purify their mana when they're cultivating, they'll eventually block up their channels and have to clear it out. Simple to do. It just requires time. Planets are not sentient like people, so the elements build up. The mana on the outside of a planet decreases as more of it gets stuck in the blocked off sections of the ley lines.

"Over the years, mana has decreased across the realms as more of the ley lines have been blocked off and people who cultivate in the lower realms have been taking it into the higher realms. Rarely does it go down the realms."

"But there's so much mana," Rugrat said.

"There's so much water in the ocean. If someone takes a few buckets of water from the ocean, no one will notice. A few million over a few hundred years, barely noticeable. Someone who saw the ocean a hundred years ago and today, they'd be terrified."

"Small changes over a long time, but a massive change none the less. Wait, so this is happening in every realm. Why try this out in the First?"

"Least amount of mana. Means that the fallout would be much smaller. If something went wrong, it shouldn't do too much damage, like uncorking bubble-filled wine."

Rugrat nodded. "Higher the realm, the more energy, the greater the possible backlash."

"If they succeeded, we were going to do it in every realm. With mana decreasing and elements increasing, the Ten Realms were losing their greatest defense against the Shattered Realms. Our Mana."

"How is mana your defense? I don't think you mean because you use it to fight."

"Mana creates stability, a cycle with the elements. It makes it harder for the Shattered to create tears, openings from their shattered world into our Ten Realms."

"So, the less mana, the more tears."

"Right." She paused, waiting for more questions. Rugrat waved her on.

"The drill was meant to open the ley lines, to shake up the First Realm. Their second mission was their downfall. To reach out and interact with the humans. Negotiations were ongoing in the higher realms between the races to stop the fighting. We were hoping to bridge the gaps in the lowest realm so they would spread up the realms."

Weebla sighed, filled with regret. "The groups in the lower realms came at them with everything, greedy for Kanesh Research station one's resources. Your Egbert, a close friend of the Station leader. He defended the station, twisted the landscape.

"By the time we heard, it was over and the negotiations with the other races were about to be signed to put the in-fighting behind us and create the Associations. The mana drill idea was dropped and no one from the Gnomes or Elves ventured into the lower realms, instead sticking to the institutions we created and in the higher realms, near the seat of our power. Our numbers were limited from the fighting, and we were tired and protective."

Rugrat opened his mouth, but he didn't know how to ask his next question.

"Spit it out, will you? You look like a fish out of water."

"What do the gnomes think about us living in Alva?"

Weebla snorted and shifted in her chair. "Mixed, as most groups are. Some people are annoyed you took over the facility and used it. They say that the honor should have been ours but was stolen by the humans. As if we were going to go back down there and turn the damn thing on after all these years." She shook her head. "Most don't care, and there are those that are glad to see that it's being put to use, that it has given you shelter. We have been watching you Alvans for a while now. Your Kanesh Academy was a nice touch. Teaching people just as those that made the station meant to do. Unknowingly, you carried out what they set out to do."

"That's a relief."

"Why? You think we'd demand it back?"

Rugrat leaned forward. "Well, you could. Be a little bit of a nasty position."

"Alva is your home; you've built and developed it beyond any of the station designer's plans. If anyone wants to try to take it, then they won't be getting any endorsement from me."

Rugrat tilted his head in thanks. "But what about these blockages?"

"Well, I'm sure that some gnomes are going to pull out the old theories and ideas, head to the First Realm and figure out what happened. Maybe we'll see more mana drills in the higher realms. With each realm, there's more mana and elements that could be blocked up. The changes to the first realm with just your drill opening a few ley lines was impressive. Do that in the Tenth

Realm…" Weebla shrugged. "Entire continents could shift, and oceans could drain or be created. Like punching through several dams in one shot."

Rekha's spell weaved through Cayleigh's blurring axes, just seconds ahead of Sam's barrage of stone spears, and hit the third fighter in the chest, encasing her in ice.

Rekha turned to the fight as Cayleigh smashed her opponent a half meter into the ground.

"The Wrekhas win it!"

The crowd cheered and started to talk among themselves as Rekha and their team left the arena.

Cayleigh waited for the door to the waiting room to close before she groaned. "What the hell was that? I hope they can give us someone better to fight after the scaling. I feel sorry for the bastards going up against us. It's like we're getting the easy ones to deal with."

Rekha took off her helmet. "The Door Kickers made it through all of their fights as well. They'll be placed in the higher-ranking quarter finals," Sam said.

"So, there is a chance we get to fight them?" Cayleigh grinned.

"I think it's likely."

Rekha sat down in a chair. She had taken the time to look into the duo. "It should be an interesting fight."

"What? You don't want to destroy them for slighting the academy? Which one did you take a fancy to? I'll do the introductions!" Cayleigh said.

Sam cleared his throat as Rekha glared.

"Sorry, fight got me all excited. Was over too quick." Cayleigh half laughed.

Sam looked at Rekha apologetically. She didn't acknowledge his look, staring ahead.

"I wasn't from an Association when I entered the academy, and I found a home here. They are both strong, but I can't let it go that they are using that strength to further their own gains and just using the Academy. Avegaaren has taught us so much. I am looking forward to the fight, but we *must* win." A fire burned in her eyes, and where her ribs met her stomach. "We have to show the people in the lower realms that we are still strong. If we don't, another war within the Ten Realms could start."

"You really think that?" Sam asked.

"I think that the sects are willing to do anything to gain power, and they have no idea the threat that the Shattered Realms present. We have fewer people trying to join the academy. The people on the frontline are decreasing every year instead of increasing as they once did."

"Don't worry, we'll wreck 'em," Cayleigh grinned.

Erik's head snapped to the side, feeling a ripple of mana spreading through his newest accommodations. He started running, blowing through rooms until he reached the cultivation room in the middle of the building. Jen and two Special Team members were rushing around a pod.

"Situation?"

"Rugrat thought it would be a great time for a cultivation breakthrough. He's opening his acupoints!" Jen sounded almost frantic as she injected a new potion into the IV bag.

One of the Special Team members adjusted a mana gathering formation in the building, the other a formation in the pod. It was thick enough to start condensing inside, the droplets being drawn into Rugrat's mana gates.

Erik used his organic scan to observe the changes in Rugrat's body. His Five Aperture Mana Heart had created a network of thin mana veins that spread through Rugrat's body, every bit as intricate as his circulatory system.

Seventy-two of these veins reached out to the surface of his skin, forming small mana gates.

Impurities from deep within Rugrat were being pushed out. Some veins were blocked, while impurities oozed out of Rugrat's pores, leaving some acupoints clear. His body purified the elements, helping to clear out more. Still, it was just a fraction of the acupoints across his body.

The changes in his body settled for a second before drawing in a titanic amount of mana. Erik grunted, feeling Rugrat's domain drawing on the mana stored within his own body.

"Everyone out!" Erik yelled.

They all retreated from of the room to the large manor that served as his and Erik's accommodation. For several minutes, mana leeched from the surroundings. As nature abhors a vacuum, it was refilled, creating mana currents and winds that tore at clothing and items not secured down.

Erik had to yell to be heard, but slowly, the draw of mana came to a stop.

"I think that should be it." Jen looked at Erik.

"First time I've been around for someone opening their acupoints," Erik said, the two of them hurrying back to the cultivation room.

Rugrat stood outside of the pod. Mana stuck to him like a fog, his eyes glowing as his mana system slowly started to fade from an inner light.

"Holy shit! I think I'm a god. That was a fucking rush!" Rugrat laughed and collapsed.

Erik caught him with air and lowered him to the ground.

"Let's run some tests on him." Erik grabbed him by the shirt and lifted him easily, grabbing a gurney that had been tossed around and righting it.

"I can't wait to see what we can learn!"

Erik faintly felt like a mad doctor, letting out a grin and shrugging before he pulled out recording instruments. What were friends for if you couldn't use them for experiments once in a while?

"And then he fainted," Erik said.

"I had just opened my acupoints. I collapsed, passed out, was rendered unconscious. Not fainted," Rugrat grumbled.

"Well, good work. Your system for increasing cultivation is one of the most advanced I have heard of," Xun Liang said. "There are few people that are willing to pass on information on their cultivation, hoarding it like some great secret. It would be easier if everyone compared information to make it easier."

"Some things change. Others stay the same," Rugrat said as the red light turned green.

"Last fight and we're into the qualifiers for the top one hundred." Erik pulled on his helmet. "Ready?"

"Oorah! I was born ready."

"Don't faint on me now."

"Shut up, jackass." The two nodded to Xun Liang and headed up the ramp to the arena.

"Well, first time facing a team with less than five people. Doesn't make them any more dangerous," Erik said.

"Begin!"

They ran forward, two for Erik and one for Rugrat, just as Erik released earth and water beasts from the ground and sky. One shot past him, joining his friend.

"Coming your way," Erik said.

"I have a domain."

Erik dodged the spear aimed at his head. The spear user created ripples of Earth that broke Erik's elemental connection and tried to break his spells.

They fought a battle of spells as he used his spear to keep Erik out of range.

"Could use some help here," Rugrat said.

Erik could see the duo overwhelming him. He tried to disengage, but couldn't do so. *Still not fast enough.*

He channelled lighting and enhanced it with mana. Frustrated lightning ran through his body, causing him to snap to the side. He hit the side of the spear as it passed by his ear.

The world turned back to full speed as Erik felt like his body was burning, flushing Earth and Water elements through his body.

*Lightning, brain.*

Rugrat was hit with a sword, dodging a kick that tore through the air before spells hammered him into the ground, killing him. His two attackers' mana barriers started to recover.

Erik released lightning through his brain and the world crystalized. He saw the spear slashing through his water beasts, the attack coming for his stomach as blades of fire and lightning surged from behind two spell formations, igniting sparks of a pillar inching toward him. Erik reached out to grab the spear, but his hand moved too slowly.

Erik felt like his body was being torn apart as he accelerated faster, sending out a flurry of jabs. The man's eyes widened in panic, fighting to dodge as hits rang out against his armor.

It was like watching the man swim through oil.

The spear user grunted from several attacks that seemed to land at the same time. The sword user silently stabbed at Erik.

He ducked under the attack, pivoting, and punched. The sword user shot backward as Erik dropped to the ground and rolled, the spear user chasing him across the ground as the sword user lost his weapon and tumbled.

Erik slapped the ground, regaining his feet.

Another bang sounded next to Erik, fire combusting, giving him momentum as he turned toward the ax user. He escaped the quick spear user's jabs.

The man created a storm of spells around himself. His speed was a half step lower, but Erik couldn't cast spells, focusing on not letting his body fall apart under the stress.

Erik yelled, running the thin thread between salvation and destruction. He weaved through the attacks, reaching out to the surrounding mana, shooting upward. He focused the elements in his hands and released them in a stream right above the man. They wrapped together into beasts.

He might be able to fight someone face to face, but fighting someone above him was really damn hard, even if he'd been the best fighter in the world.

The man down went under the beasts.

"Door Kickers win."

Erik landed on his feet, steam rising off his skin as he walked over to Rugrat who stood up, no longer restricted by the mana barrier.

"You faint again?" Erik asked.

"Next time, I hope they're all mages. I want to have some fun," Rugrat said as they walked back to the waiting room. "You smell like barbecue."

Erik sniffed himself but couldn't smell anything.

"These things have an air filter. No way you can smell me!"

"Oh, hmm, must've got some barbecue sauce in here. Snacks for later."

"Dude, anyone tell you you're nasty?" Erik said.

Xun Liang stepped out into the sparring area ahead of Erik and Rugrat as they returned to their little hideaway.

"This time, instead of throwing you into the forests or having you spar against the golems, for the next month you are going to fight against me. Rugrat, you've been working on the elements and blending them together. You're going to focus on that again. Erik, that blink step as you're calling it, slo-mo-vision or whatever, most of us call it lightning speed. Your naming scheme here, bud," Xun Liang snapped his fingers and pointed at Erik.

"You made it into the top one hundred teams in your grade. Luckily for you, you're up against some of the baddest of the bad, including the Wreckhas themselves. That would be an interesting fight. Well, not now because you need to work. Erik, make sure that you don't come apart. You're the healing body guy. You figure it out. You keep accelerating as you did for long periods of time, then you're going to be keeping yourself together with bandages and concoctions and you're of little fighting worth to anyone like that."

He smiled at Erik and Rugrat. "I think I'm going to enjoy this part the most."

"Ah shit," Erik muttered.

"Go figure out how to move without falling apart in the corner. Rugrat, walk with me."

Xun Liang guided Rugrat away. "What have you noticed in Avegaaren about how they use spells?"

"They use them a lot less. Most of them are using elements instead. They're faster to create, and that's necessary in a fight with a small unit. You don't have time to worry about grand strategy or spells."

"What are the pros of using elements compared to spells?"

"Faster casting. Even instant cast is slower than elements that you can simply project and form with your will. They're strong. You have to use more of your elemental power, but you can enhance it with your mana."

"And the cons compared to spells?" Xun Liang stopped in the middle of another training square, turning to Rugrat.

"They require a medium. Elements are projected from the body, travel through the ground, projecting from your body with mana to support them as fuel. They can be easily defeated by counter elements, or you could break the medium. Not as versatile as spells, and they are affected by the ambient mana and elements they pass through."

Xun Liang cocked his head. "Spells are affected by elements and mana they pass through?"

"Yes, but spells have a form to them. They aren't affected as much. Elements are like a bucket of water. Spells are like a hose. Which one do you think is going to have more force? Which will go further?"

A smile spread across Xun Liang's face as he clapped slowly. "Good! Very good. Elemental attacks are just that. You are exercising your control over the elements within your body, shaped by your will to create a response in the world around you." Xun Liang held out his hands to either side, a whale of water jumping from one hand and into another.

"Spells are just taking elements and mana to create a different effect. Might be easier with Alchemy, but Erik takes all kinds of ingredients and puts them together. Based on the ingredients and how he puts them together, he will get different effects. The cauldron and techniques are the spell; the ingredients are the mana and elements."

"I follow."

"Good. So then, watch." Water shot out of Xun Liang's hand, followed by a streak of lightning. The lightning struck the water and an arrow of fire appeared on the other end, hitting the target in the corner. "Many use their elements singularly. Chaining them together, you can get different effects.

Water and Earth, perfect for using Wood element. They'll enhance one another. Fire and earth, perfect for creating metal element."

Xun Liang created balls of elements in the air. They split and shifted, dousing one another, or enhancing, or creating a different effect.

Rugrat watched for several minutes before Xun Liang drew the elements back inside himself. "You don't need just spells and mana to alter and change elements."

"So, I'm going to be chaining elements together?"

"Eventually. First, you will figure out how to defeat elements. Stop my attacks before they reach you." Xun Liang threw out fire and Rugrat threw out earth, defeating the flame.

"Good. Now, faster."

# 16
## Top One Hundred

Akran opened one gigantic eye, taking in Jukxzu, who dropped through the gap in the stone, creating the roof of his cavern. His humanoid figure landed, kneeling and bowing his head, sweat dotting his brow.

Akran studied his bonded. His skin had a shine to it from his scales. Red, almost black horns reached out from between his red and white hair, framing his head.

Jukxzu didn't move as sweat stained his airy white robes. He didn't dare to use any elements to defend himself from the heat of the cavern, the pressure of being this deep, or from Akran's faint elemental leak.

Akran shifted his head, the noise like grinding stone. His head was as big as Jukxzu was tall, studying his bonded. Silver, blue, green, yellow, and red flecks shifted in his eyes and lined his scaled hide, vivid and deep, as they had become a part of him.

"Speak." His words shifted the cavern around them, causing the ceiling to shatter and crumble in places.

Akran snorted. The rocks missed Jukxzu and crashed into the ground behind him.

"All of our preparations are complete. The Academy is hosting a tournament. Many are attending, and the top one hundred fights begin next month."

"It will weaken their front line in the Tenth Realm." Akran had reinforced the cavern as his words rolled through the air and stone. "What of the head of the Imperium?"

"There are indications he has been scouting in the Tenth Realm again."

Akran's grunt sent cracks through the stone again.

"Send word to the bonded and to the Devourers. The time has come. Notify me once they are ready."

"Yes, master."

"Go."

Jukxzu called upon the fire element and soared upwards and into the roof of the cavern. The stone shifted around him as he shot upward.

"Soon." Akran closed his eyes as he drew upon the elements of the realm he rested in.

The air and ground between Erik and Xun Liang shifted and flared with elements as they attacked and defended against one another's attacks.

"Good!" Xun Liang jumped out of the sparring area, cancelling his elemental attacks as Erik followed up seconds later. He looked like he had been out for a strong walk while Erik panted, trying to bring his racing pulse down to normal.

"How long have you been here now?"

"Seventeen months since we reached Avegaaren."

"Damn, I'm good." Xun Liang grinned.

Erik looked over at the flashes of light coming from Rugrat's sparring square.

Rugrat stomped on the ground and stone pillars shot up. Lightning shattered it as flame ignited inside, turning it into a bomb as a spear of fire struck the target. He punched out with a fist. Water congealed and shot through a spell before lightning rippled through it, producing a series of fire arrows on the other side.

"I found this one waiting for you out front," Weebla said, walking in with a proctor.

He bowed to Xun Liang.

"Ah, so who will Erik and Rugrat be fighting?" Xun Liang said, walking over with Erik in tow. Rugrat was lost to his practice.

The proctor held out the scroll.

"Well, this should be fun," Xun Liang muttered.

"Who is it?"

"Read it for yourself."

Erik read the names and groaned. "A few more weeks and I could have had my body tempered with Water. If I wasn't so worried about being in the same state I got into with my Metal tempering, I could have sped it up."

"Still have twenty-four hours—Ow!" Xun Liang rubbed the back of his head, staring at Weebla. She gave him a look and turned to Erik.

"You need to do what you feel is best with cultivating and tempering. Move too fast and you will have endless problems. They are two things to take your time with."

Erik pressed his lips into a smile and bowed his head.

Erik finished tying his boots, adjusting his sand traps and the rubber band inside. He leaned on his knee, sighing, and slid his foot off the box, shaking his body, warming it up and bringing himself to his peak condition.

"What are you sighing for? This should be an exciting fight. You two will need to put up a fight with everything you have in that arena." Xun Liang patted him on the shoulder.

"Just going to miss you and Weebla," Erik said.

"Sure you won't think about joining us in Alva?" Rugrat asked.

"They don't appreciate you here, and I know that there are plenty of Alvans who would love to learn from you."

"Weebla and I like the quiet life. The Imperium isn't all that bad." Xun Liang smiled placatingly. "Even if you lose, there is a place for you here in Avegaaren."

"Not sure if I want to be somewhere where the people hate us. Even when we were doing nothing, not trying to create ripples, they came for us." Erik looked at Rugrat, who shrugged. It was what it was.

"They are loyal to their Associations. You two don't like clans, sects, and the other greedy human groups in the Ten Realms. If you had people come to your academy or went to Alva to learn everything they could from you to teach their people, what would you do?" Xun Liang's words were direct and serious, adding a gravitas that he rarely showed.

Erik made to speak, but only a thoughtful noise escaped.

Xun Liang patted them on the shoulder and smiled. "Don't be so closed off. Think of the Imperium like your Alva. The Imperium has stood for the purpose of raising fighters to fight the Devourers and Ravagers, to bring security to the Ten Realms. They've paid in blood and sweat for this cause so that others in the lower realms may do as they want. The Associations bring stability. You might have run into problems, but is that because they're assholes, or because they're angry at people taking from them so blatantly when they have given so much?"

The red light turned to green, and the door opened as Xun Liang escorted them toward the ramp.

"Will you serve the Ten Realms? Will you stand in the Tenth Realm, vowing that you will defend the Ten Realms?" His words were soft, but Erik and Rugrat heard them clearly, like thunder rolling under the cheering from the stands that quickly turned to jeering.

He pushed them lightly, and they walked toward the middle of the arena.

*I looked at them like they were just another sect, another group from the Ten Realms. Greedy hoarders.* Erik clenched his fists, a burning sensation on his cheeks.

"Fortune favors the strong. Together, we are stronger than we can ever be alone." Xun Liang's words floated on the wind to their ears.

Erik stiffened, pausing. He smiled and looked at Rugrat.

"Brother." He offered his fist.

Rugrat laughed, and they hit fists, pulling their helmets on over their grins as they walked to the middle of the arena.

"Today's first fight, the Wreckha's versus the Door Kickers."

Erik and Rugrat stopped at the starting positions. Sam and Cayleigh did as well. A blur shot across the arena, causing a stir.

Erik and Rugrat circulated their power, watching the movement. Fear gripped Erik's heart as the blur shot toward Xun Liang. He started moving as the blur resolved itself. Rekha stood before Xun Liang and dropped to her knees, kowtowing to the man swaddled in silks.

The arena grew silent as Erik came to a stop.

Xun Liang clicked his tongue and took off the glasses that covered most of his face.

"Master," Rekha's voice shook. "Your disciple greets you."

Silence filled the arena.

*Master? Wait... isn't her master... WAIT!*

Erik's eyes widened. Xun Liang looked defeated as he moved in a blur, shedding his layers to reveal his robe underneath. and took out a pin and put it on his breast.

A frosted dome appeared over the Wreckhas, Door Kickers, and Xun Liang.

"Stand, Rekha," he said.

She stood, looking up at him.

"Little rascal. I heard about you racing all over the Ninth and Tenth Realm. Didn't I tell you to go and have some fun?" He wagged a finger at her.

"Master." She turned and looked from him to Erik and Rugrat.

"Ah, let me introduce you to Rugrat and Erik. We've been having some fun the last few months."

By Rekha's wince, Erik had never felt more connected to another in suffering. He pulled off his helmet. "Good to meet you."

"But wait... Aren't you two trying to crush the academy and boost your empire's reputation?"

"They're as much emperors as I am the head of the Imperium," Xun Liang said.

"Oh. *Ohh.*" Rekha nodded in understanding, looking sympathetic, but not directing it at anyone there.

Erik frowned at Xun Liang. *Did he just diss all of us and himself?*

Rugrat pulled his helmet off. "We came here to learn how to fight in the Ten Realms."

"Don't really want to crush your academy, just learn. We do share our information with our people. We just don't think it should be locked away in the Ninth Realm," Erik said.

"S-so, what? You just came up here to fight?"

"Well, to learn how to fight. We got into a lot of fights because there were people challenging us all the time. We just wanted to be left alone," Erik said.

Xun Liang cleared his throat.

"Well, you three play nicely now, and by that I mean I want to see what all five of you can do. Hey, Cayleigh, Sam, you two are so *cute,* ah! Your great-grand-Weebla has been keeping me up to date!"

Cayleigh blushed as Sam coughed, hiding his smile behind his hand.

"And good work in keeping these two out of trouble." Xun Liang's voice dipped, making Rekha look away awkwardly.

Xun Liang clapped his hands. "So, I might disappear for a bit, but you should all get to know one another, and I want to see a big fight. Ten minutes and you'll start!"

Xun Liang stood upright, looking imperious as the frosted dome crumbled. "I wish you a good fight. I want to see what you can all do." He turned and flew down into the waiting room.

Rekha walked over to Erik, holding out a hand and shaking his and Rugrat's hand.

"Our master is a little... *different.*"

Erik smiled. "You could say that."

"I hope we can talk more later."

"Be nice to talk to someone that went through his training."

Rekha laughed. "Don't think we'll go easy on you."

"You kidding? We brought our A-game. Had a whole month to get ready for this." Rugrat circulated his elements and mana.

Their eyes flared with competitiveness.

"Good luck, you'll need it. The Wreckha's aren't like your average team." She headed back toward her group.

"You want to fight them now even more than before?" Erik asked.

"Does a bear shit in the woods?"

"You could have just said yes." Erik sighed.

"Oorah."

"That doesn't even make sense."

"Oorah. It doesn't have to."

Erik rolled his eyes, feeling his marine-ism growing, the specific aneurysm that had started once he transferred to the Marine Corps.

Mueller sat in one of the several booths that were reserved for teachers. They were all filled today as they chatted and drank, creating a lively atmosphere. All the stands were full of Imperium members, Avegaaren students, and high-ranking Association members.

Watching Rekha shoot across the arena, dread had gripped his stomach, turning to confusion when she stopped and bowed.

Her words rang through his head, sending him into a cold sweat.

*Master? Head Xun Liang? Their teacher is the Head of the Imperium?*

All the teachers were silent as the grave as the door opened. They all bowed as one.

Avegaaren's Head Serkin bowed his turban to the man who entered; the man wore a simple black robe, stitched with an almost lifelike scene of a man fighting a Devourer depicted around it. He wore the elegantly crafted cream, white and silver emblem of his office on his chest.

"The teachers of Avegaaren greet the Imperium Head," Serkin said.

"Hmm," Xun Liang said, looking around the booth, leaving the teachers bowing.

A spell cut off the sound within the booth as he paced back and forth. He waved Serkin behind him.

"Avegaaren's sole responsibility is to teach and train those that make it into the academy so they can learn to defend the Ten Realms. There is nothing in the charter that says that they must join the Imperium, or that they must be from the Associations. Over the years, the number of people that join the academy, or who have tried to join the academy, has only decreased. Even among our own ranks. While the academy trains people, we *build* teams. The Academy has become too insular in recent years, to the point where there are few people in the lower realms that know Avegaaren even exists. You will stop your petty games and honor the position of teacher you find yourself in."

The weight of that silence made Mueller wince in shame.

"Before anyone asks, I did not seek out Erik and Rugrat. They stumbled into me because they were not even given a map to the academy. I tested them for a week in the Telarri Dungeon."

Mueller shivered. The Telarri dungeon was one of the harshest dungeons with people losing limbs and being gravely wounded constantly.

"They remind me of me. They are good people and you have represented Avegaaren, the Imperium, and the Associations as a greedy group of individuals that are too scared to pass on their information to others; petty people that will disturb a student's studying to shame them."

Mueller held his footing against the wave of mana that shot out from Xun Liang.

"You shamed all three institutions. You have shamed yourselves. Erik and Rugrat came here to learn. Now, they wish to leave because they have only garnered hate. The very people we want to join our academy, you have shunned. How many others have you done this to in your pettiness? Take your seats and watch the fight, but let this be a lesson to you. Keep Avegaaren's promise above your prejudices. Stand."

He walked forward with Serkin following. Teachers parted ahead of him as he took a seat at the front of the booth.

The teachers returned to standing as the vision and sound blocking spell disappeared.

# 17

# Xun Liang's Students

A breeze carried dust across the arena. Erik and Rugrat stood side by side. They looked nearly identical except for the height difference. Sam, Cayleigh, and Rekha stood opposite in their fitted armors and open-faced helmets.

"Let's see what they can do," Erik said.

"Oorah."

"Begin!"

Sam went left; Rekha to the right. Erik and Cayleigh charged.

Buffs fell on Cayleigh from Sam and Rekha.

She hacked at Erik, but he weaved through her attacks, shooting past her as he jumped into the air. Cayleigh continued past him toward Rugrat.

Rekha fired attacks at Erik, but Rugrat broke them, his hands dancing through the air as he countered with his left and attacked Cayleigh with his right.

She weaved through the destruction coming at her from every direction, slowed but not stopped.

Erik dodged and defended against Sam's attacks. Hardened mana appeared under his feet and back, then flames as Erik channeled his Water element, changing the direction of his advance, hurtling toward Sam, doubling his speed.

"Busy," Rugrat said.

Erik watched for Rekha's attacks as Cayleigh leaped into the air. Rugrat met her with elements, the two a colorful display of power and control, of axe, mana, and element.

Erik focused on Sam's attack. He could feel the power building as he crafted a spell. Spell formations appeared around Sam, creating pillars of destruction. Erik slipped between them as they tracked him.

Mana and elements shifted wildly. A cracking noise like lightning splitting a tree drowned out everything else.

Erik dodged and gained space; something felt wrong. A roar shook the very air and ran through the ground. A shiver ran down his spine.

Cayleigh and Rugrat had spaced themselves again.

Tears cut through the sky as hundreds of beasts climbed through in a stream. A wolf with four eyes and two tentacles as large as Erik's manor stepped through, compressing into a demi-human form. He raised his hands as beasts of all varieties and malformation poured through the opening—winged, horned, furred, feathered, scaled and leathery. They dropped into the academy below and covered the skies.

"Devourers! Combat teams, ready yourselves. Spectators, regroup at the totems!" Xun Liang's words rang through the arena.

Erik and Rugrat grouped together, Han Wu and Yao Meng reaching them seconds later as tears, large and small, appeared in the sky and around the academy, mutated beasts rushing forward.

*Ravagers.*

Beasts in humanoid form stood in the sky, commanding the surrounding elements. The suction of mana into their bodies felt like they could drain the ocean.

Attacks hit the arena. The teachers' barriers lit up, defending against the attacks.

"Non-combatants, head for the totems!" Xun Liang's voice spread through the arena complex as people hurriedly used teleportation formations to escape.

While there were some fighters in the audience, being made up from the Associations, the large majority were from crafter and merchant classes, weaker students and those that had been able to make it to the Ninth Realm but not into the academy yet.

The Wreckha team shot into the sky.

"There are too many people to use the teleportation formations. We'll cover them to the totems. Get your people out," Rekha yelled back at Erik and Rugrat, flying away with her team. They crashed into a group of Ravagers, tearing into their ranks to protect others.

"Sir," Han Wu said.

"Inform command of the situation, check your gear, and get ready to move." Erik pulled out his rifle and checked it was loaded, looping his one-point sling over his shoulder and under his arm.

"Oh, hey there, baby. Papa's missed you." Rugrat lovingly patted the Beast.

"Extended line, cover the students and the civilians. Recruit those we can fight," Erik said. "Han Wu, left flank. Yao Meng, right."

They shifted into position.

"Yao Meng, have the crew at the accommodations prep for exfil immediately to the lower realm. Send messages and reports with them."

"Yes, sir. I'll relay the message."

Two Special Team members fired on Ravagers, cutting them out of the sky and garnering interest from other creatures. The team members kept firing.

"Let's go."

They flew toward where the Wreckhas and other high-ranking students were covering the spectators and lower classmates.

Erik and his people attached elements and spells to their rounds, cutting down Ravagers in a hail of tracers.

"Rolling thunder!"

They advanced into the tide of beasts, moving from cover to cover and pushed up next to the Wreckha's, who had created a field of death around them.

"You cover the air; we've got the ground!" Erik yelled.

Rekha looked at the teams cutting forward.

Rugrat fired into the ground, and it exploded several meters ahead. "Fucking termites!"

"Got it." Rekha, Sam, and Cayleigh jumped into the sky.

Erik saw an exchange of spells and elements in the clouds above. The teachers of the Academy were working in concert, wading through the Ravagers in the air.

Xun Liang ran across the roof of the house coming apart around him under the air attacks that flicked free of the wolf's tentacles. His blade snapped out, defeating several attacks as he jumped free of the destruction, landing on another building.

He picked up his speed. Blades of ice shattered buildings and the street below. Xun Liang turned left as he jumped. The world responded, his blade flashing through the curtains of ice, carving a path forward to arrive at the wolf Devourer.

Tentacles shot at him from every direction. His sword rang out as he trimmed off the tentacles, dropping them to the ground below. Flame leapt from his hand, piercing the beast and exploding.

He kicked the creature away with a wood spell and it slammed into another devourer. The wolf came to life again. Animated by the spell, it clawed and hacked at the closest Devourer.

"Come on then!" Xun Liang released his aura, hurling away an attack of air blades and smashing through several nearby buildings.

Devourers launched into the sky like sharks to the smell of blood.

"Your Ten Realms will feed our legions!" a Devourer yelled as he charged with four others.

Xun Liang sped through the sky.

Serkin's spells crashed into the enemy's spells, creating flashes of light to hide his movements. He dropped below, creating an illusion of himself running forward when he was really running on the roof below the Devourers.

The Ravagers attacked the illusions as Xun Liang jumped into the sky. Unnoticed, he melded into the elements, appearing next to a beetle looking beast. It started to turn as he slashed out with his smoking hot blade, turning the beetle's insides into steam. It exploded, tearing apart the surrounding buildings.

Serkin was holding off the Ravagers. The remaining Devourers unleashed elemental attacks.

Gritting his teeth, Xun Liang cast a counter and shot to the side, destroying one cast, the other grazing his leg, burning through his pants and taking a chunk of flesh. A flash of lighting severed the nerves before the pain could register. The animate materials stabbed into the remaining two Devourers. Xun Liang saw tears close with the Devourer's deaths.

In the streets, it was chaos. Shattered crashed into students and people fleeing in a panic.

Xun Liang shot across the sky and slammed into Ravagers. His sword cut through four and left an arc of destruction where his air blade had passed.

He channeled heat into the sewer system, filling the air with rank smelling steam around the Shattered advance.

Lightning cracked through his body, through his eyes, the god Thor incarnate as it flowed through him.

A river of light ran through the Shattered, through the mist.

Hundreds died in seconds.

Xun Liang shot into the sky, his sword blurring, blades tearing through Aerial Ravagers.

The wind turned against him, cutting at him as he called upon heat, draining it from the world, and water from the ground, from the sky. It shot to his command, flash freezing as it crossed through the aerial Ravagers and their controlling Devourer.

The Devourer diverted the shards from itself, but its sworn were shredded in feathers and blood.

Xun Liang's blade cut into the Devourer's wing. Its beak lashed out, cutting Xun Liang from the chest to his leg. He cried out, ice covering the wound as ice formed into spikes, stabbing through the bird in several locations.

Xun Liang tumbled toward the ground, using Earth Energy to fuel his body and Wood energy to speed up his healing. The element imbued attack was a poison and took much more energy to heal.

He opened his eyes, recovering from his tumble. He shot forward, coming just feet away from the ground and back up into the sky. He reached out; a tree tore itself apart into a spear, and metal from a fence into a point. He hurled the spear, imbued with the power of flame. It crashed into a tear, taking it out and halving the Devourer coming through.

Xun Liang rained down weapons of ice upon the tear, collapsing it.

He cast fireballs that threw Ravagers aside like bowling pins and left craters in the school grounds.

*Danger.*

His body reacted on instinct as he dodged and weaved through the elemental attacks coming from three directions. Devourers converged on him. *Looks like they brought friends.*

He blocked attacks with counter elements and his sword. He blew his hair from his face, blood coloring his teeth, his life sustained by Wood and Earth elements.

His heart didn't beat, but even now his body was repairing.

Xun Liang shot to the side. He blew a hole through a building which came apart around him as the Devourer's attacks landed. He turned in the middle of the block of houses, coming out in a direction different from where he'd aimed.

They roared and chased.

*Two-star Devourers, at least.* He needed to kill them. If they were to get loose, there were few people in the Ninth Realm that could deal with them. The good news was that he only sensed these remaining Devourers.

Xun Liang diverted down streets filled with Ravagers. They roared in anger and then fear as the Devourer's attacks followed him, killing with impunity.

Xun Liang sensed teachers, students, and people of the Ninth Realm. Each of them was a fighter, using whatever weapons they had, banding together to confront the Shattered.

The wounds took a toll on his speed. He breathed for the first time and his heart started to pump again, the savage wound starting to close.

He created several illusions, splitting up into every direction, using one to go to the ground. He dropped. The ground shifted, swallowing him up, and closing without a disturbance as he used his senses to see the converging devourers. He moved through the ground as easy as a fish through water. He launched attacks of every element at the Devourers from every direction in his domain.

Two Devourers fell under the attacks as he shot out of the ground. He gathered the heat and air upon his blade, and slashed out, leaving a line of plasma that bisected another Devourer.

Attacks fell upon him as spells shot out from around him, crashing into their attacks. His blade was a flashing wall as he closed with a Devourer, the shockwaves maiming and killing Ravagers caught too close.

He grabbed its body and roared, charging forward. The Devourer came apart under their attacks. Xun Liang threw the remainder of the carcass and drew the elements into his body, enhancing him totally.

He could see teachers spreading out in a wave of chaos. Each man and woman worth a sixth realm army were being pushed back.

He dove into battle, losing an arm to a fire attack. Poison got into his wounds as he fought as savagely as his opponents, taking wounds to claim their lives and tears.

Xun Liang killed one of the two two-stars with a stunning punch that launched it toward a grand library. Xun Liang ripped off the metal gates, creating a massive spear that stabbed through the creature and separated into several more, forcing the Devourers to defend as he hurled out lighting, heat, and water, ravaging the remaining Devourers.

Xun Liang dropped to the ground and called upon Water, but he wasn't fast enough. The fire element Devourer detonated himself, burning through Xun Liang's defenses, hurling him across the sky, through the outer wall of the library, several rooms and bookshelves, coming out on the other side through a fence, leaving a torn trail through the cobblestone street. Xun Liang pushed up from the ground, coughing blood. He tore off his upper robe, little more that tatters. The blast had taken half his face. He pulled out healing and stamina potions, pouring them over himself like water.

He hissed at the pain of his wounds rewinding in slow motion. Chugging another potion, it came out the side of his cheek. He used his one good eye to look at where he had come from. The three remaining Devourers had landed and were moving toward. him. Two were missing limbs; one had a nasty wound along her side.

They had given up their Demi-human forms for their stronger elemental bodies.

Xun Liang gathered his power. If he dropped his elemental enhancement, his body would start to die. He threw powder on himself. The star rated concoctions kneaded flesh and bones together.

He blinked, his missing eye returning.

The Devourers roared and charged.

Xun Liang raised his sword and yelled. Around him, stone, dirt, and metal rose from the ground, joining his charge. Water swirled forward, taking on his features as air versions descended like the lord of air's avenging warriors.

The Devourers roared in anger, focusing their attacks on Xun Liang.

His blade was liquid light, shimmering between attacks. Elements shot out to counter attacks, creating a wall of destruction ahead of him as he diverted attacks that detonated buildings, cleaving through stone, dirt, and down to bedrock.

The Element Incarnations arrived and interposed themselves with one another. Metal skeleton and dirt muscles, threaded with wood, stone skin, air joints, and blades of fire. They combined together in the tens, then in the hundreds.

He cracked his teeth, mana and elements draining from him. They charged, a sea of element given form.

The Incarnates died in only a few attacks, but there were *hundreds* of them. Their swords struck the Devourers, converting allthe elements and mana that made up their body into a blast of destructive and twisted chaotic power, their bodies collapsing to deliver those final blows.

The first Devourer fell, then the second.

He reached out for mana. It lashed out at a Devourer, stabbing through them, skewering them. The creature jerked backward. Xun Liang smiled through broken teeth.

Two Incarnations were consumed in their attacks, using the opening to end their opponent.

Xun Liang dropped to his knee. He checked the area with his domain, coughing from his wounds.

He drew back the energy from the Incarnates and felt dozens more tears open across the academy. He looked around wildly, and pulled out potions, covering himself in them and tossing on powder, adding in elemental and mana recovery concoctions.

*Four Star.* Xun Liang groaned. He couldn't think of the pain, lest he be lost in it. His eyes fell on the latest Devourers as soon as they stepped through the tears and shot into the sky.

One had large gem-like eyes and rings running down its body, looking like some kind of bug. The other was like a minotaur but with an extra set of arms; both were four stars. The wolf had been a three star, the ape and beaked also threes. Their power was immense.

He felt them looking, searching. The two of them were brimming with power.

One waved their hand, and the ground rose to their command, consuming several buildings, crushing them and their occupants.

Xun Liang had no more elements or mana stored within his body. He had barely finished off the level two- and three-level Devourers, and they had been heavily wounded.

Three stars were a whole magnitude stronger than level twos, and there were three of them and they were *fresh*.

He knew his limits.

But if they lost Avegaaren Academy, it would leave the Seventh Realm open to attack. Anyone that completed the Eighth Realm Trial and reached the Ninth Realm would be fed right to the Ravagers and Devourers. More importantly, they'd lose anyone that could fight the Ravagers and Devourers and anyone to teach them. Even if Avegaaren fell, the knowledge must not die here.

Xun Liang reached deep and drew on his power. There was but one more option.

*I was so hoping to see those three graduate. I wanted to see Rekha's smile.* In a small part, deep in his heart, a part he would rarely hope to himself through his centuries of living, Rekha was like the daughter he'd never had.

He laughed as tears appeared at the corners of his eyes, then yelled, drawing his domain in, pulling his elements and mana together. Waves of power struck his domain, but he gathered it.

"Your Tenth Realm will fall as you will. Akran will reward us for your head!" the minotaur roared, then charged, the bug followed.

*This is Akran's plan. He must be in the Tenth Realm.*

He was at peace, focused internally. His elemental core cracked and spread, power burning through his channels, through his acupoints, fusing and changing.

"He's ascending!" the bug hissed.

The two increased their speed as Xun Liang breathed as if reborn. His body burned with power, pushing past limits he had not known as the world responded to him.

His body started to collapse, like one would if their tombstone was claimed, the power charging into his body counteracting it. "Die!"

Incarnations in the thousands formed, creating a sea that charged the Devourers.

The Devourers roared in outrage as the first attacks met them, chaotic attacks raining down on their bodies.

"Xun Liang!" Serkin yelled, his clothes torn and bloodied.

"Get away. We can lose Avegaaren, but we must not lose our students! We must raise people to defend the Ten Realms!" Xun Liang's voice spread through the Academy as he rose, a war god ascending. He no longer commanded the elements; they were an extension of himself.

He felt his elements fighting one another as he crudely forced them together, mana, elements and body becoming a single entity.

It was like trying to put out a candle with gasoline, making it burn faster so that it would eventually stop burning.

Xun Liang's body radiated light as he burned up from inside. He didn't have the balanced elements or mana and his body was falling apart under the stress, but he could tap into more power than he'd ever had before.

He flicked his sword and turned into a streak of light, entering the melee.

His attacks met the Devourers, the force throwing Incarnations through the sky that cleared nearby buildings and Ravagers exiting the tears.

Xun Liang's face was expressionless, beyond physical pain, in ecstasy as he deflected attacks and countered their elements. His own sword distorted and burned from the power channeling through it, leaving savage wounds. Each aimed to cleave and kill.

More wounds appeared on his body. He lost his arm to the bug, but he didn't need an arm to use his domain. It gave him an opening as he appeared on the other side of the bug, crackling with lightning.

"My student taught me that one." He laughed as destruction surrounded him and charged back in.

The Devourers, creatures who had lived for centuries, that had tamed three elements, had thousands of sworn Ravagers, even other Devourers under them, showed an unfamiliar expression—fear.

He cut the bug's eye and took an arm from the minotaur.

Xun Liang grinned and charged in again. Elements and mana raged around him as he tore into the two Devourers while they cut into him.

He was hit; he had braced for it. The last of the power inside him broke. His legs had fallen apart and his remaining arm, holding his sword, collapsed.

He hit a roof, then another, and crashed into a street, throwing up the flagstones. He coughed; the Realm seemed slower now.

*So, this is it.*

He saw Rekha charge into the sky with Sam, Cayleigh, Erik, and Rugrat following.

His right eye tracked them to the two Devourers. The teachers and a one-armed Serkin surged from their fights, led by a wall of spells, throwing the wounded minotaur and bug.

He felt scared for them, wanting to protect them.

"I call upon my wish. Ten Realms, take my power. Heal my master Weebla's old wounds and add whatever remaining cultivation I have to hers."

| **Your power will be used to heal your Master: Weebla** |
|---|
| Any remaining power will be drained from you and given over to her. You may only make 1 wish to the realms. This will use up your wish. Do you agree? |
| *YES/NO* |

He took one more selfish moment to watch his students fighting together in the skies above Avegaaren. Tears blurred his vision as he felt the coldness of the ground, his body collapsing under the sheer power he had called upon.

"Yes," he said before he allowed the fear to close around him. "Weebla, protect them as you protected me! General Battleaxe."

Power leaked from his body, but it gathered in titanic force, an external source compressing it and directing it.

It shot off like an eel of light, passing through buildings and walls without affecting them.

A tombstone shimmered in the middle of a street, with only a few bloodied rags remaining in the upturned flagstones.

Everyone was working together, trying to clear a path to the totem. Fighting was getting thick and heavy as Erik dodged a blast of flame. He cut off the Flame element with his Water element and his beasts of stone tore free of a nearby building, crashing into Ravagers, drawing their attention away as someone activated a spell scroll. A pillar wiped out the Ravagers, Erik's metal beasts, and another ten meters of street.

"Move!" Rekha yelled, ducking under a Ravager and blasting it with fire, killing it.

The totem gates opened as the guards within defended. People ran through the corridor of fighters into the totem. Many joined the walls to man mana weapons, sending spells and bolts into the enemy, pushing back the Ravagers.

"No!" Rekha yelled as she shot up into the sky.

Erik turned to see Xun Liang drop out of the sky. Two Devourers laid into the teachers that had been backing him up. The battle was turning against them, and quickly.

Sam and Cayleigh shot into the sky, following Rekha.

"Yao Meng, Han Wu, defend this point!"

Erik and Rugrat flew upward.

Rekha unleashed a spell, hitting the minotaur Devourer and knocking him back across the sky.

Erik accelerated, neck and neck with Cayleigh.

Buffs fell on them both from Sam and Rugrat.

Erik tossed her a concoction and drank one himself. Power thrummed through his body. They clashed with the minotaur head-on. Erik tried to dodge, but the minotaur was too fast, his attacks too strong, to throw him off his game. The passing of his fist caused Erik's muscles, blood, and internal organs to shift out of place.

He coughed, striking the minotaur, who snarled as Cayleigh attacked him from the other side.

Between the two of them, they could tie him up.

"We'll hold him back; you hit him!" Erik yelled.

"Buff Rugrat!" Sam yelled. His and Rekha's power diverted into Rugrat as he tossed back a potion.

Erik and Cayleigh locked the Devourer in place with their bodies and elements.

Erik got hammered in the side, feeling several things break.

They grunted and groaned as Rugrat fired. His first round was met with elements, creating a shield around the minotaur. The second got further, breaking the shield. The third hit the minotaur in the chest. The fourth and fifth punctured through.

The minotaur was thrown free of Erik and Cayleigh as he started to expand.

"Lightning and fire!" Rugrat panted, shooting out a thread of water and running lightning into the minotaur. They found the shrapnel inside the minotaur.

"Erik, use your storage ring!" Rekha yelled.

Erik flew over, holding his side and using his storage ring. It didn't work several times before the minotaur disappeared.

They looked around as Ravagers rushed toward the tears closing across the realm.

Three charged Erik. He created beasts of water, fighting them off as he retreated.

He felt something shift like a release as his control started to increase rapidly over the elements. *No, no, I can't temper my body here!* Erik focused his water beasts before he cried out, breaking through that last thin barrier between him and his Water body.

Erik dropped, feeling something wrapping around him as his body drew in the Water element hungrily. His power grew as the Water element became a part of him. That power thrummed through his veins, carried upon the air, and beneath his feet. Instead of simply being the power around him, he could reach out and touch it.

He opened his eyes, finding Rekha and Sam killing Ravagers that came close as Rugrat rendered aid to Cayleigh.

Erik pulled out a revival needle and stabbed it into his leg.

"What happened?"

"She took a hit for you when you dropped to the ground," Rugrat said.

"Cheap shot." Cayleigh's breath caught in pain at Rugrat's work. "Got to finish our match."

Erik took over, healing Cayleigh. "Not pretty, but should be good."

He used a revival needle on her. She hissed as it hit her blood stream. "Cheers."

Erik reached out and helped her up.

She tested her side. "Good to go."

A shockwave passed in front of them.

Erik thought he saw someone fly overhead between the buildings.

He took in the street they were in. "The other Devourer?"

"The teachers got him." Mueller, their home room teacher, was looking worse for the wear as he landed and checked on them. "We're moving to the totems. Gather people together to retake Avegaaren and send those that can't fight down to the lower realms. Will you help us?"

Erik looked at him, biting off his first response. "We'll help."

"Thank you." A building exploded, hit with a stray spell.

"We can gather our guards. They're good in a fight and can move through the streets," Erik said as other teachers landed behind Mueller, mostly wounded.

Erik looked at Rugrat to take up the conversation and moved to the walking wounded.

He worked on one man with a gash on his side, smacking his hand out of the way as he bandaged him, and then hit him with several healing spells and a stamina needle.

The teachers were stiff around him, leaving him to work.

"We're heading out!" Mueller yelled. "Rugrat will lead the way. We'll gather reinforcements and push back the Ravagers."

Erik quickly finished up his work as Rugrat walked over to him.

"I can't raise anyone on comms."

"We'd best hurry," Erik said.

They flew into the air, along with the Wreckhas and the teachers that were not too wounded or missing team members.

Erik saw the fighting at the totem A section exploded, covering the totem in smoke. Flashes illuminated the smoke and dust. A wave of defenders turned attackers as they carved through the Ravager lines. The Ravagers broke, running back to their tears.

The teachers cast their own spells where the Ravagers were running, collapsing several buildings as Erik and Rugrat landed.

Han Wu and Yao Meng stepped forward, covered in dust.

"Well, one clear totem," Yao Men said, reloading.

"Might need a new wall and ground." Han Wu shrugged, looking at where the charges had gone off in the midst of the Ravagers.

"Let's check everyone over and then we'll push forward," Erik said.

"We're good to go now," Rekha snarled, getting up in his face.

"We've got wounded, and we have people that don't have groups to fight in. We organize them and push forward, or else we'll be going in without a plan," Erik said.

She twisted her lips.

"He's right, Miss Bhatta," Mueller said, getting her full-bore glare. He didn't back down. "Even your teammate will need some time to adapt after her wounds."

Cayleigh grunted and made to talk, but Sam stopped her.

"Fine, we leave as soon as you are ready."

"All right, let's get everyone inside. Water, stamina potions. Make sure everyone gets geared up, have people check for any injuries," Erik said to the team leaders.

They nodded and passed orders, everyone moving inside the totem defenses.

Thankfully, the worst injuries needed only a few minutes of Erik's care. Most had armor and gear in their storage rings and quickly pulled it on over their clothes.

Erik remembered the sight of Xun Liang fighting the Devourers, killing three and critically wounding two others with only his sword and no armor or formations to help him.

Erik checked his notifications.

| Quest Completed: Body Cultivation 5 |
|---|
| The path to cultivating one's body is not easy. To stand at the top, one must forge their own path forward. |
| **Requirements:** |
| Reach Body like Divine Iron |
| **Rewards:** |
| +48 to Strength |
| +48 to Agility |
| +48 to Stamina |
| +80 to Stamina Regeneration |
| +1,000,000,000 EXP |

591,087,113,543,978/1,168,160,000,000,000,000,000 EXP till you reach Level 105

---

**Your personal efforts have increased your base stats!**

Stamina +24
Agility +24
Strength +24
Stamina Regeneration +60
Mana Pool +10
Mana Regeneration +10

---

**Title: Strength of Water**

You have tempered your body with Water. Water has become a part of you, making your body take on some of its characteristics. You have gained:

Legendary Water resistance.
Increased control over Water mana.
Physical attacks contain Water attribute.
Can completely purify the Water attribute in mana.
Physical Domain

---

**Name: Erik West**

*Level: 104*
*Race: Human-?*

Titles:

*From the Grave III*
*Blessed By Mana*
*Dungeon Master V*
*Reverse Alchemist*
*Poison Body*
*Fire Body*
*Earth Soul*
*Mana Reborn V*
*Wandering Hero*
*Metal Mind, Metal Body*
*Sky Grade Bloodline*
**Strength of Water**

Strength: (Base 162) +88          2750

| Agility: (Base 155) +120 | 1650 |
| Stamina: (Base 165) +105 | 4455 |
| Mana: (Base 647) +134 | 8132 |
| Mana Regeneration (Base 670) +71 | 475.24/s |
| Stamina Regeneration: (Base 302) +99 | 90.32/s |

He checked his stats and pushed it to the side, using his Alvan wide channel.

"Change formations to linkers and add tabs." Erik took out two tabs, putting them under his vest's side. They said STEP DOWN in Neon green letters.

He checked his IFAK, making sure there was a step down, and an extra revival needle, closing it and securing to the back of his carrier.

He walked over to a Special Team member, helping one another to change out the formations on their armor.

Mueller had all his gear on, checking on the students manning the defenses alongside people that had just come to have a day out and watch the fights.

The Alvans were all wearing the same gear and were changing out small formations hooked into their armor.

He thought he saw someone familiar and did a double take. Kujo Hikokie, in his red armor, approached Erik who was working on another's back, not looking at him.

Mueller circulated mana as Hikokie snapped his arms to his side and bowed to Erik.

Erik finished with the other man's armor as Mueller slowed his pace, ready to move if he needed, but wanting to see what the two men would do.

"I thought that you were shaming the academy and looking down on us. I am sorry for the trouble I caused."

"We all make mistakes."Erik exhaled. "I can kind of see how you would think that we were screwing with you. I know that I might feel the same way if people did what I did in my academies. So, will you stop bowing? You won't be able to face anyone looking at the dirt," Erik said, helping him stand up and clapping him on the shoulder. "No hard feelings. You were protecting your home. Takes real honor and pride to admit that you were wrong. It's made me realize that I'm prejudiced too, against others who aren't Alvan. Looks like we both have something to work on."

Mueller smiled and headed up the defenses where the Wreckhas were waiting.

Cayleigh and Sam were talking in the corner while Rekha looked over the defenses at the academy beyond talking to several others. Buildings had been flattened, the manicured gardens and parks ruined, while Ravager bodies fell apart as their elements reduced what was left.

She finished talking to other students organizing the defense and walked over.

*She hasn't taken any time to go through the loss of Xun Liang. She doesn't have the time.*

"Are we ready to go?" Rekha asked, her voice tight.

"Just a few more minutes. Wanted to gather you downstairs. the other teams are organized now."

She gathered her trio and followed him back down. The other teams made their last preparations, looking toward Professor Wahida, who would be leading them.

"All right, we're going to move to the West where most of the tears are. Our primary objective is to find and escort people to the totems or add them to our forces to clear Avegaaren. Warships and external support will be coming. What we do now will help the students and others in the academy who are trapped. I have team groupings and the places you are to check."

She moved to a map on the ground. The team leaders gathered around as she pointed out the different objectives throughout the city and the totems they would check and establish as strongholds.

Weebla grunted, hitting the wall behind her, and sitting on the broken stone at the bottom of the wall. She took out a recovery potion, feeling squeezed dry.

*It's been so very long since I could feel the power moving through me like this*

Her eyes blurred as she looked away, bartering with herself, and trying to not think of the pain and the way she had been healed.

Her sound transmission buzzed as she accessed it.

"Weebla?" Eli'keen said.

"The Ninth was attacked. Five Devourers attacked the school. Xun Liang must have killed them before he…"

"What happened to him?"

"I don't know, but he made his wish to the Ten Realms, transferred all his power to me, and healed me."

"Akran has appeared with nearly a hundred Devourers. They're attacking across the Tenth Realm, making them unable to close the tears Devourers created from the Tenth to the Ninth realm. The bases in the Tenth can't hold."

"You're talking about losing the Tenth Realm."

"We can lose the Realm, but we can't lose the people, or we'll have no way to retake it."

"Every minute the Shattered consume mana in the Ten Realms they get stronger."

"I know, Weebla, I know. But if they remain in the Tenth, they'll just die. We're stretched too thin."

"How did this happen, Eli'keen?"

"It doesn't matter how it happened. What matters is how we deal with it. Every minute Akran's forces are in the Ten Realms is another minute they get stronger by consuming mana. We have to defeat them before they become so lodged in the Ten Realms we can't force them back out."

Erik killed another Ravager in a hail of rounds as he walked forward. Ice shot down from the sky, stabbing through a Ravager jumping from a roof. Another running along a wall was stitched with stone darts, landing next to a team member who put in a dozen rounds before it reached her feet and pushed forward.

"Take cover!" Rugrat yelled. Everyone ducked as mana cannons tore through several blocks.

Erik looked over the wall at the carnage. Magical attacks struck the ground. Warships appeared in the sky, slowly flying forward, raking the ground with attacks.

A ragged cheer rose among the defenders, teachers, students, and combat experts, wounded and tired from the fighting.

A man on a flying mount landed among them.

"We're clearing through the academy and from the city. The city is largely secured. It seems their attack was focused on the academy. Head to the totems and get some rest. Forces from the Tenth Realm are teleporting down.

Once we've secured the Ninth, we'll retake the Tenth."

They continued talking with the teachers as Erik opened a channel to the special teams and Rugrat. "Send a messenger to Alva if we have them. Tenth Realm got taken by the Shattered. Imperium is working to retake the Ninth. Intel is for the council only. We're going to head for the nearest totem and dig in, get the non-combatants out. We'll go from there."

# 18

## Stronger Together

On the afternoon of the second day, Erik sat with Rugrat inside a building they'd taken as an overwatch beyond the totem.

They looked up as Weebla came down the stairs.

"Weebla." They rose to greet her.

She waved them back down, looking tired. "They found Xun Liang's body. I saw him. He's dead."

The spark of hope in Erik's chest died as he let his head fall back, his helmet digging into the stone as he hit it a few times. He'd seen him fighting, but hadn't seen him afterwards. He'd hoped.

"Fuck." Rugrat rubbed his face.

"Rekha?" Erik asked.

"I just talked to her. She's up there, not sure how to…" Weebla moved her hands around, a lost expression on her face.

Erik took off his helmet as she gazed at her hands. He knew the expression; she was missing someone she'd never replace. There was a gaping hole in her world, and she hadn't processed it yet.

Erik signalled Rugrat toward her.

It wasn't any easier on Erik or Rugrat, but they'd done this before. They knew what was coming and the ways they would deal with the pain. It didn't make them stronger or tougher, and it didn't make them cold. If anything, it hurt more each time, like a piece had been torn from them. It just meant that they could take on more of the pain to take care of those that didn't know how to deal with it.

"Take my seat. I'll check on Rekha," Erik said.

"Come on, I've got some tea to warm you up." Rugrat said as they switched places.

Erik headed up the stairs to the roof. Fires smoked across the academy; the warships had at least calmed down. He found Rekha looking over the battlefield with her sword out and her staff at the ready, next to the roof's battlements.

She turned at Erik's arrival. "O-oh, sorry, just, ah, I thought I heard a Ravager out there. Just uhh." She laughed and sat down on a box.

"Just wanted to check on you. Here's some water." Erik moved up in her line of sight, placing himself so she wouldn't be looking right at the fighting or what was behind her.

"Oh, thanks." She made to reach forward, glancing at her sword and staff.

"I don't think you'll need those to drink." Erik smiled. "Here, I'll trade you and even clean it up." Erik moved to take her sword, waiting for her to put it in his hand as he offered her the canteen.

She laid down the staff as Erik used a clean spell on the sword.

Rekha drank from the canteen, quickly starting to take huge gulps as Erik put her sword down beside her and crouched in front of her.

She panted, taking off her helmet wiping her mouth with the back of her hand. There was a hollowness in her movements and an emptiness in her eyes.

"Did Weebla…?"

"Yeah, she did." Erik grimaced, looking away.

Rekha tried to hold back her crying, but the sound escaped between her lower lip and her teeth, a cry that came from deep within as she dropped the canteen, looking lost as tears ran down her face.

"Hey, hey, hey. Don't worry. You're all okay," Erik said, pulling her to his chest. She grabbed onto his vest, crying, wailing as Erik held her, patting her armor.

Her cries redoubled as she tried to muffle herself in his chest.

He didn't know how long she cried for, but it left her tired and empty and no longer able to cry anymore.

"Good thing you drank that water. You must have cried it all out," Erik said, realizing his knees were cold and wet from where the canteen had drained its last remains.

He hid it and pulled out some thin soup for Rekha. "Have some of this."

She looked at the soup, frowning before she started drinking it.

"Mmm!" She let out a surprised sound as she started drinking faster and ate the meat and vegetables within. "That is a most strong stamina potion."

"Called soup where I'm from." Erik grinned and took a seat with her, slowly drinking a coffee, the bitterness and warmth comforting.

It was in moments like these he gained a hankering for a cigarette.

He took a deep breath and let it out slowly, rubbing his grimy face.

"When I first came to Avegaaren, I caused a lot of problems," Rekha said, looking at the steam rising from the soup. "I came from the Bhatta family. We had rank and position in the past, but we were on the decline. Everyone was trying to make alliances and bring back the glory days of the clan. It was largely patriarchal, so my father, when he had four daughters, had to figure out a way to make the greatest use of us." She rolled her tongue around her mouth and spat to the side. "He promised us to different men."

She fell silent, looking over the battlements. "I thought that if I became stronger, I would make my mother and father proud. I could get us the position we wanted and then me and my sisters could create our own path. My father didn't tell me differently as I trained, cultivating and tempering." A deprecating smirk spread across her face.

"My father used my increasing cultivation as a way to get more interest and suitors for me. I found out in the end. In my training, I had never been taught how to fight. I would be followed in the lower realms; the Eighth Realm was the only place I could go. I passed through the Eighth Trial and fought to enter Avegaaren for two years. My family found out where I had gone. By then, I was in the academy, so they accused the Academy of holding me against their will." She snorted and looked into her soup, a pure smile breaking through.

"Xun Liang was getting demands to return me to my family. He silenced everyone and walked over to me. I was so nervous. You know what he said? 'Those are lovely tiles, but my face is up here.' I was so nervous looking up at him and finding him standing there like some scoundrel schoolboy." Rekha chuckled. "He asked me what I wanted to do. I told him I wanted to learn how to fight. He attacked me and I defended before he told me to follow him.

"My father demanded to know where I was going. Xun Liang kept walking. 'Just going to teach her to kick your dumb ass,' he said. Isn't that what a teacher's supposed to do?'"

Erik grinned, picturing it as she looked up at him, her smile fighting the sadness underneath.

"So Weebla and he trained me. She introduced me to Cayleigh, who led me to meeting Sam. Gave me a home, trained me. He was more of a father than mine ever was." She looked away as the tears fell.

"He was a good man," Erik said.

She nodded as Erik shared the story of how he and Rugrat got lost, meeting Xun Liang and Weebla on their first day in the academy.

The afternoon turned to night as they sat together sharing stories, sharing memories of a life that had touched so many.

"You sure that she's going to be good?" Rugrat asked as he walked with Erik toward the totem.

"She needs the sleep and we have work to do. Weebla, Sam, and Cayleigh are with her," Erik said.

"All right."

"Also, there's something I need to do before I go back to Alva," Erik said.

"Where are you going?"

"Kushan. I need to talk to Ziyaad al-Saade."

"Leaving me with all the fun of talking to the council?" Rugrat smiled.

"You've got this." Erik hit him on the shoulder.

"Jeez, thanks." Rugrat bumped fists with him as their teams separated. Rugrat moved with Han Wu's team, watching Erik and Yao Meng's team disappear in a flash of light before another overtook Rugrat's vision.

"All right, time to do the job. Egbert! Need a transport!" Rugrat yelled up in the air.

"Damn taxi service," a voice mumbled as they appeared in front of Alva's government offices in the new dungeon headquarters.

George appeared in a flash of light beside him with a wide grin on his face.

Rugrat grinned as he felt a similar connection. "Hah! Look at you! Formed your mana core and tempered with Earth now!" Rugrat laughed, smacking George on the shoulder.

George scratched his hair and looked away, embarrassed but proud of what he had achieved.

"Won't be long before you're beating Erik and me in cultivation."

"Well, about time you caught up in levels," George said.

"Lil' devil."

"Got a feeling you're not here to do the paperwork that's piled up while you've been gone."

Rugrat felt George's amusement through their bond.

Rugrat blew out a breath. "Anything happen while I was gone?"

"Not much. Everyone is training. The dungeon and the empire expanded. More schools. There were a few groups of demi-humans that joined as well." He used a sound cancelling spell. "The old Sha Fleet has disappeared, undergoing renovations. We've got warships being completed in different locations across the realms. The crafters went all out on them. Is what I heard about the Tenth Realm right?"

"What you hear?"

"That the realm got taken by some creatures not from the realm."

"Yeah, they're called the Shattered. Come in Ravagers and Devourer types. They took the Tenth and hit the Ninth." Rugrat's voice dulled, looking away.

George patted him on the shoulder and gripped it. "You lost people." George didn't need to ask; he could feel it through their bond.

"They attacked everyone. Didn't care. Killed my teacher, a good man. He took on a half dozen Devourers, but they'd mastered multiple elements. He took out most of them, but…"

Rugrat felt the savage hole that seemed to have torn through his very soul. Each death, each loss tearing through the part of his soul they had melded with.

George patted him on the shoulder. "You taught me that life goes on. It sounds like he died doing what he felt was best."

Rugrat looked at George. He had grown up quickly.

Storbon nodded to Rugrat, gathered himself and headed inside. People turned to watch as he walked through the halls, still wearing his battle-stained gear, fresh from the Ninth Realm.

He ran his hand through his hair, trying to clean himself up some and calm his nerves before knocking on Delilah's door and opening it.

Their eyes made contact as the words slipped from his mouth. She ran around her desk, grabbing his hands, checking him, looking him over.

She sighed, gripping his hands tight. Storbon reached up to move errant hair behind her ear. Her eyes caught him as he stilled.

She looked down. As if realizing she was holding his hands, she quickly released them, turning away, hiding. He could see her bracing herself, clearing away whatever had just sparked between them.

"Delilah." His words paused her movements as she sunk into herself more. "I…" His voice was rough. "Well, that is…" Storbon looked at his hands. "Aw, fuck it. Delilah, I like you. I'm interested in you. I don't want to put you on the spot, and I am sorry if that scares you. I needed to get that off my chest. Don't worry, I won't bug you about it again. We don't need to talk about it. I can deal with it."

He looked at her, seeing her shoulders shaking. His insides turned over as he reached out to comfort her, his hand stopping, fearing she might shy away from him. *Shit, I didn't want this.*

"Delilah?" he said in a small voice.

She turned, wiping her face, the smile clearing the clouds in her mind. "Good, because I like you too." She reached up on her toes, grabbing the top of his carrier and pulling him down to kiss him quickly.

She giggled at his expression as Storbon touched her face.

"Well, then." He coughed as Delilah released him and bit her lower lip, blushing.

"Priority message. The Ninth Realm is being evacuated to the Seventh. There was a second attack!" Egbert's voice filled the room.

"Shit!"

Ziyaad al-Saade finished up his inspection of the latest round of repairs and remodeling to the crafting district and the mountains on the western side of Kushan that had been the worst hit.

It had taken nearly two years to fix all the problems, but that wouldn't bring back the people he had lost.

"Sir, Erik West and his Special Team have arrived. They are requesting an audience with you," an aide said.

"They bring war to our city, don't listen to a word of our plans, and we're *still* at their beck and call," Ziyaad hissed. "This would have been minimized if they had taken the time to listen."

He waved at the mountain and flicked his hand in dismissal, shaking his head. "I will meet with him."

Ten minutes later, he was in his audience hall.

*He looks like he came straight from a fight,* Ziyaad thought as Erik left his guards behind and walked toward him. Ziyaad forced himself to not shift in his chair.

Erik bowed deeply to Ziyaad, making him sit up in alarm. A ruler never bowed like such in front of another. "Ziyaad Al-Saade, I have done wrong by you and your people. I wrongly thought that you were trying to use me and my people for your gain. Your people fought with great honor to defend their homes. Due to my words and actions, we did not listen to what you said, and you knew that the enemy would attack your western cities. I painted your actions with my past experiences instead of taking the time to talk with you, to learn what an honorable and good man you are. My actions drove Alva to overrule others." Erik shook his head. "I am sorry."

"I—" Ziyaad wasn't sure what to say. He glanced at the hall filled with people from across the city, and with people from beyond his city walls.

He moved from his chair to Erik. "Please, stand." He helped him upright.

He held Erik's arms, seeing clarity in his eye instead of the cloudiness of schemes that filled the eyes of many he met with. Ziyaad patted his arms.

*I can see it now. How this man sparked an empire.*

He took his hands away from Erik's arms. "Is there anything that I can help you with?" Ziyaad asked.

"No, I just wanted to apologize." Erik's face pinched together. "I've come from the Ninth. The Shattered Realms led a sneak attack, hitting the Tenth and Ninth hard. Now is the time we need to work together instead of falling apart with our differences. Thank you for your time, Lord Al-Saade." Erik bowed his head. "I have to return home to prepare."

"Go with God and may he shine down upon you."

"And to you as well."

They bowed heads to one another.

Rekha woke up suddenly, looking around the room for Erik.

"He's not here. He had to go down to Alva to deal with things there," Cayleigh said from where she sat, glancing out of an arrow slit at the academy beyond.

"Oh," Rekha felt her stomach tighten. "Wait, why would I be looking for Erik?"

"You talked all afternoon and all night. He looked after you and brought you here to get some sleep. Had me and Sam promise to look in on you and be around when you woke up." Cayleigh smiled. "Longer than I've seen you talk to anyone. Thought you might be interested."

"Did he say anything else?"

"He seemed concerned for you." Cayleigh winked.

Rekha growled even as her heart jumped in her chest.

"There's a lot to do. Ravagers have been spotted across the realm. The Imperium has started gathering everyone in the major cities, clearing groups are moving with the fleets to clear out the Ravagers and Devourers hiding across the realm."

Rekha got out of the cot. Using a cleaning spell, she quickly changed into clean clothes. Cayleigh helped her with her armor. She was nearly done when her sound transmission device rang.

"We're being invaded by people from the lower realms. We need support immediately!"

Rekha looked at Cayleigh. She pulled tight the last bind she was working on as they ran through the defenses, looking into the area around the totem. Rekha pulled on her helmet as people started appearing. They all wore the same gear.

*Erik and Rugrat's gear.*

"Hold back," Rekha ordered over the channel.

She got to the defensive wall as the Imperium and school forces stared at the armed and armored men and women.

A man stepped forward and pulled off his helmet.

"Hi, I'm Captain Gong Jin. We were sent to support you here in the Ninth."

"How did—" Rekha looked at them all as more appeared through the totem.

"When we learned about the truth of the Eighth Realm, a lot of people took time to think about why they fight. Erik and Rugrat scouted ahead. They said you needed support, so everyone that thought they'd make it past the Eighth Realm, or had already, has come with me to support you."

"Stand down. They're here to support us," Weebla said through the sound transmission channel.

"Well, thank you," Rekha said, the words awkward on her tongue.

"No worries," Gong Jin said. "Wanted to coordinate with you on where to place my people."

"Certainly."

She spent the morning organizing Imperium units. The Alvans added to the security of the Academy. People were recovering the dead's belongings to be sent to their families as they advanced to clear the academy.

By the afternoon, Rekha was still tired, but they were recovering. The fleets were now scouring the remote areas of the Ninth to clear out the last Ravagers.

She sat down, sharing a stamina potion with Weebla. "So, what now?"

"Now we need to iron out our defenses and then we can think about retaking the Tenth Realm. The longer the Shattered are here, the stronger they will become."

"What about the Imperium?"

Weebla reached out her hand, gathering power and then releasing it. "A new Head will have to be picked as soon as possible."

"Would you?" Rekha's voice was a strangled thing.

"I'm even worse with politics than Xun Liang." Weebla smiled, a small, sad thing. She forced out a sigh, pushing on. "I'm a Gnome, and while I'm strong, it has been a long time since I have needed to fight."

"That shouldn't—"

"The Imperium is not as strong as it once was, and they will need a face to deal with the other sects and clans. There are only a few that are Gnome or Elven and they will listen to me and Eli'keen. Humans, there are many and few that work together." Weebla shrugged.

"How could they take the Tenth Realm?" Rekha said.

"They have numbers and dozens of planets on their side. While we think of them as dumb beasts, they can live for hundreds of years, and they can plan. What has happened has happened. We must deal with it and not forget it." Weebla reached out her small hand and gripped Rekha's wrist.

Rekha took strength from the gesture, putting her hand on top. "What about the Alvans?"

"A good ally to have." Weebla smiled as she drank from her stamina potion and sat back, trying to get into a comfortable position in her armor.

Rekha smiled and leaned forward, drinking her own stamina potion.

A klaxon broke the silence.

"Tears!" someone yelled as she threw the stamina potion into her storage ring and stepped up to the totem's walls with Weebla.

Tears appeared around the academy, in the cities, and in the distance. There were a few to start, and then dozens and then hundreds.

Rekha felt the blood drain from her face.

"Pull back all fleets to the academy. Emergency teleport. Evacuate all civilians!" Weebla ordered as Ravagers ran through the tears, their roars carrying across the Ninth Realm.

Weebla pulled out her map. Rekha saw Sam and Cayleigh hurrying over and studied the map. There were tears *everywhere.*

"This must be their second wave, their push on the Ninth," Weebla said, communicating with the different leaders without activating her sound cancelling. "Yes, I understand, but we're too spread out. I agree that the warships and the Tenth Imperium forces will help, but while we hold the Ninth, we only take up around fifteen percent of the total planet. That leaves the rest for them to gather their forces for an attack."

Weebla continued her one-sided conversation on her sound transmission device. "If the fleets can hit the tears when retreating, then yes, but we can't hold. Everyone has been fighting for the last few days. We control too little of the ground and our forces are spread too thin. We must pull back to the Seventh. There, we can call upon the Sects and the Clans to help."

She waited, frowning at whatever response she heard. "I will act like you didn't say that, Savare. If you say it a second time, I'll duel you and I'm stronger than the last time fought." Rekha felt the hairs on the back of her neck rise at Weebla's tone.

"The Sects and Clans will have to help us. If they don't, it will be their homes under attack next. If we die here, we'll be useless to the Imperium. Retreating to the Seventh Realm gains us time—time to train, time to plan, instead of off-the-cuff ideas. I have been placed in command, so hear my orders. We will withdraw, destroy anything that could assist the Shattered, and kill as many as you can."

Rekha ground her teeth, gripping her sword tight. She wanted to argue, say that they could turn the tide.

Looking out of the defenses, she saw the Shattered, rushing toward the academy. Spells crashed into the oncoming force that returned with their own attacks.

Creatures tore out of the ground under the defenders. Others howled and dove from the sky, or ran across the broken landscape, gaining speed as they exchanged ranged attacks. The spells turned into a wall of destructive light as the distance shortened.

Units on the front lines were too dispersed. They withdrew through the streets, covering one another with spells.

Rekha stepped onto a casting platform, feeling it resonate with her mana system. She aimed and started dropping spells on the leading Shattered.

Ships appeared above Avegaaren.

"Dammit," Sam hissed, casting beside her.

She spared a glance. The once proud warships were streaming fire, blackened with damage from fierce fighting as they cleared the attackers that had teleported with them and opened fire on the Shattered breaking through Avegaaren's walls.

"East!" Cayleigh acted as the spotter for the mages filling the casting platforms, raining destruction on flanking Shattered.

"Devourer!" Rekha called out, feeling a familiar elemental resonance as a beast launched into the sky for the warships. Ravagers swarmed around them, hit by magical attacks, and falling to the ground below.

As they thinned, the Devourer could be seen through the gaps. It shot out a stream of water, rocking the nearest corvette's barrier, coloring it rapidly. Formations flared to regain balance as the Devourer dropped toward the ground, followed with attacks.

Several other Devourers charged into the sky, focusing on another corvette on the other side of the formation.

They entered its barrier and unleashed attacks of flame, stone, metal, and water.

Rekha felt her stomach twist. She drew upon her mana as she animated the metal inside the buildings behind the retreating Alvans. Golems of metal tore free and laid into the Ravagers, killing a few dozen, but were overwhelmed by numbers as their mana was drained from them.

Rekha felt frustration, almost futility at her attacks.

Cayleigh directed attacks. She, Sam, and the rest of the mages followed her coordination. The totem-teleport hubs were bastions of fire as those that had been clearing or defending the outer walls collapsed inward in savage street to street fighting.

Rekha and her fellow mages cast again and again. Some fell from sheer exhaustion, but others quickly took their place.

The fleets created an aerial defense, moving together, trying to cover one another as Ravagers and Devourers charged them from the ground and the sky. Tears appeared in the sky above Avegaaren and in open locations across the school grounds.

"They must have drained the formation defenses," Sam yelled.

"Full pullback to the teleport hubs! Now or else the tears will cut you off!" Weebla yelled.

The diminutive woman was on her own platform, hurling out a spear of fire, hitting a Devourer and making it explode. The wounds made them flee as she unleashed a rain of ice that tore through buildings, streets, and Ravagers, leaving a block clear of standing structures and beasts.

The defenders rushed into the teleportation hub. The Alvans were at the rear, holding the gates.

A frigate dropped from the sky, its damage too heavy to sustain flight. It crashed into the ground, crumpling as spell formations appeared around it and shattered. The entire mana stone stores of the ship and the ambient mana of the surrounding area *ignited*.

"Get down!" Weebla yelled.

Rekha ducked behind the parapet, looking through an arrow slit in morbid curiosity as the ship exploded, tearing apart the surrounding area in a sudden and terrifying wave of heat.

Rekha looked away from the light as the force slammed into the teleportation barrier.

She looked back. The broken ship lay across the ground. She couldn't reconcile the area she saw with what it had once been.

Shattered ran toward the burning wreck of the frigate, and started to fill the broken landscape.

"Come on!" Cayleigh grabbed her and Sam and jumped. Rekha got her feet under her as they dropped onto the teleportation pads.

The last defenders ran to the teleportation pads.

Rekha saw Weebla's spells hurl back a Devourer diving from above, tearing great wounds into the beast, which healed as fast as they formed.

Light overtook her senses, and she found herself at one of the totem islands. People appeared on pads across the island, rushing the totems at the center of the island.

Rekha looked at the teleportation pads.

*Come on, where are you, Weebla?*

Others streamed through the teleportation pads, pushing past her. She pulled free of Cayleigh, who was trying to pull her toward the totem.

The air was hot as a bloodied Weebla finally appeared on the teleportation pad.

Rekha caught her, lowering her to the ground. Rekha's heart twisted in place as she frantically cast healing spells. "Dammit Weebla! Open your eyes! Come on!" She pulled out healing potions, pouring them through the cracks in Weebla's armor to get to the wounds below.

"Grandma." Cayleigh dropped on the other side of Weebla, administering her own healing concoctions.

The frantic fear was a lead stone in Rekha's stomach.

Weebla let out a rasping breath, breaking the stone in her gut as Rekha turned Weebla on her side.

"We need to get going soon!" Sam said.

Weebla's eyes fluttered open.

"What are you still doing here?"

"I can't lose two of my family in as many days," Rekha hissed, pouring out the last of her healing potion.

"I'll cover you," Cayleigh twirled her weapons, standing.

Rekha picked up Weebla with a grunt.

Sam let loose a volley of arrows at Ravagers flying for the island.

Rekha hugged Weebla tight as she ran toward the totem. Cayleigh let out a yell as Ravagers started to land on the island.

Rekha reached the totem. "Let's go!"

Cayleigh unleashed a wave of fire, creating the space she and Sam needed to run back to the totem. Light surrounded them, leaving the Ninth Realm behind. She could feel Weebla breathing weakly as they appeared in the Seventh Realm.

"Stay with me. I can't lose you too! Healer! I need a healer!"

Thank you for your support and taking the time to read **The Ninth Realm**.

The Ten Realms will continue in **The Tenth Realm.**

As a self-published author I live for reviews! If you've enjoyed The Seventh Realm, please leave a **review**!

Do you want to join a community of fans that love talking about Michael's books?

We've created this Facebook group for you to discuss the books, hear from Michael, participate in contests and enjoy the worlds that Michael has created. You can join using the QR code below.

Thank you for your continued support. You can check out my other books, what I'm working on, and upcoming releases with the QR code below.

Don't forget to leave a review if you enjoyed the book.

Thanks again for reading ☺

Made in United States
Orlando, FL
16 June 2024

47958810R10117